Praise for William the Patriarch

"7ese characters come alive as real people who show the complexity of their lives and times. Who knew Puritans were this interesting?"
—Sally Borden

"A fascinating recreation of life in early colonial America . . . steadily, carefully, expertly, Nancy moves us from the quotidian to the eternal, a steady march up to the final chapter of the book as if encouraging us to break down the fence between the mundane world and the eternal one. 7e book ends in a most amazing final chapter which I will not spoil by describing except to say it brought me near to tears timeless and very moving."
—Excerpts of Book Review by Philip Shaddock

"7is is true 'slice of life.' When can I read the next one?"
—Susan Titus

"Lets the reader experience living in a newly-settled area in the frontier of western Massachusetts surrounded by Indigenous people who could be quite hostile at times. 7e community of Puritans, too, impose a strict, unforgiving way of life on its members, in addition to administering the local government . . . I loved the opportunity to get a glimpse into the inner life of our country's early Puritan immigrants [and] can't wait for the next.
—Excerpts of book review by Karen Stankye

WILLIAM, THE PATRIARCH

Book One of
The Watertown Chronicles

Nancy Shattuck

This is a third edition of a novel, *William, The Patriarch*, Bo
One of *The Watertown Chronicles* by Nancy Shattuck, Detro
Michigan. The third edition replaces the Ardent Writer Press seco
edition (the proprieter retired and released
the manuscripts.) Based on author's research into her own fami
roots that started in Massachusetts in the late 1600s, *William, T*
Patriarch, is Nancy Shattuck's re-imagining of her own family's tri
and life through the fictional Sherborn family. All rights reserved
Nancy Shattuck. Excerpts of text may be posted online
only for a noncommercial use, provided quotations do not exceed
total of over three hundred (300) words.
Cover art and composition the work of The Ardent Writer Press usi
Photoshop techniques. The painting on the cover of William, T
Patriarch is by Philip Shaddock. The background lithograph for
the cover is in the public domain and is by Reinier Nooms, Dutc
1623-1667 entitled *Harbor Scene with Landing Boat, 17th Century.*
rights to said painting are owned by Philip Shaddock. Compositi
and cover, as well as Mr. Shaddock's painting, are covered by t
same grant for noncommercial use noted above.
Photo of Nancy Shattuck is by Devenand Ale.

Library of Congress Cataloging-in-Publication Data

William, The Patriarch, Book One of *The Watertown Chronicles*
by Nancy Shattuck

p. cm. - (Independent Press) ISBN 978–1–969319–45–7

Library of Congress Control Number 2020939377

Library of Congress Subject Headings

New England--17th century--Fiction.
New England History--Colonial period, ca. 1600-1775--Fiction.
New England--Social life and customs--Fiction.
FICTION / Historical / General.

BISAC Subject Headings

FIC014070 FICTION/Historical/Colonial America & Revolution
FIC014000 FICTION / Historical / General
FIC008000 FICTION / Sagas
FIC000000 FICTION / General

Third Edition, 2026 (Copyright Nancy Shattuck © 2017)

CONTENTS

ACKNOWLEDGMENTS

I began this project as a single historical novel, but as I wrote, the voices of the family emerged, each offering a divergent point of view on what happened in the years surrounding King Philip's War. They convinced me that history was more than a collection of facts; and I decided to follow where these voices might lead. The result was a series, *The Watertown Chronicles*.

I could never have progressed this far in the project without the aid and encouraging support of the members of my writing group, The Detroit Writers, who slogged through two entire novels as they streamed from my laptop to print. I owe thanks to Anthony Ambrosia, Dr. Anca Vlasopolos, Robin Watson, Alinda Wasner, Dr. Claire Crabtree, John Gallagher, Charlotte Varzi, Carol Campbell, and Patricia Abbott. Hopefully, they made short work for editors Doyle Duke and Steve Gierhart of The Ardent Writer Press.

Early in the project, I was able to travel to Watertown and Groton in Massachusetts to begin my research. The wonderful receptions I received at the main libraries in Watertown and Groton, as well as that of The American Antiquarian Society (AAS) in Worchester, Massachusetts are unforgettable. In Watertown, the librarians enthusiastically led me to a room where they pulled dusty boxes from shelves and opened them for the first time in perhaps years: we found original land grants and titles written in calligraphic script. In Groton, librarians led me on a wonderful search for books on early Groton. The AAS ushered me to a reading room where tables are covered in felt cloths and books are read on book stands. They also were helpful in giving me access to digital archives. Imagine reading the Watertown and Groton council meeting minutes, which name the attendees and record the events of a day in 1666.

Also, early in my project, I was fortunate to meet Dr. Susan Parrish, who teaches history at the University of Michigan, at a Washington University alumni dinner. She recommended that I contact AAS and turned me on to Slotkin's Regeneration Through Violence: The Mythology of the American Frontier1600-1800. Likewise, Philip Shaddock, who succeeds Lemuel Shattuck as the chief genealogist for the family, recommended Bridenbaugh's Vexed and Troubled Englishmen 1590-1642 and Cities in the Wilderness. I must also extend special thanks to Philip because he has written an exceptionally fine book review and added it to his website. Susan Titus and Dr. George Wieland too have sent books such as Starr's Social Transformation of American Medicine and some on Puritan family order. I would also like to thank Dr. Anca Vlasopolos and Sharon Luckerman, who wrote recommendations and reviewed my application to AAS for an artist grant.

Likewise, I must extend my thanks to those first readers of William, The Patriarch, who were able to point to ways to improve its historical relevance, the scriptural verity, and to avoid anachronistic license. Thank you, Philip Shaddock, Susan Titus, Dr. Thomas Anderson, Dr. Nancy Owen-Nelson, Karen Stankye, and Sally Borden. Last but never least, I want to thank my family readers, Polly Shattuck and Shelli Brown, who have been so encouraging.

I dedicate this book to my father
Claude Emerson Shattuck

PREFACE

This project, to breathe life into the New England colonial past, was an exercise in "reading between the lines" and working where inductive and deductive logic cross paths. I've taken my direction from historian Ronald Takaki, who wrote *A Different Mirror: A History of Multicultural America* (2008). He uses microhistory to illuminate the larger issues of the American story. What makes his history so readable—the minutia—will hopefully serve the same purpose in this fiction. The irony of writing fiction about a white European family and paying homage to an historian of Japanese-Hawaiian ancestry who imparted American history from the immigrants' point of view is not lost on me. Too often the 'founders' of New England are not seen as immigrants now. However, I seek to add them back to the lists at the same time I tip my hat to including gender-driven views that have been excluded in past histories. Last, I seek to imitate Takaki's skill in reconstructing history from cultural objects that in themselves are unimportant.

William Sherborn, the fictional immigrant who arrives in Watertown, Massachusetts is the one character to which all the others fall heirs. He's the kingpin for eleven following narratives. To construct his persona, I extrapolated what facts I could from Lemuel Shattuck's book, *Memorials of the Descendants of William Shattuck: The Progenitor of the Families in America That Have Borne His Name (Boston, 1855).* Sherborn's prototype William Shattuck was a voting member of the Watertown council. As such, he had to be a professing, covenanted Puritan, a member of the church, and own land. In the Massachusetts Bay Colonies, to be a full member of the church, he would have professed an epiphanal conversion to his faith. Someone professing such a conversion usually lived in devotion to Puritan principles, however imperfectly.

I was able to establish his status in the community from the Watertown Council records; the meeting minutes date back to its beginning in 1630 and have been released in digital format. Thus, I could see from mentions what services he had performed for Watertown as well as get a feel for the changes in the society as the council leadership evolved.

Likewise, I used the will published in 1672 to build Sherborn's character and the relationships with his wife and children. We know from Lemuel Shattuck's book that William Shattuck wrote and signed the will in sound mind on his sickbed, eleven days before he died. He had waited to the last to write this will. It was signed by adjoining neighbors (according to the Watertown map of original allotments), who were by his own words, 'loving friends.' The will was executed by his wife and witnessed by the Council Clerk.

I took poetic license with the will, deriving from it the relationship that he had with his wife Susanna, and even her character. She was a unique woman of her time as she signed the first prenuptial agreement when she remarried after William's death. One could assume she had some say in William's original bequest. In his will, he grants her the use of his house on the hill until his two youngest sons turn twenty-one. That statement is followed by a badly worded clause he will give her four pounds a year "if she marry" or "if she marry not." I play with the language to create a conversation between the two on his sickbed, when Susanna bargains with him to keep the house if she marries again.

The will also informed me that he had favored his son William junior, as might be expected of a father whose son follows in his footsteps. He split his Waltham farm and meadowland between the older boys, Philip and William junior, but sweetened the bequest to the latter with his "loome and its appertinences" and a young horse. William junior was employed in Captain Prentice's cavalry at the time, and the horse could have been specially trained for military use.

I derived a troubled relationship with his oldest son John from the will as well. William gives John a cash equivalent of the land he bequeaths to William junior and Philip, but only after his mother's death, and then, annually in four equal parts. John never appears in Council meeting minutes or on the church member rosters, which is notable for the oldest son. John only names his *third* boy after his father. I took these as signs that John had a poor connection to William. A letter from Reverend Sherman to Magistrate Danforth in Boston and Daniel Gookin's account of a meeting in Charlestown, also belittle John's character, which could change his Puritan father's affections

Oddly, William bequeaths three pounds to his married children, to be distributed a month after his death, but six additional pounds to his "son" Samuel Church (in fact his son-in-law). His sixteen-year-old daughter Rebecca had married Samuel Church, a man twice her age, with only one child issuing before the couple disappear from records. The facts were rich with implications any novelist would leap to convey.

For the rest, I've sought to uphold some historical accuracy without replicating it. The inventory for the will helped establish how the house might be furnished and the tools they might use, as well as expect for their class. I haven't attempted to reproduce the differences in language, though I may slip in an occasional 'aye' for an England-born character, or 17th century syntax. I use the names of people who occupied the town during the period, changing names only if needed to clarify the text. It's difficult to write conversations when all the characters share the same name—both of William's close friends are named John for example—or when a family may have three generations of 'John' or 'Mary' in the same room at once. In instances when

I don't have biographical information, I have invented the townspeople's characters and descriptions.

Drawing on my childhood experiences, when I briefly lived with a family who practiced a Christian fundamentalist faith, I have tried to construct the religious life that the family might have led. I weave this into my research on Puritan mores and published sermons from the period. Also drawing on childhood experiences (living on a farm with no indoor plumbing and attending a one-room rural schoolhouse), I aim to reproduce from memory this colonial family's life conditions.

Although I followed a twentieth century Native American (NA) shaman for many years and can draw upon ritual ceremonies such as Lakota sweat lodges, Yuwipi ceremonies, baby blessings, and sun dances, I confess that I have little knowledge of east coast Algonquin ceremonies that were practiced in the seventeenth century. I did find a journal description of an Algonquin sweat lodge. I know that Indian excavations in Mexico have sweat lodges and draw from that inference that sweat lodges were universal in NA history. Likewise, I presume some other rituals might have been practiced in the past. Unfortunately, little of aboriginal culture has been recorded, though the captivity narratives do help. I cannot claim I am writing a cogent NA history.

The project has been for me a thrilling adventure, in that marrying the facts of history to the extraneous scraps of information I'm using to build the characters is like solving a picture puzzle; the facts of our history provide the picture but fitting in one interlocking puzzle piece (the tip of a feather against a blue sky) is the work at hand. I can hope that these novels share not only what I learn but my joy in searching for historical truth.

INTRODUCTION

illiam, The Patriarch is the first book in *The Watertown Chronicles*, a saga of one of America's immigrant families. William, an early emigrant to Massachusetts, his wife, and their ten children live through the pivotal period in colonial history that surrounds the devastating King Philip's War of 1675-76 in New England. *The Chronicles* comprise the twelve stories of these individuals, beginning in 1666 with the birth of the tenth sibling and ending with Samuel's wedding in 1686.

Though William, the Puritan patriarch, dies before King Philip's war begins, he serves a colonial system that gives rise to the war. He is also the progenitor of the individuals who fight in and survive it. In the first book, the actions of the Watertown settlers alter the face of Indian lands, and the factionalism of European nations fracture the Indian alliances. In the subsequent books, William's family reap the war that their father, a man who bowed to the Puritan ways, has unwittingly sowed for them. King Philip's war ravaged more than half the New England villages, destroying eleven; its death toll was more than one thousand colonists (two percent of the fifty thousand New Englanders) and three thousand Indians (fifteen percent of the twenty thousand Algonquin Indians). After victory, the colonial government either executed or sold the remaining Indians into slavery, annihilating the East Coast native population, which was already fewer than half that of Europeans before the war started.

This war was also pivotal in colonial history. The Royal Charter for The Massachusetts Bay Colony was unique in that it didn't specify England as the seat of the governing board of stockholders, and board members bought out any stockholder who chose to stay in England. Unlike any other charter colony, The Massachusetts Bay Colony conducted regular meetings of company officers and stockholders—required of all colonies—in Boston instead of England. The officers resided in New England.

Beginning in 1630, the Puritans set up a theocracy in the Massachusetts Bay Colony. "Freemen"—white male church members who owned property and paid taxes—elected a governor and a single legislative body called the Great and General Court, made up of assistants and deputies. Although the colonists' hunger for land has often been attributed to greed, clearly land ownership was more importantly a key to suffrage and social standing. Likewise, the doctrine of 'divine providence' was as much a ploy to keep settlers from returning to England as it was a religious belief. After the war, the colony lost this independence; in 1685, King Charles II revoked the Royal Charter and placed Massachusetts under the Dominion of New England, appointing a governing body.

It's difficult to wrap our minds around those years of rising tensions between the emigrating colonists and natives because the complexity of competing nations and shifting alliances is unparalleled. The new colonizers were still tied to the wars and rivalries of the European nations they'd left while immersed in those of the Indian nations surrounding them.

English, French, Spanish, and Dutch immigrants were culturally more diverse than the Indian nations, tribal identity notwithstanding. European nations didn't share a language, dress alike, or even eat the same food, though they shared technologies. The Massachusetts tribes were by comparison homogenous. Christianity did unite Europeans, even as the Protestants splintered the ways to worship. Some Massachusetts colonists made it their mission to convert natives to the Puritan faith, to unite with them. However, that intent politically divided the tribal people, complicating their alliances even more.

The English colonists banded together to meet their unified interests, forming the New England Confederation, a military alliance of Massachusetts, Plymouth, Connecticut, and New Haven. However, internal conflicts over boundaries, uneven contributions to the armies, and funding diminished its efficacy by 1662. The confederation no longer conducted regular meetings when the war began. Though it officially declared war on the Wampanoag and their allies in September 1675, conflict and resentment continued to erode its operation in the theater of King Philip's war.

The names of the Indians who were the chief players in King Philip's war are emblazoned brand names and place-names familiar to us, but featureless. One can buy Wamsutta towels, for instance, but never know that Wamsutta was the son of *Massasoit* ("great chief") Ousamaquin, who helped the Plymouth colonists survive their first winter. Nor would anyone know his importance in history, that his brother King Philip wanted revenge for his death.

The *Massasoit* Ousamaquin was a friend of the Plymouth settlers until his death. His treaty with the Governor was one of friendship and support; the colonists and the Wampanoag tribe even allied to fight the nearby Narragansett people. Ousamaquin's sons and successors were given Christian names. Wamsutta, the oldest son, took the name Alexander; Metacom, the next son, took the name Philip.

The treaty between Ousamaquin and Governor Prence of Plymouth unfortunately did not outlive its makers. After Ousamaquin died and his son Wamsutta became *sachem* ("chief"), Governor Prence, threatened by the French and Dutch, began to make unreasonable demands on the Wampanoag people, who resisted. After

King Alexander (Wamsutta) mysteriously died while in the hands of the British under suspicious circumstances, King Philip (Metacom) began to build a fighting force. In 1671, Governor Prence responded by insisting King Philip sign a new treaty in which he declared he would sell no more land without the approval of Plymouth, would surrender all of his guns, and pay tribute and fines. While Governor Prence instituted the moratorium on Indian land, conflicts continued, mainly over arms. However, after Governor Prence's death in 1673, the new Governor, Josiah Winslow, removed the moratorium and began to use lawless practices to pressure natives to sell land. At this time, Philip sold Wampanoag land recklessly to purchase guns and ammunition. He aimed to win back his lands, thereby ridding himself of the Europeans who waged war among themselves and pitted rivaling Indians against one another.

The conflict began in early summer when Governor Josiah Winslow executed three of Philip's men, accusing them of murdering a Christian Indian interpreter and spy in 1675. King Philip responded immediately, attacking Swansea in June, an act which coincided with a lunar eclipse. The Indians took this as a good omen and continued their offense; the New England Alliance officially declared war in September. King Philip's War raged for eighteen months before the Indians were routed or sold for slavery in the West Indies.

The war nearly destroyed the economy; in the aftermath taxes rose so high colonists suffered hardships to pay them. Thousands of refugees who had lost their homes and all means of livelihood crowded into the towns the war passed over. The colonial government struggled to settle their debts to soldiers who'd fought in the war. Promises of land for pay weren't met until the eighteenth century, and land was often paid to the now-deceased soldiers' offspring. Charles II's brother, King James, dissolved the Massachusetts Bay Colony charter in 1691 and consolidated Massachusetts,

New Hampshire, Plymouth, Martha's Vineyard, and Nantucket into The Province of Massachusetts, appointing a governor from England. With this loss of independence, thus began the ninety-year march to the revolutionary war to sever ties with the motherland.

While this short history of the war is based largely on Euro-centric views, I may revise it in the future. Since I began this project in 2017, publishers have begun to release a plethora of new historical accounts that tell a fuller story, from a tribal native's point of view. These accounts encompass both oral histories and Wabanaki *awikhigan* ("written instruments") and promise to bring seekers closer to the truth of our shared history.

Watertown, Massachusetts in the Seventeenth Century

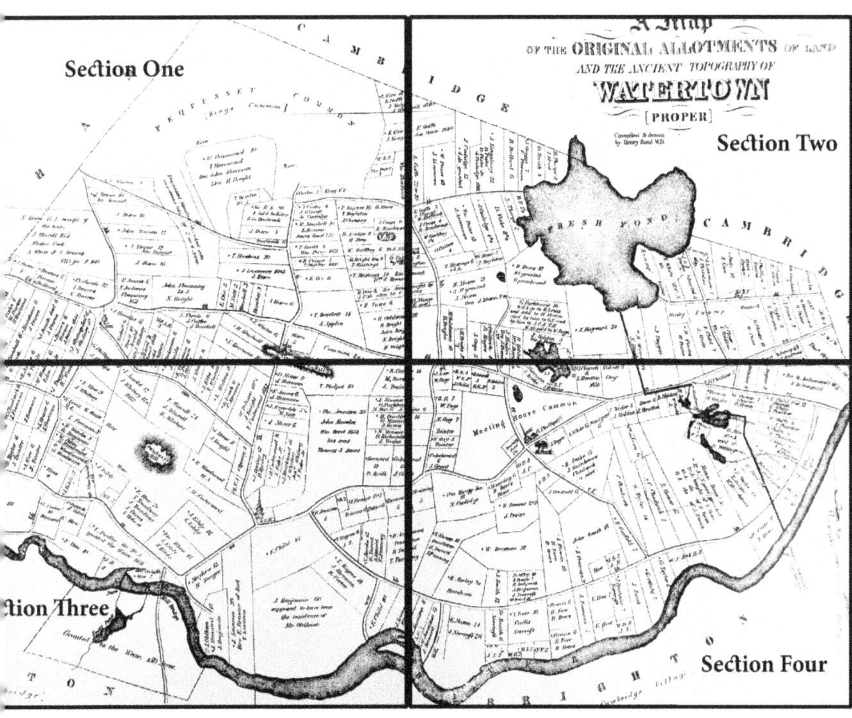

A Map of the Original Allotments of Land and the Ancient Topography of Watertown [Proper], Compiled and drawn by Henry Bond, M.D.

Note: The Sherborn/Shattuck's land is located to the right of the Pequuusset Common at the intersection of streets hh and jj (Hill Street and Road to the Pond). The homestead is perched near the crest of a steep hill labeled P.H., with a view east to the Fresh Pond and across Cambridge to Boston. The meetinghouse is one mile south on Hill Road in the commons.

Watertown Map on Successive Pages in Greater Detail
Sections One, Two, Three, and Four

Explanations to the Map

The mark "+" prefixed to a name denotes an original grant. Two or mor
names on a lot show successive owners of it. The location and relative siz
of the lots are shown here, but the shape is conjectural because the earl
records indicate only the bounds and the acreage.

Key to the Streets

aa   Mill Street: Cambridge Road: County Road: Mt. Auburn Street

bb   Bank Lane, a part of it now Walnut Street.

cc   Water Street, to the landing.

dd   Pond Road. ee Busby's Lane.

ef   Ancient Road.

ff   The way from the meetinghouse to Pastor Sherman's Arlingto
Street.

gg   Back Road: North Road: Country Road from Cambridge t
Weston: Belmont St.

hh   Hill Street: School Street.

ii   Stone Street: Pequusset Road: Common Street.

jj   Road to the Pond: Washington Street.

kk   Concord Road: Lexington Street.

ll   Bowman's Lane: Common Street.

mm   Ancient road without a name: Orchard Street.

nn   Cartway to the Meadows.

oo   Ancient road without a name: Hagar Lane: Warren Street.

pp   Boundary between Great Dividends and Small Lots: Warre
Street.

qq   Way to the Little Plain: Way to Dirty Green: Howard Street.

rr   Sudbury Road: County Road: Main Street.

ss   Cartway betwixt lots: Way to Beaver Brook: Pleasant Street.

tt   Driftway: Gore Street.

uu   Driftway to the marsh.

vv   Driftway opened to Washington Street in 1708.

ww   Crooked Lane.

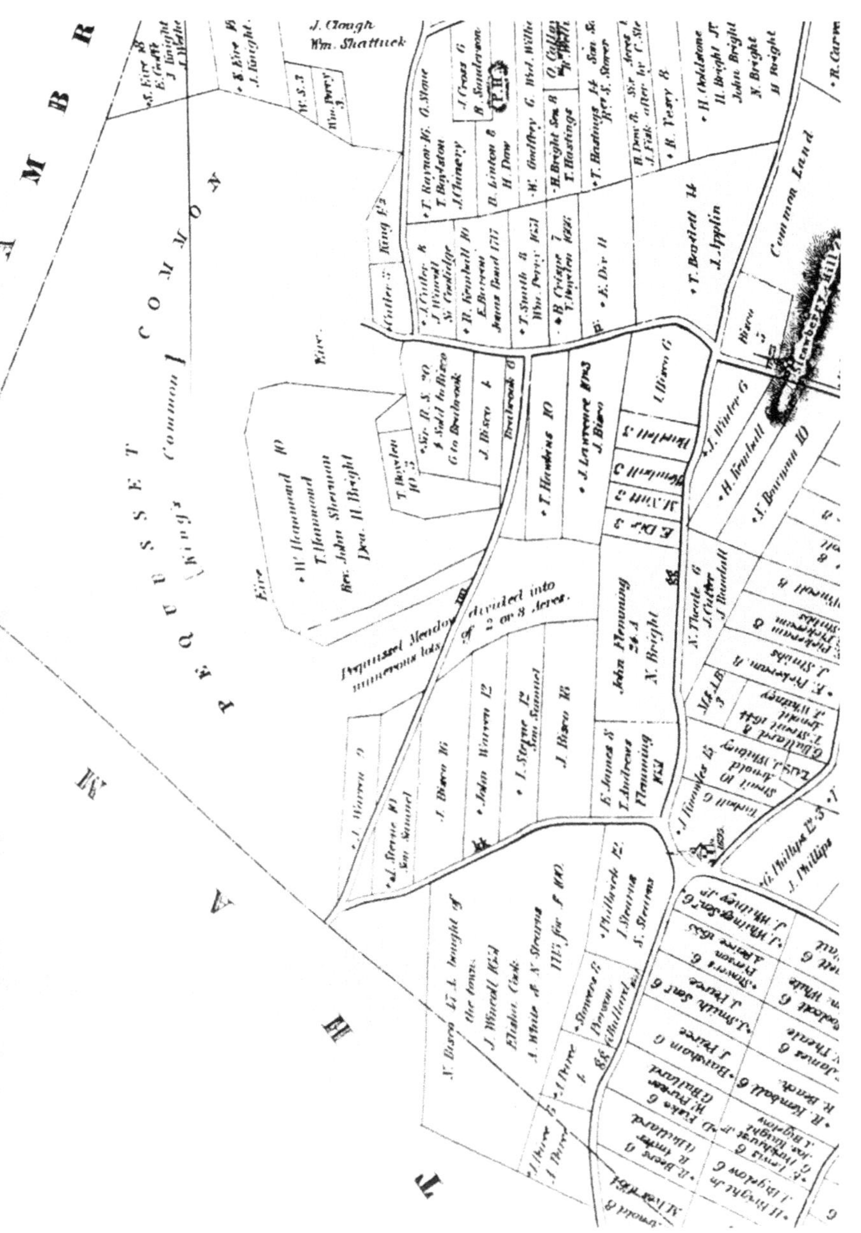

Old Watertown
Section One Detail

Old Watertown
Section Two Detail

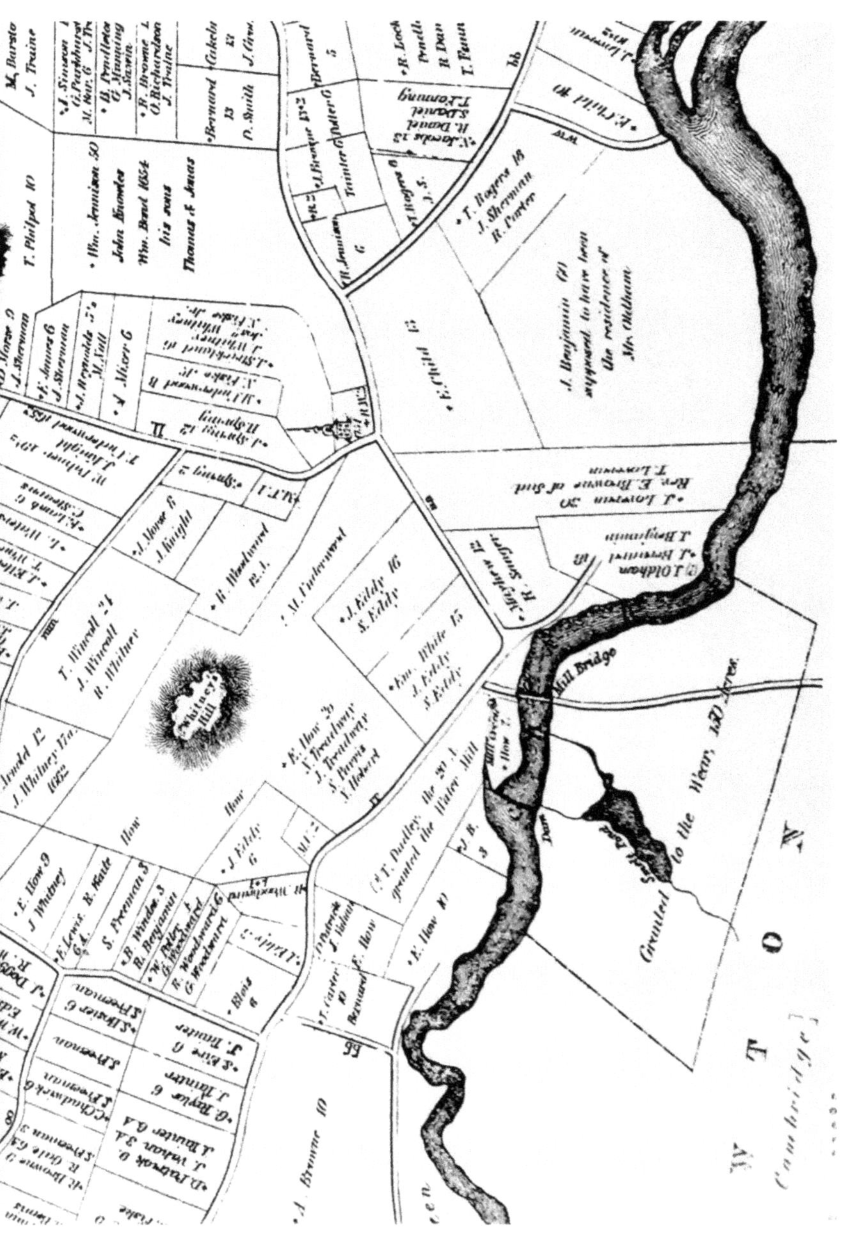

Old Watertown
Section Three Detail

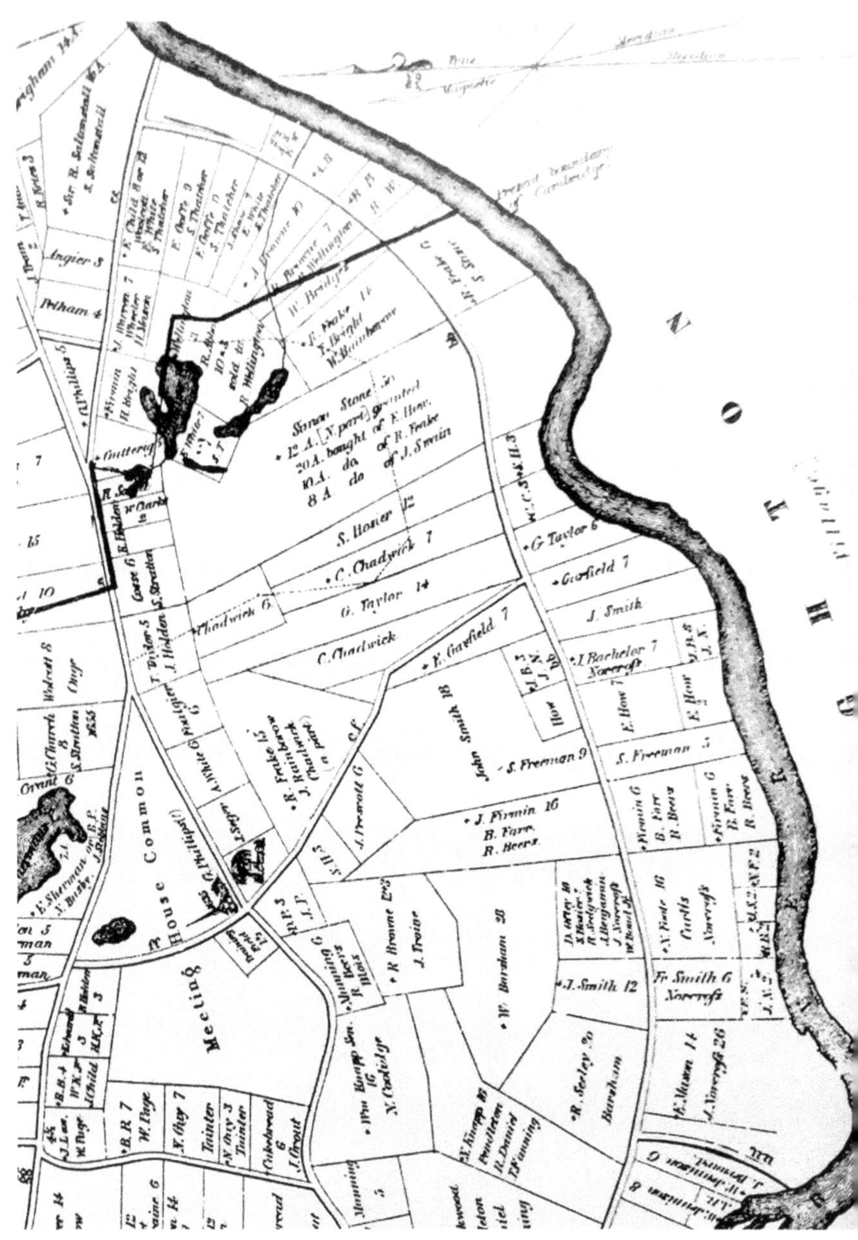

Old Watertown
Section Four Detail

*The way that can be gone
is not the eternal way ....*
—TAO TE CHING

Chapter One

FAVORITES AND FAVORS

Watertown, July 1666

It was early morning, and already, both rider and horse were sweating. William rocked in the creaking saddle, calmed by the rhythmic sound of his grey roan's hoofs on the dry dirt road. Grey Coat (his horse's hair was so shaggy it looked like a cloth coat), had become Old Gray since William first rode his gelding from the market in Watertown. In 1642, William had been young, too, just turned twenty, newly married and a father. Twenty-four years later, he'd witnessed the growth of the Massachusetts Bay Colony, but even more, a dissolution of English customs that threatened his sense of order.

He turned to head down Hill Street, toward his daughter Mary's home. He was due at the Watertown council meeting at Representative John Sherman's house this morning but needed first to ask her help. Since the three eldest children had married and distance interposed, remaining head of his scattering family was more difficult.

William would never admit that he favored one of his nine children over another. As Puritan head of the family and spiritual guide for their souls, he must behave as impartially as God, the stern Father did. As one who had accepted God's covenant, William was His emissary. Not only must he obey God's laws as he'd promised, but he must exact promises from his family, friends, and community too. William could only impart what he knew to his children, show them God's grace, lead them to their own covenants with the Lord.

In his heart, though, he couldn't deny Mary, his second born, every favor. First, she had the beauty of his mother—Mary's namesake—whom he'd seen last when he was eighteen, when he'd boarded the ship *Recovery* to cross the Atlantic in 1640. He'd never seen her again; she'd died in England ten years afterwards. William couldn't help staring at Mary while she wasn't looking, noting her fine features, the flawless peach-brightened cheeks, the blue eyes rimmed with indigo, the thick brown locks streaked with chestnut and blond. No man could help noticing her, praise God.

He was unaware that this link of Mary to his mother masked another inconsistency in himself. They embodied his attachment to his birthplace in Somerset, England. Since his migration to Watertown, he'd harbored a deep longing for the domestic neatness of the Somerset countryside, the peace of grazing sheep, the security of knowing his place in the world. That his land holdings and status in Watertown far exceeded any he might have had in Stogumber didn't matter.

Sunday's sermon gave no comfort, either. Pastor Sherman had pointed out that last year's black death plague in London followed right on the heels of restoring the monarchy and reestablishing the Church of England and its Papist ways. The pestilence that killed a hundred thousand sinners, the Reverend preached, could only be God's punishment; whereas, the Lord showered his favor on His faithful Puritan colonists. While William acknowledged providence was evident in Watertown, his longing sprang from a simpler source. He had no taste for the frightening wilderness, for the endless challenges faced to build a new England, or for the burden of wrestling with his spiritual doubts.

Even after twenty-six years, the Nonatum Indian's moccasined, sometimes naked presence unnerved him. Though Boston's Reverend Eliot had succeeded in moving this Massachusetts tribe to the praying Indian town, Natick, they still fished at the weir or showed up at the marketplace. Although the fur trade was no longer viable in Massachusetts—it had moved north—Indians now traded land for European-made goods, especially guns and ammunition.

The wooden houses of Watertown would always feel impermanent compared to the stone and thatch buildings of his youth. St. Mary's church in Stogumber, a medieval stone structure with a tower, inspired worshippers with its carillons. William could not compare it to Watertown's one-room, one-story frame meeting house, where congregants nailed bear and wolf head trophies on its wall. A street prosperously paved with cobbles, the narrow thoroughfares where one could walk to buy any number of commodities, the markets, the fairs! Watertown with its sprawling settlement of farms on muddy roads, lots still darkly wooded, the lonely distances to neighbors, might never reach the mark. Most of all, he wanted his children to see his England before they'd become permanently provincial.

William was not alone in wishing his children were more English; the complaint was universal in his church. The generation born on Massachusetts shores, who could not imagine what their parents from England knew, resisted old world ways, especially when old customs made no sense in the new world. The young had even more cause to break with their parents. While the Puritans dominated the civic and legal governance of the Massachusetts Bay Colony, emigrating Englishmen were as often lusty Elizabethan adventurers as Puritan pilgrims. The children could easily fall under the influence of these hypocritical and disobedient settlers. Keeping his family in line with his covenant was not simple.

To admit Mary was his favorite, would be to expose his true commitment to England, which his brethren in Watertown would believe hypocritical given his covenant with the Church.

William's observations of Mary had a greater purpose than this attraction, though. He was sure that Mary had the second sight, just as his mother had. He'd convinced his wife, Susanna, that this trait was at the bottom of Mary's spiteful jealousy of her older sister, Suzanne. Mary had lost her compass in this strict Puritan community, and without self-knowledge, must forever flounder. Her soul was in jeopardy. Indeed, Mary had become so conservative and conventional after she wed the son of a wealthy and powerful family in Watertown, William was losing his certainty. *Has she lost her gift?* he now asked himself. He hoped he could support her growth.

William reined in his horse and dismounted at Mary's house. It was large by Watertown standards and had painted shutters that brightened the weathered grey boards. To the side of the house chickens strutted across the garden, brooding and clucking as they searched for seeds and grubs. A dog barked in the back. He crossed the yard and clapped the door knocker loudly. Mary's servant, a red-haired, freckled Irish lass, opened the door and stared wide-eyed at the gray-haired, broad shouldered man standing before her. Despite the heat, he had dressed for business: boots, breeches, waistcoat and hat. She recognized him at once.

"Goodman Sherborn, we're not expectin' you! You're here to see Mary?" she said in a thick brogue. The Browns had only recently bought her indenture from Captain Greely, and she was still 'fresh off the boat' as colonists would say.

"Yes, Rose" he said. "She's here?"

"Follow me." Rose dared not delay a member of the family, though she knew Mary would scold her. Not expecting visitors, her mistress was still in her shift, and so were the children; her mistress insisted on formalities.

Rose turned and hurried to the great room at the back of the house, where Mary groomed her just-turned-four Lydia, and where two-year-old Elizabeth played. Mother and daughters, the three, wore their lightest cotton shifts; she would have them keep cool if possible.

William saw Mary redden, looking as surprised to see him as Rose had been at the door. Self-consciously, she patted her hair, searching for the missing and necessary head covering; she smoothed her chemise, looking for at least an apron to cover herself. Rose grabbed Lydia when she cried 'Grandfather' and tried to run to him. She took over the work of combing her hair. Mary scooped up Elizabeth, frowning at her servant before she turned to her father with a smile.

"Father! I wasn't expecting you. I'm sorry I'm so unprepared. I'd have dressed …" she apologized, then added in concern, "What's wrong?"

"I haven't much time!" he answered. "You're well as you are. I couldn't wait. I'm on my way to the council meeting and thought I'd stop in for a moment. I have a favor to ask."

"What? Please, will you sit?"

William clumped across the wooden floor to the settee and sat leaning forward, hands braced on his knees. "Your mother and Aunt Joanna asked me to come."

Mary's face registered apprehension. His mention of these two names together could mean only her mother's pregnancy. Aunt Joanna—her mother's best friend, not an aunt—was the midwife who would deliver her baby. In truth, Aunt Joanna delivered all their babies, even her next, due two months after her mother's. She set Elizabeth down and took a seat across from him.

"Since Suzanne has moved to Groton, Joanna has no one to assist her." William examined her face, expecting her guarded reaction. The whole family knew Mary was jealous of her sister, a competent midwife, and Mary did not disappoint her father's expectations. Her lips tightened, as though she knew what he would ask. Indeed, he knew that she knew everything from this point forward.

"Yes, well?" Mary never publicly revealed what she knew; she was terrified someone would take her psychic gifts as the Devil's own. Her intuition was acute.

"Joanna has asked that you come. She needs your help with the lying in, too. A month, most likely."

"I am no midwife to assist the birth."

"Joanna has a reason for asking. She's fearing scarlet

fever, too many cases lately. And Boston reports an outbreak of smallpox. She says she needs a second pair of hands to prevent contamination." He spoke the truth, though he also knew the two women were scheming to ease Mary's jealousy. "God knows, extra hands are best. You owe your mother that."

"Of course, I can help while she's lying in. I'll not refuse, father." Mary decided that he relayed her mother's, not Aunt Joanna's request. She resented her mother for sending her father to ask. *She doesn't have the courage to ask me herself,* she thought. *She knows I'll never refuse him.* "You may depend on me."

"Good, then. I'll send Will to get you when the time comes."

"I hope I'll see you before then. Will you have a bite to eat while you're here?"

"No, I must go. I don't want to be late." William rose and strode from the room. Inwardly, he congratulated himself on a successful mission as he remounted Old Gray and headed south to the council meeting. It would not be the first time his wife had asked him to make a special request; the feelings between Mary and her mother had soured that much. They were not exceptions to human nature he reasoned; women were emotional, and neither mother nor daughter could control these feelings. God had made them women, so the scriptures taught. William must be both guide and protector.

··

Chapter Two

THE SELECTMEN

Watertown, Same Day 1666

Mary Brown lived near John Sherman, but William had a lengthy ride before him in a town where roads undulated around steep hills, woods, springs, ponds, and marshes. He descended from Mary's to Cambridge Road and turned right past Corporal Bond's forest. At his left, houses faced Bond's woods across the road, where he often saw Indians at the fringes. Today, none appeared crossing the dense undergrowth. But looking for them by habit, the thought came to him. They're like animals; they use the same narrow trails and show the same stealth. They even call animals their relatives.

William had never had an occasion to speak with an Indian, but his wife, Susanna, who'd been born in Plymouth to Puritan saints, had tried to explain their ideas. She'd often taken their side when anyone spoke ill of Indians; consequently, William had repressed his opinions to keep peace in the family. He continued to wonder that Indians could see no difference between themselves and beasts, especially since some of them became Christians and lived in English houses, wore English clothes. They mystified him.

Another sharp turn down Bank Lane, toward the Charles River, led to John Sherman's homestead on the right. John Sherman, the earlier settler of the two Shermans in Watertown (Reverend John Sherman lived near the meetinghouse), held the distinction of being Watertown's representative to the Massachusetts Bay council in Boston. What is more, he'd been a venerable selectman on Watertown's council most of his fifty years.

William dismounted, handing the reigns to Sherman's indentured servant, a limping boy of eleven, who led the horse to the adjacent grazing yard. William chuckled, realizing the boy wore only one shoe. *Where's his other shoe?* he thought. He stepped through the large green door of the two-story, gabled house with shuttered glazed windows framing it. He greeted his host, a man with a powerful physique, a testimony to the work of many hardy Watertown pioneers. A trimmed goatee and light-brown, wavy, shoulder-length hair framed his round face. The silver buttons on his waistcoat and buckles on his shoes revealed his social rank.

He gestured William inside, speaking low. "Good you are here, William. I must ask a favor." He took his arm and drew him aside.

"Of course," William said.

"I had to fill in as Highway Surveyor when Goodman Payne broke his leg, but it's too much. I can't continue. Would you let me announce you as a replacement for Payne? You have the experience."

William nodded, granting he'd served as selectman for the position before. The last time he served, his partner had died midyear. He'd taken the double load for a month before the council appointed a stand-in. For that reason, he answered, "I don't think that I can spare the time, either." All the selectmen took on extra work for their communities, but he'd expanded his land holdings, buying out bordering properties of Clough and Sanderson, his former neighbors. He now felt overwhelmed, especially since John and Philip were no longer at home to help.

"I see. We'll talk later." He squeezed William's arm and left to greet John Coolidge, who waited at the door.

The seven acting selectman and principals crowded the few seats in the parlor. William took in the group, standing at the back, which was his proper place in Watertown society.

The East Anglian settlers who had followed the Reverend Phillips to Massachusetts in 1630 were his neighbors, but not his peers. They had given William land when he'd come in 1640 from the southwestern English province, Somerset, because he shared their profession. New England needed weavers, and the Watertown society, who came from England's Stour Valley in the northeast, were weavers. In England, both weaving communities had suffered from slowing trade, though prosperous Somerset held out against the depression longer.

The Watertown surveyor—Abraham Brown, the younger brother of the powerful Elder, Richard Brown— had granted William one acre for a homestead and three acres for planting, though the acreage turned out to be hillside. Reverend Phillips and Elder Brown—the two most powerful men in Watertown after Saltonstall abandoned his colonial venture and returned to England— had ignored William's possible temperamental differences. He descended from Celtic Britons in the southwest, whom the Anglo-Saxons often caricatured as independent to quarrelsome, and so mystical, they bordered upon the heretical. However, the Anglian fathers had lost many residents who had given up their harsh colonial lives and returned home to England. So, they even ignored the young man's ensuing marriage to Susanna Andrews, whose parents had been separatist Saints in Plymouth, those who wanted to abolish, not reform, the English church!

The Watertown elders had not only generously allotted William a homestead, but also nominated him—after he'd accumulated enough land—to the rank of a voting freeman despite his drawbacks. He'd been selectman several years, too. Still, his twenty-six-year residency and growing, never-possible-in-England prosperity had not moved him to the center of Watertown society, even after his daughter Mary had married Abraham Brown's son.

William scanned the room from his place at the back to locate his allies. He nodded at Richard Norcross; the schoolmaster was a great friend to his wife, Susanna. His nearest neighbor, John Livermore, never missed a meeting, even in years when he was not a selectman. He didn't see Deacon Hastings anywhere this morning.

John Coolidge, his closest neighbor now, sidled up to him. "I couldn't help overhearing Sherman's request. Why did you turn him down?"

William chuckled and turned to him. "Did he ask you to speak to me?"

"Yes," John said. William knew the men claimed a family relation through marriage. John Sherman's mother, now deceased, had been a sister-in-law to John Coolidge's mother.

"I don't want more work right now."

"What work? There're few months left before the council selects the new officers. There's no new road laid out, and nothing to do once the snow falls. You could handle a downed tree."

"All good reasons; I'll grant I've given a poor excuse. Perhaps this one will improve it—I see no present benefit."

"Is not being selectman enough for you man?" John scoffed. The two men chuckled and turned toward the room. "The way I see it, you might get some advantage working with Corporal Bond."

"Might be," William said, staring at the burly man who stood near John Sherman. He too represented Watertown at the Boston courts. "You think I should accept?"

"I would."

"I'll take your advice." William worked his way to John Sherman and told him he'd changed his mind.

Sherman called the meeting to order, and one by one, each selectman reported his activities in the past four months. John Sherman and his partner were one of the three teams that oversaw the children's education. The Reverend Sherman had complained of several instances of disrespect at Sunday meetings. The council had responded by pairing up to canvass the community and assess each child's instruction. It was the law in the Massachusetts Bay Colony that all children learn religion and capital laws properly. All must be literate in the English tongue and be able to calculate. All must fit the Puritan mold. Unfortunately, not all parents agreed. Those who needed their children's labor might protest. Puritans and adventurers alike held a practical view of education; many argued against book learning in favor of apprenticeships.

Richard Norcross, Watertown's schoolmaster, did not join the assessing teams, though he followed these reports avidly. As Watertown's only appointed teacher, he taught both the grammar school and the Greek and Latin school that prepared youths for college. The council considered him more ally than opponent. The assessors maintained that the problem began when parents, for economic or cultural purposes, did not send their children to the public school, but apprenticed boys or sent their girls to dame schools to learn housekeeping. Master Norcross would agree about the latter, as he had long criticized the girls' education. He thought girls needed grammar school at the very least, and Greek and Latin just as boys did for the best. He didn't believe women were incapable of logic and reason, nor did he find it true in his own family of seven.

John Sherman reported fining two families for withholding their children from school attendance. The council fined Goody Rachel Cooke, who ran a dame school near Cambridge, and ordered her to amend her reputed separatist ways.

John Sherman, who'd stepped in to replace Goodman Payne as highway surveyor, teamed with Corporal Bond to report on Goodman Samuel Benjamin's fence. They had taken up the matter from the previous year's highway surveyors, who'd been unsuccessful in correcting the man. He'd refused to take down the fence that blocked the road to the river.

Corporal Bond, a burly man with a thickly curled beard and bushy eyebrows, stood for his report. "Captain Mason, John Sherman, and I went back to check the road, and he'd not taken the fence down."

Goodman Payne said, "We warned him a year ago! Watertown granted him that land only if he kept that road open."

"His indenture contract clearly stated an acre," Richard Norcross said. "We checked. The acre was partial payment for the seven-year bond."

"He has a full acre," Goodman Payne said. "We asked him to leave the road crossing open. The problem is he fenced it in."

"We don't count swamps as acreage. Perhaps we should add roads to the list?" Richard Norcross suggested.

"All we asked is that he remove the fence," John Sherman said. The men in the council nodded, offering their support. No one was listening to the teacher's assertion. "We told him we'd be back in a week, and if he didn't do what we asked, we'd do it for him."

"He said he wouldn't," Corporal Bond said. "Then he said he wouldn't thank the town for the land they gave him, either." He postured, his thumbs in his pockets, shoulders back. "We took down the fence!"

The council voiced their approval.

"He's ordered to pay the fines," Sherman added. "William Sherborn has agreed to replace Goodman Payne as highway surveyor for the rest of this year, and he'll work with Corporal Bond to collect."

Corporal Bond nodded, acknowledging William across the room. The council members murmured their approval, but William's heart sank. Unlike the rest, he had heard Richard Norcross and knew he was right. Now Sherman had charged him with collecting fines from Samuel Benjamin, a man who must know that his only fault was poverty that led to bondage. He'd worked through his seven-year indenture, but he still could not claim full rights. Granted he was not a freeman yet, a voting member of the church, but he had good company, over half the town who were in the same ranks. William shook his head, now regretting his decision. His new partner, Corporal Bond, clearly supported this harsh view.

The town had granted William just one acre for homesteading and three hillside acres for his farm when he'd first arrived. *How can they know what one acre means when each of them holds more than one-hundred acres?* he thought. *John Sherman must have four-hundred! They quibble over a man's one acre?* He tempered the letdown with the thought, *God has a purpose for me.*

Next, the council approved the bounty for wolf and bear heads. The clerk was to pay two men ten shillings each for wolves and another fifteen shillings for the bear. They'd already tacked the heads on the meetinghouse wall, to encourage the congregation to fight the wilderness—snakes, foxes, and birds—that threatened their common good.

Everyone quieted when Thomas Trimble stood to read through the report he held in his hands. "You know I've completed a new survey of land grants. I found the original survey had many errors; Watertown has three-hundred acres of commons that were previously not accounted for."

The selectmen murmured, shifting in their seats, concerned the survey might affect their own titled grants. "Gentlemen," he asserted. "I've found the following land in the eastern common. There's land on the backside of old Goodman Stratton's; a swamp near Walter Allen's house; a parcel of marsh by Deacon Thatcher's lot; a small piece of land adjoining William Sherborn's farm."

William had already spoken with Goodman Trimble about the piece that extended into marshes at his farm. William had bought a lot from John Clough that included a marsh that his title didn't count as acreage. It was land that couldn't be improved. The selectmen grunted their approval at Trimble's findings. No one would miss the acreage he'd found, nor did it seem much use to Watertown, which now owned it. No one contested the new boundaries and the land that reverted to the Watertown commons.

John Sherman raised the last piece of business, financing the repairs to the bridge by the mill. Everyone had agreed that the bridge needed to be widened to allow carts to pass; however, the estimates of the improvements made the cost of the repairs staggering. What's more, no one wanted to raise the town rate to pay for it. Too late to discuss it, the council members decided they'd postpone the topic until the next meeting. Pearce moved to close the meeting, all agreed, and John Sherman pounded the gavel to adjourn.

Though no one commented on the money assessed for the bridge, William was sure others shared his unease. He felt the cost would raise the taxes too high, and the business took thought.

He left the house, following John Coolidge into the yard. The man was stout, with a full dark beard below a round face with large eyes. Sweat beaded on his forehead and stained the back of his shirt. "John," William said, "I have your bricks."

He signaled to the groom. The indentured boy no longer limped. William noted, he'd found his other shoe. He quickly led their mounts.

John steadied his horse. "Good. I have two bales of wool ready for spinning. You'll be needing' it now?"

"Susanna says she'll take all you have. I don't know how she does it, even with her helpers, but she'll spin the lot."

"I'll bring them today," John said. "I'm headed to the mill to pick up some corn now. Say, I wonder if you've heard more on Reverend Phillips' boy and the girl in Groton."

"I don't know anything."

"I thought you might. John is the one who reported the crime."

"John? My son?"

"Yes. My wife heard it from Reverend Sherman's wife. A rumor about the Phillips boy and a Mary Daniels. John said a man he worked with in Groton said he'd seen Phillips molesting Mary … well, 'uncivil behavior,' whatever that means."

William's face fell, and he shook his head. "Is the girl expecting?"

"I don't know the details."

"I haven't talked to John since he's been working in Groton. Not that he'd say anything anyway."

John Coolidge nodded sympathetically. He knew William's oldest son had turned away from the church and what it meant to him; the estrangement had saddened his friend.

"Well, I heard that word got to Boston, and the magistrates will try Phillips in court. Hard case for a minister's boy, well, not a boy now. Just thought you might know if John has to testify."

"I don't know when John's coming back, but when he does, I'll find out what I can. Corporal Bond is always up on what's going on in Boston. Maybe I'll talk to him."

"Told you he'd be good to know. Glad you took my advice?"

William grunted a reluctant 'yes.'

"So, you have the serge for me? Goody Coolidge won't take no other but yours. She says it's the best in all New England." John Coolidge mounted his pony with surprising agility for his build.

"I do, but it's not the best," William said. "You've seen my son's broadcloth! Will junior has a gift. See you later." He slapped Coolidge's horse on the rump, and the man rode off toward the mill.

Chapter Three

A LIFE WEAVING

Watertown, Same Day 1666

William mounted Old Gray and followed the cleared roads the two miles up the steep incline of Hill Street, down a shallow valley, and then up to his house on the road to Fresh Pond. When he'd settled the horse, he entered his workroom. The loom occupied nearly all the space floor to ceiling, and the raw materials that he would use to produce the wool serge he was known for lined the walls.

Twenty-six years ago, when he'd arrived with the clothes on his back, two spinning wheels, his loom, and the little currency that was left of his inheritance after buying passage, William began his trade. He'd worked from the barn of a neighbor until he was able to raise a roof for his wife and child and build a small workroom off the back of that first house. Ironically, he'd succeeded because of the British tariffs on the colonists scrabbling to build their villages on the rocky Massachusetts shores. Few could afford imported textiles; the colonists decided to weave their own. He was grateful to the Watertown powers, weavers from East Anglia, who enticed him with land. Elder Brown had explained: "We need weavers like you to make our own textiles now. We can promise you smuggled sheep and flaxseeds." Indeed, William found that flax seeds were so valuable, they replaced Indian trade beads as the new currency in Massachusetts.

Another crisis arose four years later: to build their trade, the colonists needed more weavers, but new immigrants from England had trickled to nothing after England's civil war began. William took on apprentices to meet Boston's new laws; now teaching youngsters to weave, he collected fees from his apprentices as well as his trade.

Seven years more, when he'd begun his second generation of young weavers, William could no longer buy local yarns. The many new weavers caused a shortage because it took four people spinning full-time to supply enough yarn to employ one man. With this new colonial need to import raw materials, England again took advantage. After the commonwealth cause had beheaded King Charles, the new governors took on punishing ways. William was shocked when the Navigation Act of 1651 restricted all colonial trade to the British ships and navigators, and the British raised the prices on imported spun yarn. William had to spend his teaching wages on raw materials imported from England.

The ingenious colonists retaliated with new orders, seeking to replace the English trade with homespun wool and linen yarns. William voted for the law that provided the four spinners for each weaver. In the Massachusetts Bay colony, it was compulsory—local selectmen assessed each household for able bodies who could spin, then ranked them. A full-spinster household must spin three pounds of cotton, wool, or flax every week for thirty weeks. Woe be to the quarter-spinster, half-spinster, or full-spinster household—for that's how the selectmen named them— that did not meet its monthly quota; the council fined each household twelve shillings for every pound short it might be.

In this way, William found he could work at full production with no shortage of orders. In the next nine years, he'd been able to increase his land holdings, buying out his neighbors, Goodmen Clough and Sanderson, nor did he stop at enlarging his farm by more than sixty acres. He bought another farm at Stonybrook in nearby Waltham. By now, besides weaving, he and his sons farmed and made bricks from clay pits he'd gained from his land purchases.

His son Will worked with his apprentice Jacob, a thin youth of ten, who'd become a live-in apprentice when he was only eight. Will, already taller than his father, guided Jacob's hand over the heddle as they warped the thread on the huge loom. William was happy to see they'd made progress on this most demanding of tasks for the weaver. His students must avoid errors at this stage of weaving; the complexity needed focus.

"Goodman Coolidge will be here this afternoon to drop off two bales. He'll be needing four yards of the new serge. Jacob, you take care of that."

"Yes master," Jacob said and disappeared.

"Father, we're close to finishing. Could you look?"

"Glad to."

Will left the loom's bench to make room for his father, and William sat to examine the set up. "Will, Jacob missed this heddle." William pointed to the row of metal eyes that separated the warped threads—the ones running the length of the weaving. Jacob had missed threading yarn from the feeding spool through one of them.

"I know, but I thought with yarn this fine it wouldn't show."

"Son, show? A fault in a weave weakens the cloth." The error was serious because the foot pedals controlled the rise and fall of the warped yarn through which they wove the shuttle; the missing thread would create a fault from end to end. "You'll need to show him how to fix it."

"Yes, father. He'll need to cut here and reattach to string the heddle."

"Good. Not much time lost! Knotting! How'll he make it strong?"

"Double knot?"

"You don't know?

Will sighed. His father was so exacting. "Double knot," he barked out.

"If you don't know, ask! Never let pride block your chance to gain knowledge. If you know, own it!"

Will raised his head in attention: "Yes, Father."

William reached for the wool yarn and handed it to Will, who would show Jacob how to mend the mistake.

Jacob reappeared with shears, rope, and a measuring stick. He arranged a cloth across the long boards that flanked the wall on the left of the loom. The serge bolt was light, and Jacob lifted it to the table easily to measure the cloth for Goodman Coolidge and tied the bundle neatly.

"Master Sherborn, anything else?"

"Come here." William stood and motioned he should sit down. "You need to correct this problem."

William moved Jacob to the seat and pulled Will behind him. "Continue."

William left the boys to finish their warping and went to the yard to sort out the bricks he and Will had carted from the clay pits yesterday. The clay pit was so close to his titled property, the town called it 'Sherborn's clay pit' and granted him the right to make bricks and sell them, more income for his growing family. When he finished, he went to the house to see about his lunch.

Susanna worked in the great room, hampered by her large belly. She was in her eighth month. She greeted him cheerfully, but bent slightly, massaging a spot on her belly. He knew she was getting impatient now; it had been so with all her pregnancies. He must take care to smooth over any friction.

"There's ale in the pitcher," she said. "Bread and cheese? I can warm it."

"No need," he replied. "Too hot."

He sat to pour a tankard of ale and sliced the thick loaf and a hunk of yellow cheese. As he chewed, he could hear a ruckus at the back door: the hens that pecked for grains scattered each morning there were clearly disturbed. *Gawk, gawk, gawk*, they sounded in chorus, flapping their wings in short flights. Joanna appeared in the back door trailed by the youngest Sherborns. "Father," the girl nodded respectfully. Her younger sisters, Rebecca and Abigail, pulled the giggling four-year-old Benjamin between them by his hands.

"Abigail, leave those hens alone." William knew that his youngest daughter, who was charged with all matters to do with the chickens, took out her resentment on them. For the life of him, he couldn't understand why feeding them, gathering their eggs, and making sure they were secured in the coop each night, should engender such disdain. Yet, more than once he'd found her chasing them for no reason, calling them 'stupid.'

"They were in the path," Abigail answered. "making a mess. I just moved them." She grinned at her sister Rebecca when he wasn't looking. The two were close enough in age to form a colluding bond.

"No back-talk young lady."

"Yes father."

William turned to Joanna. "Hungry?"

Joanna nodded to him and held up the bunch of carrots she'd brought, the feathery tops cascading like a bouquet. "Mother, here's your carrots."

Susanna, pleased, pulled one out, brushed off the dirt, broke it in two, and handed the end to Benjamin. He gnawed on it happily, barely nibbling enough to feed a mouse.

Joanna sat next to her father, slicing the bread and slathering the piece with butter; she cut it in two and handed pieces to her sisters. Then she cut one for herself, adding a thin slice of cheese. The younger children stood at the table, silent for once with their mouths full.

"Abigail," William said, "go get your brother and Jacob. They're in the shop."

When the children had finished, they ran back to the yard.

"What happened at council?" Susanna asked. "Did Master Trimball talk about the land grants?"

"He did. He's found three-hundred acres of common land that wasn't assessed right."

"Humph. Did John Sherman have any punishing words?"

"Now, don't be criticizing our Representative."

"Banish the thought. "She flashed a lopsided grin; she instinctively disliked the man. Susanna's dislike was instinctive, perhaps because she sensed his insensibility.

William winced when he couldn't arrest the day's memory of John Sherman's and Corporal Bond's treatment of Samuel Benjamin. *The road shouldn't have counted as his acreage. And I volunteered to step into Sherman's place*, he thought. *I thought him better than that.* He changed the subject quickly. "The mill bridge needs replacing. They are thinking that they will raise the town rate to pay for it."

"How much?" she asked.

"Estimate is high. No one would talk about it. It's unthinkable."

"When will they decide?"

"I suspect the next council meeting," he replied.

William brushed the crumbs from the table top. "I don't want to upset you, but you need to know. John Coolidge heard that the Reverend Phillip's boy is being tried in Boston. Our John reported he'd harassed a Groton girl to the pastor in Groton. Word passed on to Reverend Sherman."

"John! Doesn't sound like something he'd do. I mean, he doesn't go to church here, so why would he report bad behavior to the minister in Groton?

"I share your surprise, especially that his accusation traveled to Boston."

"I'm assuming Reverend Sherman heard it from his daughter. She's married to Reverend Willard in Groton."

"Maybe Richard Bond has heard something in Boston; I'll be working with him now. I'll check, but I want to hear it from John's mouth when he comes home."

He greeted Will and Jacob, who came for their lunch. They sat down on the table bench and cut bread and cheese Will gnawed on the tough crusts with relish. "Hear what?"

William usually answered Will's questions; the boy had always had more questions than his brothers and sisters. William believed it was a sign of intelligence, though Philip was the scholar. He didn't answer this time because he felt it was wrong to talk about Will's brother behind his back.

"Nothing you should hear," he replied.

Will shrugged, though he could hardly contain his curiosity; he was aware his father disapproved of his older brother. "We'll finish the weave tonight," he said.

"Good son. You can start a broadcloth in the morning."

Chapter Four

THE PROPHETS

Watertown, August 1666

A Kelly-green hedge bounded the field in England where William Sherborn ran, and he headed toward the thatched roof that showed above it. He could smell the green plants that wrapped his ankles, bleeding cool beneath his bare pounding feet; he urgently needed to reach the cottage. Someone had left tools scattered in the yard.

The closer he came to the cottage, the more ground the menacing force lost. Suddenly, he was safely inside a room with a great loom; large-paned windows flooded it with enough light to see his father, John Sherborn, at his loom, his face venerably lined with age. He watched him lean forward to run the shuttle through the warped threads; saw him pull the reed, tamping the weave. Then he saw the patch of uneven woof that spoiled the yard of cloth. "Father," he said, "stop. We need to go back; you've ruined the cloth. See here, the woof?"

His father paid no attention but continued with machinelike precision; he stepped on the food peddle to reverse the heddles and passed the yarn shuttle through the new tunnel that opened. Once he'd drawn the filling yarn through the warped yarn, he reached forward and pulled the reed to tamp down the weave. The dream sped forward, and now William sat at the loom, frustrated by having to undo his father's mistake, feeling as he had the year before his father's death.

He didn't linger on this feeling for long though. In his dream, a child again, he stepped out of the high box pew at St. Mary Magdalene's church in neighboring Taunton after the Sunday service. He was dimly aware of the painted ceiling with the gold gilded angels peering down on them from the vaulted ceiling. Then he heard the twelve bells of the carillon pealing, his spirit soared, and he ran through the open doors, down the church steps. His mother ran after him, calling in anger. He felt happier than he'd ever felt before.

William started up from his sleep, woke with an overwhelming longing to go back to his dream, to again see his home in Somerset. He rolled over, burrowing his head into his arms. *I don't want to wake*, he thought. He tried to go back to sleep but couldn't; he could hear Susanna in the next room building up the kitchen fire for porridge. Though he went to bed soon after dark fell, he could never sleep through until dawn. He rolled to his side, swung his feet to the wood floor, and quickly dressed. He'd dreamed of Somerset before, but never had woken with such longing.

"Good morning," Susanna said when he'd joined her in the great room.

"Morning," he mumbled. He longed to tell Susanna of his dream but had failed before. Susanna didn't understand. Born in the colonies, she had never seen England or crossed the ocean. He'd never complain because he'd been such a novice when he'd arrived. His wife was as much his guide and adviser as his companion. Colonial ways were so different from those in his home, England.

"We need wood," she said.

William grunted and headed to the back lean-to, reminiscing as he pulled logs off the stack by the wall, splitting them expertly, rhythmically, on the chopping block. He felt the dream tapped into a tight ball of unease lodged in his chest. His father's death had precipitated his emigration. *I wouldn't have left, otherwise*, he thought. William's father had willed his property to his oldest boy, as was usual, and when his brother John had moved his family into the homestead, William had been barely a man, just eighteen. His mother had no problem with the adjustment, but William felt alienated.

The conflicts dividing the two Protestants in England—the Anglicans and the Puritans—had deepened his unease; he felt it could reach the pitch of a civil war. At eighteen, filled with the Puritans' religious zeal, William was a perfect candidate for colonial recruiters. When he saw the circular nailed to a tree—an advertisement for the Massachusetts Bay Colony that promised land to those who had certain skills—he knew he wanted to emigrate. He'd leave the brewing civil war in England and a town where he'd become an outsider, for a place where he belonged and was needed. He'd eagerly embraced the opportunity to join his brethren in this great experiment, in this community that would live by God's laws and needed him and his weaving. Every way the wind blew carried him across the ocean.

His mother (now a widow with two grown daughters and two sons) grieved his decision. Conversely, his brother John encouraged him to go. While both brothers were in the cloth business, John was a merchant, not a weaver, and gladly settled William's bequest: some cash, the loom, and two spinning wheels. He understood William's desire for security and blessed his passage. William had sailed with his settlement, just enough for his fare and provisioning his first year.

She never forgave me for leaving, he thought, chips from the splintered wood flying as he drove the wedge into a log. He'd never forget the sound of his mother sobbing, her last embrace. He gathered the kindling in his arms and toted it to the hearth where Susanna worked.

"I'll ask Jacob to renew the stack." He didn't bother to sit down but accepted the bowl of porridge Susanna held out for him and spooned it down as he stood. "Tell Will I'll come later. I need to check the sow."

"I'll tell him." Susanna turned and gestured toward the spinning wheels. "I'll be finishing the new bale today, with Jo's help."

William nodded, lifted the bail of the table-scrap pail, and strode from the house. Keeping pigs was not easy; he couldn't build a pen secure enough to contain them. Pigs had the intelligence of Devils, he often thought.

Fence them in, and they'd root under the fences; roaming freely, they could devastate a garden in an hour. It was no problem for Watertown folks because they fenced their gardens. But Indian neighbors complained of the settler's cows and pigs roaming freely through their unfenced plantations. Everyone thought pigs were dirty, but they were the cleanest barnyard animal, another sign of superior intelligence. They never soiled their own beds but shat in one corner of their pen. They bathed, too, rolling in dust; the greasy caked soil would flake from their now clean skin.

The grunting began as soon as the sows and baby pigs saw him, and they were at the feed trough before he emptied the pail. He inspected the peg and tethers that attached to their nose rings. The tethers limited their range within the pen; they could not damage the fences that way. His year as the council's hog greave had taught him well. He would never pay a fine for wandering pigs or cows. He checked the swelling body of the sow that was due to deliver soon.

The dream again came to mind and its aftermath: his aching desire to return to England. *It isn't as if I'd be the first*, he thought. When the civil war had ended, and Cromwell took up the protectorate, scores of his neighbors had braved the anger of the congregation, sold their homesteads, and embarked for England. He'd wanted to follow them, but Reverend Sherman had reminded him of his covenant and opportunities to buy land arose as more attractive. Then, six years ago, the Puritans' good fortune had reversed. Cromwell died, and the English restored the monarchy. The new king, Charles II, wanted to rein in their independent colony; he had other plans for his British subjects occupying a new continent. Still, he mused, *maybe brother John needs me. If there's another Indian uprising? I'd save them from that!*

William crossed the yard and left the scrap pail by the door before he entered the workshop where Will and Jacob bent over their tasks. Fortunately, he was swept up in the matters before him, and the dream receded until he said his prayers that night. He decided that he needed spiritual guidance deciphering this dream; it would do no good to brood on it. What's more, returning to England could not be his decision alone. Reverend Sherman would bring it to the Watertown parish, and those party to his covenant would need to agree.

That Saturday, he saddled the horse and climbed the hill that led to Reverend Sherman's house at the edge of the meetinghouse common. A heavy summer rain soaked him and turned Hill Street into a temporary mudslide, and even Old Gray struggled to keep his footing. He counted the minutes between thunderclaps; the lightning was not in striking distance. His best friend, a boy in Stogumber, had lost his life crossing an open field in a storm, so William respected the elements.

William had a warm acquaintance with the minister because, like himself, Reverend Sherman did not hale from East Anglia but from Essex, which like London's Middlesex, was settled by Viking Saxons. He too was a newcomer to Watertown, though he would never be an outsider like William because he was councilman John Sherman's cousin, related through their mothers. His congregation knew him to be an astute scholar and scientist (he'd graduated from Oxford University), and they trusted his vision and authority.

The maid showed him into the reverend's study. The tall man pored over the manuscript for his Sunday sermon at his high desk, pen and ink in hand, spectacles perched on the end of his nose, which made his hairline recede even farther. William could hear the voices of children and a woman sharply reprimanding them. While Puritans tried to repress their children's natural excess, they were rarely successful. Here, God had blessed the reverend with more children than any man in Watertown, and William wondered how his wife managed. William stood in the doorway, holding a dripping hat in his hand.

"I hope I am not intruding."

The Reverend rubbed the ink from his forefinger with a cloth kept on the desk for that purpose, set his spectacles on the manuscript, and strode to the door to greet his guest. "Not at all. I'm revising my sermon, a task I dislike so much that I value any interruption." He smiled and took William's extended hand in both of his own. "And you, William, are hardly an interruption in any case. Please, sit down. Let's talk."

With this warm greeting, William at once felt at home. "I don't want to waste your time, but I need your advice." He sat on the settee, and the Reverend, now serious, settled on the facing bench.

"Is it your family?" he began. John Sherman had the dubious position of gate keeper for men's souls in the community. The church body had elected him and paid him as God's emissary and guide to spiritual and moral integrity. He was not a mere teacher, as his salary made most obvious, for Watertown paid him four times as much as the schoolmaster. He oversaw a flock who'd elected to cross an ocean to establish a Godly community in a wilderness, though their Moses was the now deceased Reverend Philips.

"No, not directly. It's a dream I can't get out of my mind. The Bible tells me that dreams are the spirit's wisdom, not human wisdom. But I fear I'm not spiritual enough to decide its meaning."

"Ah, you speak of Corinthians. Yes, many Bible passages tell of dreams. We take our lessons from the likes of David and Daniel. But while the scriptures tell us that dreams and visions have a place in our spiritual lives, we cannot take them so seriously that they interfere with more practical matters. Otherwise, we should all be praying in the desert and do nothing."

"It was so clear. I dreamed of my boyhood in Somerset, England. I saw my father and mother and woke with such an intense longing to go home that I am ready to take my family on the next packet to England."

"You won't be the first to find 'home' means your past and not your future. Immigrating from England to this wilderness was hard, but surely, you see your success here." His only defense to talk of returning to England, which if allowed unchecked would tear the fabric of their precipitous settlement, was to remind them of God's Providence. And drill deeper to find more subtle counterarguments. "What were you doing in the dream?"

"I was running from something chasing me. I ran to a cottage. Empty it was. Then, I saw my father, weaving. He'd made a mistake in the cloth but wouldn't stop. I had to correct his work."

The Reverend folded his arms and tilted his head inquisitively. He wondered what motives were driving William. Though it was true Watertown had lost one in six settlers over the years, they'd had reasons: collapsing finances or health. *Was it William's livelihood?*

"So, it's a dream related to your work?"

"A warning. Am I making a mistake in my weaving practice? Did I make a mistake coming to the colonies?"

Reverend Sherman couldn't help but note the leap from occupation to emigration. William was rationalizing. Many who'd come for the parish's blessings had returned without letters of dissolution because they were clearly making the wrong decision. To break one's covenant with God and the congregation for greater financial gain was simply not acceptable.

He tried another tack to sound him out. "You've heard the news from England this year?"

"Do you mean the plague? Yes, of course. I've heard the accounts. Terrible! You've told us that a hundred thousand died. But no danger now, and I want to know what family survived."

"God led us to the Massachusetts Bay after thousands of Indians died of smallpox. Ironic, isn't it? Now you want to fill the places left by those who suffered the Black Death in England?"

William shifted uncomfortably in his seat. "I have money and can buy land there," he confessed, but added "I buy land here, but every acre compounds the work. I have to hack life out of this infernal wilderness."

The reverend drilled him for more information. "Is there more?"

"Yes. I was with my family at the Anglican church in Taunton, where we visited relatives. I was seven. They were Anglicans then, before they joined us in Stogumber, and took the Puritan faith after Anthony Stroke came to Stogumber to speak. In my dream, we were leaving the church and the bells pealed. Oh, the bells! You wouldn't believe the bells! Twelve in the tower, a carillon. Each bell struck the heart. I'd forgotten how beautiful. In my dream, I was soaring, running down the aisle. I was happy even as my angry mother chased me down the steps. Have I made a mistake? Am I losing my faith?"

"I see now. You fear backsliding. In some ways, leaving our Puritan community to go back to England is like abandoning your faith in our project, is it not?"

"I didn't see it that way. Yes, if my father and mother were Anglicans. But they were staunch Puritans."

"Ah yes, your angry mother, chasing you?"

"Hmmm." William knotted his forehead.

"Would your mother have occasion for anger if you did return to Somerset?"

"My mother passed and my father, too, but I want my children to see our England—the village life, the shops and markets, what being English means. They cannot imagine it."

"Isn't Susanna due for another child soon?" the Reverend said, asking questions the judging parish would ask.

"Yes, she is soon to deliver, next month."

"Our practical lives do enter our dreams, such as the working dream where you are at the loom. Mothers and motherhood enter this dream as well."

"You are saying?"

"You will split up your family if you return, and I must put this to the congregation. Mary will not bring her husband to England. I'm sure of that. Your Daughter Suzanne is in Groton now?"

"Yes, I would have to leave Suzanne, Mary, and John. Probably Philip, too. He's serving an apprenticeship. But

I still have the five youngsters and the new baby. It would form them as proper Englishmen. They lose our ways here."

"I'm saying that your dream might be telling you that you cannot return to Somerset while your wife is due, or even afterward. You cannot ignore these responsibilities and expect God's grace."

"You're saying I should stay until my child is born?"

"I hate the thought of what the congregation will make of your defection."

"But my faith?"

"Returning to England will break the covenant that you have set with God here, and you are longing to go but forgetting the distance that separates you. Do you remember your voyage here? Are you willing to face those dangers, the months of discomfort? Would you subject your wife and children to this voyage, cross the ocean again?"

William suddenly appreciated the pastor's reasoning as he remembered his voyage to the colonies: the near-starvation rationing, the seasickness, the beginning of scurvy. A young man he'd been, not yet twenty, and adventurous. The voyage was hard then, but now, at his advancing age? He was forty-four. What is more, Susanna had never even been on a boat let alone the open sea.

"I see what you mean. I'd endanger my family. Anything could happen. And …" He paused and rubbed the back of his neck where his soaked collar began to itch. "Susanna and I are old enough to experience the voyage as a great hardship."

"I hope that helps you decide."

"Yes, thank you for your help."

William left the ministers house and stepped into a fresh world, still dripping from the morning rain but steaming in the sunlight. Old Gray waggled his head, huffing in greeting.

Chapter Five

DISTANT DRUMS

Watertown, September 1666

William and the men gathered at John Sherman's house for the September meeting stood in a circle around two citizens as they debated hotly. Young James Pearce, sandy blond hair curling to his shoulders, towered above his opponent, the elder Thomas Trimble, a thin man bent with age. The men were arguing about raising funds to replace the bridge near the mill, and the problem had become complex when James Pearce suggested funding the construction without raising taxes. Because Thomas Trimble, the surveyor, had corrected land grants and found another three-hundred acres of common land, James Pearce maintained that Watertown should sell the land to raise money for the bridge. He reasoned those seeking more land would benefit as well as the townsmen paying taxes.

Any reconsideration of land grant borders was bound to bring dispute. William knew the resentment firsthand as the township had granted him three acres on a hillside as well as his one-acre homestead. Too young to know better, he'd accepted the grant and didn't think about paying taxes to both the township and colony for unusable acres. It was land! Colonists who knew better bargained with the town's surveyor. They argued the surveyors should not consider swamps, marshes, and uplands as acreage because they objected to paying wealth rates for unusable land. Thus, a man granted ten acres might have title to fifteen, counting the swamp and slope lying within his boundaries; grant borders were subjective. Re-assessing the borders, the surveyor could reclaim these uncounted acres for the township commons, and with land grant borders shifting, James Pearce saw an opportunity to appease the titled colonists. Let them buy their land back. What's more, he second-guessed Trimble's survey; he bet it was as subjective as the original land grants had been. He figured much more common land was available than Trimble reported, and the township, rife with wetland and steep hills, owned a revenue gold mine.

"We don't need more common land," Pearce argued. "Private ownership creates prosperity." He and several others believed that Watertown needed to move away from the traditional English system that dated back to early Christianity. "Isn't it the possibility of owning land that brought us to Massachusetts?"

The older Thomas Trimble did not agree; he believed the admittedly medieval practice of allowing public access to shared pastures and meadowlands promoted prosperity for everyone. Commons served as a safety net that smoothed out the ups and downs of everyone's fortunes. In fact, the surveyor thought that only keeping this balance would allow the entire community to thrive, rich and poor alike. They'd fought the battle in their homeland, England, and it continued in Watertown.

"The land was *given* to new arrivals. How can we put a price on it?" Trimble argued.

To Pearce's surprise, prior holders of the newly-freed land—many of them progressives like himself—rejected his proposal. They weren't happy about buying land they'd previously been titled to. What's more, these landowners decided they wouldn't be paying for land; they'd be unfairly assessed to pay for the bridge.

William liked Pearce's idea. *I'd buy land, bridge or not,* he thought. *There's no land to be had in Watertown.* His last land purchase, Stoney Brook farm, was miles away, in the next township. However, he was silent to honor his connections to the Brown family; the original surveyor was a member of the powerful Brown family. He felt he owed his daughter Mary's new family loyalty.

Pearce wasn't going to give up his proposal, not when it meant money from his own pocket. "No one will miss the new commons. We should sell the land."

"I say it's shortsighted, at best." Tom Hannigan thrust one shoulder into the ring surrounding the two men. "You'd be robbing our children; we're a town that's growing fast. It's their land, not ours."

The man behind him raised on his toes, seeming to tip into the ring. "I agree with Pearce. And we wouldn't have to police collecting taxes, either. The sale'd be quick."

Corporal Bond spoke as one who'd benefit. "Yes. We all want bordering land." William couldn't help nodding.

"Wait, wait." The surveyor signaled 'halt' with his hands. "There's not enough revenue from land even if we sold every acre! We'd still need to raise the rate."

William Perry butted in with: "No more taxes! The rate's already been raised to pay for the ammunition we need."

Jonathan Fox sidled closer to dark-bearded Perry as though to face him on an issue they had argued before. "The bridge is a need. Ammunition is not." Fox, an older, square-jawed, muscular man, who had campaigned to end conscripting sixteen-year-old men in their colony, hadn't ended his objections to the military-minded.

Fox's son, who was eligible at sixteen for the militia, supported his father. "Right. Who says you need guns and ammunition to correct a drunk Indian?"

"…or a thief?" Richard Norcross chimed from the back. Last year, George Briscoe's servant, John Nunnunipe, had stolen seventeen Greek and Latin books from his schoolhouse, and though the bailiff had recovered them, an important book of poetry and a Bible were still missing.

William marveled at how fast the discussion had changed from the bridge to defenses. When he'd first come to Watertown, every man over sixteen counted as local militia, and William had drilled with the rest several times a year on the Meeting House Common. Now, conscription had ended, though a boy of ten could enlist. Nevertheless, any man over eighteen was expected to keep his guns ready in an emergency, when conscription would again be necessary. *Ammunition is a need,* William thought.

Perry, a vigorous young, tall man, who townspeople said had ears for news in every joint—he frequented Captain Richard Beer's ordinary—buttressed his first argument. "You don't think that we need better defense? We've all heard the suspicions about Alexander's death."

Fox interrupted. "You mean Sachem Wamsutta?"

"Right," Perry replied. "His brother King Philip—that's Sachem Metacom to you—thinks they poisoned Alexander, treated him like a traitor for selling land to the Dutch. His braves think so, too."

Fox ignored Perry's protest. "The Plymouth treaty didn't specify who he could sell land to. Sachem Wamsutta wasn't breaking any law. Why would Governor Prence punish him? Rumors!"

"Not Prence. He's always been fair…" William Perry replied.

Tom Hannigan broke in loudly, "You call sentencing white men who kill an Indian *fair*? Indian vermin!"

Perry raised his voice to overcome interrupting Hannigan. "It was his *deputy*, Josiah Winslow. He can't steal enough Indian land."

"The white men were guilty; seemed fair to me," Richard Norcross challenged Hannigan.

Hannigan avoided his challenger and joined the mainstream: "Prence ordered his deputy to bring Wamsutta in. Wager that."

William Perry sputtered, "You're wrong, but that's in the past, anyway. Metacom signed a *new* treaty; Boston will arbitrate any disputes between Metacom and Plymouth. But Metacom is two-faced. He's playing along with Plymouth but gathering men."

Jonathan Fox reasoned with him. "You're peddling fear. What for? Chief Massasoit was our friend for thirty years, an ally. His sons are, too."

Richard Norcross turned to William Perry. "William, you'd not be suspecting King Philip if his father was still alive. But there's the rub."

"Right," said Corporal Bond, who'd stayed out of the argument despite his insider status in Boston. "He's dead. But we should take advice from Plymouth! In April, Prence and Winslow decided the Dutch are such a threat that they've asked towns to maintain watches. Everyone must keep arms ready and plan evacuations for women and children. Plymouth knows the Dutch will recruit Indians, too."

"Plymouth is south, on the front. Not likely we'll have battles here," Fox argued.

"We can't ignore good defenses," Bond insisted. "We also contribute the most soldiers to the New England alliance if there's trouble. And don't forget, it's the law for every man in Massachusetts Bay. You own a gun; you load it; it's ready to shoot. The law!"

John Sherman pounded the gavel sharply three times. "Gentlemen! We are losing sight of our purpose. Order!"

"So, we don't need to raise the rate. We've got the land," said James Pearce.

Thomas Trimble shouted at his opponent, "I have surveyed the land, and I'm telling you there are only about three-hundred acres not accounted for."

"There are more than one-thousand acres, I'll wager." James Pearce was of the mind that Trimble should have retired many years ago; he was sure that Trimble had surveyed and replotted land judiciously, sparing his cronies.

"You can take this up with Boston." Thomas Trimble cleared a path from the circle.

"You can bet that I will," James Pearce threatened.

"Gentlemen! Take your seats!" John Sherman again slammed the gavel on the table.

As William turned to the back of the room to take his seat again, he caught sight of Will Junior, standing in the doorway. Will gestured, his hands describing the arc of a big belly in the air above his own; he mouthed, 'Now.'

Richard Norcross, having noted Will Junior, grabbed William's arm as he passed by. "Tell Susanna that we are sending her our prayers. God be with you." He had taught eight of the Sherborn children as well as most of the children in Watertown of school-age for the past twenty-six years, and Susanna was his friend and staunchest supporter.

William joined Will and said, "You need to go get Mary now."

"No need. Mary came this morning; she knew to come! And she had me fetch Aunt Joanna."

William suppressed an "ah hah" that would reveal his surprise at Mary's efficiency. He mimicked Will's nonchalant acceptance that, of course, Mary would know.

William would never call Will Junior his favorite because he lost all sense that Will was a different person; Will was not only his namesake, but also close in temperament. Will's weaving, even at a young age, surpassed his own. With pride—though he fought it because that was the Devil's way—he saw Will channeling his Flemish forbearer's famed art. As a boy, William's Somerset relations told him a family myth of an ancestor who'd come to England three hundred years before, when King Edward III passed laws forbidding the export of wool and import of cloth. The king had imported the unwelcome Flemish weavers, who fled the Hundred Year War, to build the English cloth trade. William ignored his son's other talents: breaking horses and figuring, which Will had inherited from his mother.

While William and his son led their horses into the yard, Will couldn't help being curious about the melee he'd seen at the meeting because his father's face was still creased with concern. "What was that about?"

"Repairing the bridge at the mill." William checked the saddle cinch, patting Old Gray on the withers as he straightened the gear. "James Pearce wants to avoid any town tax. He wants to pay for the repairs by selling off common land."

"You mean sell all the grazing land, the meadows?" Will sounded alarmed. He weighed the reins in his hands as he paused in his preparations.

"Just the extra three-hundred acres Trimble found when he surveyed again."

"That's different." Will tugged at a strap hindering his stirrup and steadied the horse. "Whoa, boy."

"But old Trimble won't hear of it. He's for saving the commons for Watertown. 'It's for our kids,' he says. About ten acres of it adjoins our east border."

"What we bought from Goodman Clough? Can we buy it?"

"That's the idea." He put his foot in the stirrup and swung his leg over the saddle. Will followed his example, and the two headed toward Cambridge Road at a walk.

"Watertown owns it now? It's open grazing land?"

"Right."

"But if Watertown sells the land, uses the money to build the bridge, the buyers are paying for the bridge!"

"Will, sometimes I think you take after your mother more than me! You've got it!"

"Who do *you* think's right?"

"I can't take sides in this because Trimble's new survey finds some irregularities in the first survey. Don't forget that your sister's father-in-law was the surveyor who's at question here."

"So? I don't get it."

"Some think he was paid off for those 'mistakes.' Of course, Trimble's already getting some complaints on his corrections."

"You think he was taking bribes?"

"It's not for me to say. I'm no judge in the matter."

"So, what'll they do?"

"James Pearce is going to Boston. He's going to ask the court to order another survey from an independent surveyor. He's sure we can claim more land for Watertown."

"I guess there's always them that want to point at corruption."

"That's right son."

"So, we stay out of it?"

"For now," William concluded. "Let's go."

He urged his horse to a full gallop as they reached Cambridge Road and made their way home.

Chapter Six

THE LAST CHILD

Watertown, Same Day, September 1666

William and his son entered the shop to find that Jacob was sweeping up lint. He set the straw broom next to the pile and greeted them.

"Good, Jacob." William said. "Will, I want you to finish what you can on the loom. Jacob, we will need more yarn. Start spinning, and I'll join you later."

William left to make his way to the great room, where it was oddly quiet except for intermittent talk and moans issuing from the birthing room. The door was open, but Mary blocked his view. He accepted that men were not welcome in a birthing room and respected his wife's privacy. He leaned over the hearth, adding wood to the fire there.

Not long after he'd arrived, their neighbors Martha and Biddy arrived.

William greeted them, taking their baskets and motioning to the hooks where they could hang their shawls. "Goody Godfrey ... Goody Payne. You are just in time," he said, nodding politely to each.

"God willing," Biddy said, removing her shawl. Always practical, she hung it neatly, and noted the large pot sitting on the hearth still half-full of the rabbit stew served at lunch. "I brought some bread and cheese for later."

"And venison stew," Martha added. "You'll be wanting dinner. Where are the girls?"

"Jo took the children to the Coolidges' for the night. Will's seeing to the chores." William took the basket from her, removing the wraps to set the bowl to warm near hot coals on the hearth.

When Mary heard them, she quickly enlisted their help and closed the door. It was too quiet then, and William made his way to his workshop to work with the boys. It would do no good to worry.

When he came back to the great room for a snack, Mary slipped through the door, looking devastated.

"What news?" he asked. "How is she?"

Mary shook her head, her face a mix of rage and anxiety. She could barely answer. "It's bad. The baby's breeched." Then she burst into tears. Mary deplored her emotional outburst, as it proved what the scriptures said of women. She didn't want to believe she was unreasoning and thus inferior to men, but she had to admit that in pregnancy, she was more emotional. Righteous anger all the way to grief, she was moved to tears. She choked out, "I wanted to help, but Joanna made me leave. I can help. I can learn. I know I'm not as good as sister, but I can learn, too."

William instantly recognized her grief. Mary's jealousy had reared. He knew that every life decision she made since her birth had been to compete with her sister, even her marriage to the wealthy Brown boy. He had a hunch that Mary's problem stemmed from Reverend Sherman's sermons, which cast suspicion on any knowledge that wasn't gained through the five senses. He was a man of science who published hundreds of tracts. To him, what wasn't fact, was the Devil's domain. His rebuke of natural, God-given second sight, his claims that only the Devil could grant such capacities, caused more harm than good. He had made Mary, for one, fear her own nature. The Sherborns were descendants of Celts, and the clairvoyant gift threaded the fabric of their ancestral memory. The British scorn of the Irish, also Celts, whom they considered barbarians, skipped over the small pocket of Somerset citizens. They had practiced their second sight free of censorship.

William took both of her hands in his own. "I know how worried you are. Joanna needs someone who's more reasoning than you right now."

"She wants Suzanne, not me."

"Dear, dear. Joanna's beyond talking about your sister; she asked for your help because she cannot help your mother without you. She worries that your mother's in danger because she's treated scarlet fever. She told me."

Mary's mind flashed back to the birth room, realizing that Joanna's instructions did mention it.

"If I had one dream for you, one wish, I would want you to understand that you are equal to your sister in every way. This jealousy eats at you, but I know you don't see it."

"I'm not jealous!"

"You are. Every reason you give has Suzanne's name on it. Just now, you said Joanna wanted Suzanne because you're not good enough. I'm right! When you get into an argument with your mother, you always think she's mad at you because you aren't Suzanne. Sit down. Let me tell you something."

Mary deferred to what her father was telling her because she knew her emotions might cloud her vision. Her father was rational, wise even.

He pushed her gently down to a bench at the table. "Your mother and I don't go to Suzanne when we want to find out what anyone in this family is thinking. We go to you. You have some inner knowledge, some second sense. You see into hearts; you see the future."

Mary stared at him intently. He had never spoken to her like this before; that was the Devil's way. He was mistaken. Reverend Sherman had made it clear that those who harbor unnatural visions see what the Devil offers. *Normal natural vision does not see into the future; God gives us eyes to see, ears to hear,* she thought. *I hate these visions.*

"Father, don't say so. That's blasphemy. I pray to God to dispel this evil!"

"The second sense is no sin!" he argued. "If you think that's blasphemy, you're no daughter of mine."

"What are you saying?" she said, horrified.

"Mary, I'm saying that God gave you second sight to save you. God gives you this cross to bear for his greater glory."

"Reverend Sherman says it's the Devil's work."

"He has never found that in the scriptures. It's a notion born of his own love of science. Mark you, I'm right: the scriptures do tell of seers and prophets."

"Father, I mustn't compare myself to these; pride is a grievous sin."

"Many seers felt as you do, humbled. You must read your Bible again. God has given you a second way of seeing. Do you deny it?"

Mary could not argue with him; in her heart, she wanted to believe he was right. He made sense. She would have a fight to keep her gift on a Godly track. She quieted, silent with this new thought.

"How long before you put that competitive, jealous Mary to pasture? Let her go. Let the Mary I know come out and live her beautiful, rich, and righteous life!"

Mary squirmed, uncomfortable with unaccustomed praise. "Stop."

"No, I won't stop until you give up this foolish jealousy of Suzanne. And your mother won't stop, either. We've spoken many times about it, and I must tell you the only resentment she holds against you is your jealousy, which she condemns. You break a commandment when you covet. Give it up. Your mother's your greatest ally. But you don't see it."

"Really?" she stammered, wiping her tears away.

"Try it. Just stop. Go back in that room and help your mother. Every time you want to compare yourself to Suzanne, stop. Remind God, 'I'm your daughter, Mary,' and be certain when you say it. Defeat the Devil."

"I could try."

"Good. Go back. Now, tell me, what is Joanna doing for her?"

"The baby is sideways, and Mother can't push it through."

"And Joanna, what does she say?"

"She's trying to move the baby with massage, but father, it's not working. If her water breaks, it will be impossible."

"We need a surgeon, then?"

"Yes, but Joanna said there're none available right now."

"I see." His shoulders slumped with the news. "Then we must pray."

Mary went back to the birthing room.

As he was a man, William had never entered the birthing room. He knew from the wails issuing from inside that his wife was in great pain, but he'd never witnessed a birth. He'd never realized the fetid interval that came between the last day of her clumsy pregnancy and the exhausted, pale woman who presented the wrinkled but clean infant. Just weeks ago, though, he and Corporal Bond were called to an emergency on their way back from a road inspection, and Goodman Adams had run out to stop them. His wife had just died in childbirth, and he asked them to help him move her. The midwife and neighbor led the men to the birthing room, where the stout woman lay. They had closed Goody Adams eyes, but she was lying, gray, face twisted, in her bloodied shift. Blood-soaked linens were crammed between her legs or thrown to the floor, and blood still dripped from the bed. William was overcome by the smell and the sight of her stillborn infant. The gray mass hastily crammed in her arms was splotched with the birth gore, still attached by the greasy umbilical cord twisted around his neck. These specters rose in his mind to sharpen his remorse. Once set in that direction, his memory wound down a path worn smooth by the time his tenth child was due. In their small community, many women had perished giving birth. No matter what adamant assurances his wife gave him—'you can be sure Joanna will let me suffer no such end'—William couldn't rest. Before Goody Adams, Reverend Sherman had announced the deaths of five in their parish. Among his fellow council men, two had been widowed in the past year.

He could not shake the feeling that he was responsible. The idea that God was about to punish his family for some lapse of his own sent him searching for the reasons. He mixed the conversation that he'd had with Reverend Sherman with the images in his dream, and then wrestled with the implications. The Reverend had been right; he couldn't break his sacred covenant with God.

Dear God, he prayed, his hands clasped in prayer, *forgive me and bring this child into the world. Deliver my wife from this trial.* He continued his prayers until the sun had set and the dark corners of the room grew larger, as though they fattened on the anxious secrets he whispered to his God. At some point, William put more wood on the fire and lit a lone candle to send a circle of warm light to defend him against the dark.

When he heard the cry of the new infant, William wiped tears of gratitude from his cheeks, but his apprehension was not relieved until Joanna opened the door and beckoned him. He had to see his living, breathing wife before he could admit the joy sent by the grace of God.

Later, when his son Philip had returned from Cambridge, where he served a seven-year apprenticeship to Dr. Daniel Stone, a Boston Physician of good repute, William began to relax. As Philip threw himself into the task of helping the women clean the borning room, William supported the efforts of neighbors Biddy and Martha, who prepared a late evening meal. At supper, William learned that while God had delivered his Susanna from this trial, He had more work in store. Mary told him that her sister, twelve-year-old Rebecca, had repeated a rumor that Joanna Morton, Susanna's midwife and best friend, was a witch. The rumor, Mary said, had already circulated through the schoolhouse; children repeated it. The more she described the details of Rebecca's genuine terror, the more he knew he needed to act. In his lifetime, the Boston magistrates had executed a midwife for witchcraft; Joanna was vulnerable to rumors. He must act to quash this lie immediately.

....

Chapter Seven

DEVIL, BEGONE!

Watertown, That Week, September 1666

When Susanna had rested enough, William sought his wife's advice on clearing Joanna Morton's name. Susanna sat in bed, holding the swaddled Samuel close; she'd dozed and nursed by turns these two days while Joanna took over managing the household and Mary attended to her mother's person. William sat on the bed, noting that Susanna's color had returned, and the slight puffiness caused by recumbence had erased lines in her face and a decade of hard living. Wisps of hair jutted from her white cap. She looked so vulnerable, like a little girl.

"The mere mention of Sam and Alice Stratton took me back to the first trial," William said. "Do you remember Goody Jones' hanging?"

"I do," she said. "And I fear for Joanna. I've said it before: our midwives are in jeopardy when they cannot restore their patients to health. We must do something."

"The pastor not only hanged an innocent midwife, he prosecuted the Strattons." Sam and Alice Stratton were his first customers and still bought his woolens, though less often as they were in their eighties now.

"I remember I was still nursing baby John."

"Where'd we live then?"

"Our first house. Remember living in the basement?"

"I do. We dug out the cellar, put up a fireplace, and added a roof and chimney. I didn't have room for my loom! I had to rent Goodman Adams's barn to set it up."

"How long before we had walls?"

"More than a year before we raised the frame for the house."

"Yes. We had walls, a roof, and you built the lean-to for your loom. Mary had just begun to walk, and Suzanne was four. The Strattons ended in jail, didn't they?"

"Yes, he put them both in jail."

"For something Goodman Adams said … what was it?"

"When the Pastor announced the hanging at church, Sam said, 'Goody Jones is no more a witch than my cow.' I agreed with him, just didn't say it out loud."

"Oh, yes, I remember now. I was shocked when the whole congregation backed Reverend Martin."

"He jailed them, then let Alice go."

"Did you know of any bad feelings before?"

"None. Might've been me."

"Teaches you to keep your own counsel."

While he was a devoted Puritan, William did not accept the authority of any human; all were born to degrees of sin in his way of thinking. His inability to give the reverence due authorities, especially one of the church, bordered upon heresy. It wouldn't be the first time Susanna reminded him of the colonial mind-set—every citizen was responsible for correcting his friends. She'd had to explain to him that Massachusetts was not like England. No one was free of prying neighbors, and loose words or spontaneous thoughts had repercussions. Her corrections had felt like a rap on the knuckles, though he'd never admit he took her advice that way. The Boston court acquitted Samuel Stratton, but not before Reverend Martin fined Sam five pounds. *What for?* William thought. *Blasphemy?*

"They'd never have hung Goody Jones for a witch but for Hopkin's book. A more dangerous man never lived. King James's pawn, but he claimed to be a Puritan. Going to save us all from witches and the Devil."

"I cannot say."

"I'm glad of that. My family will not be reading his poisonous lies by my permission."

William had tied the murder of Goody Jones to Hopkin's book on witch-hunting in East Anglia. It came out the year before the first witchcraft trial in the colonies, where a wise clergy had previously relegated witchcraft to folk myth and tolerated witches as delusional at worst. William, who'd left Somerset when the civil war was brewing in England, thought Hopkins was the right hand of Parliament, not an agent for God's covenant, even if Cromwell did appoint him. What's more, he was a lawyer, a most dangerous man to turn witch-hunter; his book modeled interrogations as treacherous as the Spanish Inquisition. Interesting book if you studied the occult, but laws to live by?

"I plan to speak to Reverend Sherman this Sabbath. Joanna has asked that Mary come with us, too. She thinks that her second sight might help."

"I think that's wise. The slander links to a child's death. Grief is a powerful force. But Mary must be discreet if Reverend Sherman is in your party."

William felt better about Reverend Sherman than about others. Their pastor was a noted skeptic when it came to supernatural subjects; science proposed causes for natural events that bypassed Devils. The Reverend was so enamored of science that he even claimed that astrology was valid because it studied the movements of planets and stars, God's creation. He often said those who believed in magic were more sinners than possessed Devils. He approved of Indians reading and writing, of converting them to Christians. To William, the Watertown congregation was most fortunate to have Reverend Sherman.

As much as William valued safety and sought security, he would never fall prey to the hysteria of his fellow citizens who saw every shadow imprinted with a brown-skinned Indian sent by the Devil. He knew that confronting slander was the best way to spread truth. That, and that alone. So, the scriptures taught. Nevertheless, he agreed with Susanna's caution.

"I think you need not worry there. Mary's fear of his opinion has always determined her behavior. Have you talked to Rebecca? Has she spoken more of witches?"

"She has not. Mary and Joanna have been watching her closely."

"We'll find who started it." William bent to kiss the sleeping baby and warmly squeezed his wife's hand before he left the room.

The week passed quickly, punctuated by an expected but overdue visit from John, who brought news of Groton and a letter from Suzanne and Joseph.

On that day, William, Will, and hired hand David were in the back twenty cutting barley, stacking it in sheaves. William paused to wipe the sweat off his forehead when he noted Joanna at the edge of the field, waving and calling, 'John's here.'

He turned to David. "You keep going. I'll be back soon. Will, you come with me."

The two made their way to the house, Joanna leading the way with Benjamin riding piggy back. Everyone was gathered in the great room. Susanna sat across from John at the table boards. Mary sat with her sisters nearby on the settee, where she'd obviously coerced them to sit like little ladies, hands in their laps, straight backs, and quiet, too.

After everyone had welcomed John, they sat at the boards. William let the conversation flow, though he had only one item on his mind. While he was curious to hear more about Groton, he wanted most to hear John's account of his accusation of the Phillips man.

They exchanged small talk about buying land in Groton and Watertown, and he noted that Mary remained silent when they spoke of Abraham Brown, her father in law. He was sure that she was feeling protective, and he changed the subject.

William turned to John, narrowing his eyes warily. "Corporal Bond tells me your name came up in Boston. I didn't get the details." By now, William had heard reports from Corporal Bond as well as his neighbor John Coolidge.

John bent his head, stared down at the table smiling. "Nothing important. John Ong—I work with him on the meetinghouse—told me he saw Jonathon Phillips behaving uncivilly with Mary Daniels. I thought Reverend Willard should know."

"Jonathan Phillips? Reverend Phillip's son? He lives in Watertown, not Groton."

John raised his head, eyes glittering. "Yes, but he had business in Groton. Everyone knew he had his eye on Mary Daniels, and John Ong said he witnessed him go after her. I can't give you details. Just said it was bad. Seemed to me he shouldn't get away with it. I told it to Willard; I guess he reported it to Boston."

"It went farther than that. Missus Willard told the story to her father here in Watertown. Reverend Sherman notified the magistrates in Boston to get to the bottom of it. Are you going to testify?"

"I don't know why I would. John Ong told the story. He's the rightful witness. He was too afraid to say anything, so I stepped in."

William had listened critically but found nothing that might cause him to chastise his son. Perhaps he was changing his ways and would join the church after all. "We'll just have to wait to see how this rolls out. Susanna, do you think we can hear that letter now?"

***

At sundown the next Saturday night, William set aside his work; he'd not begin again until the Sabbath passed at sundown. He enjoyed this weekly respite from the heavy and continuous labor of his weekdays. This morning, before sunrise, William had greeted his family and helpers at the table, where they breakfasted on hot porridge sweetened with honey or maple syrup. Once they'd eaten, they'd headed to their morning chores.

Rebecca bent over the spinning wheel, making up their colony-mandated weekly quota of spun wool for her and her mother. If she didn't produce their full share, William would pay a fine. Joanna milked the cows, cleaned their stalls. She then handed them over to the shepherd who led them to the pasture in the Pequusset Common. Abigail gathered eggs and fed the chickens. Will Jr. groomed the horses and cleaned their stalls before he joined apprentice Jacob at the looms. Susanna had ventured to her feet, but still avoided any strenuous labor, even when Mary returned to her home for the Sabbath. David, his hired hand, was harvesting the grains, scythe cutting wide swaths in the fields. William had worked with his son and apprentice at the loom all morning.

After chores and lunch, he turned hands to the seasonal work; in September, harvesting and preserving food for both people and livestock occupied everyone. Winters were always longer than imagined. This day, he had joined his servant David, bringing Joanna and Will to join in harvesting the corn; two had cut the stalks, and two had bundled and stacked sheaves. Then they'd fill the crib with the shucked cobs. They had yet to harvest the hay, but that could be done well into October. Before dusk, they'd secured the chickens, pigs, horses, sheep, and cows for the night, letting the children muck out their barn and lay fresh hay. An hour after sundown, on most days, he could no longer keep his eyes open, nor did he try. The nights were pitch-dark, and night hunters prowled the forest, no time for good men to be abroad. Every morning, he began the cycle again, every day but the Sabbath.

In the dwindling light, William went to the door and stepped outside, where the western sky flamed above the hilltop and set the oaks and maples on fire as well. The chill of the autumn night reached his skin, though he was warm enough in his flaxen shirt and woolen doublet. Birds that would normally be murmuring to sleep in their nests had already migrated south, so it was profoundly silent. He heard only the lowing cows and a lone turkey gobbling in the distance. Later, he'd hear the screech owls' tortured shrieks and wolf packs' lonely howls. Or a predator's soft hoots and a victim's scream.

He shuddered as thoughts of mortality assailed him; the news from London was dire. A conflagration had destroyed more than three quarters of the city; what's more, the Exchange, the center of New England trade, had burned, too. Following so closely on the heels of the plague, the second disaster reminded him that God could punish as well as provide. Was not London comparable to Israel, and the fate of Anglicans, to the fate of the Israelites? He bowed his head and prayed. 'God grant me wisdom; let me not stray from your righteous path.'

Turning, William walked to the great room where Susanna shuffled about, lighting lanterns and candles for their evening bible study. The heat radiated a cozy smell of autumn, a mix of wet wool permeated with sweat and the lingering aromas of food. Mary had returned home for her Sabbath; her family needed her, but she would return on Monday for one more week to help with Susanna's lying in.

The large family Bible now occupied its usual place on the board table, close to the light from the hearth, already opened to the place marked the last Wednesday. The hearth projected reflections of dancing red flames on the closest walls. The children gathered on the benches near the fire, lumps hunched in homespun sweaters, murmured as they passed around the tankard of heated cider that Susanna had bartered with Biddy Payne, who had apple trees. They sipped the treat appreciatively, turning the tankard to drink from their own place on the rim. Benjamin nursed his own cup of warm milk, which Susanna spared only for the youngest. He would be fast asleep before they'd finished this lesson.

....

Chapter Eight

A CANDLE GIVES LIGHT

Watertown, September 1666

William took his seat at the head of the table to begin their lessons in prophesying. He thought the children needed to read the Old Testament, a history of the agreement that God made with the Israelites, His chosen people. The stories told of the Lord's love, but more importantly, of his wrath and punishment when they sinned. William didn't believe his God would ever raise humankind's status to the chosen again, even though he'd joined the church, a sign he was chosen himself. Though Jesus promised a new covenant with God through his grace, true Puritans felt they could not take that as granted. They knew they had much to learn from the Jews to keep that covenant, to avoid the fate of Israelites.

William smoothed the open pages of the great book. "Abigail, will you read for us tonight?" Abigail, who was nine, needed practice as she was the last to learn to read; her older brother and sister gladly conceded this task that all had performed in their time. Abigail read well, unlike Rebecca who stalled whenever she came to a word she could not pronounce. Abigail could sound out the words so they all could follow the story, even if she didn't know their meanings.

Susanna, who sat near, raised the candle above the book where Abigail stood squinting to read the sacred text. Her mother had opened the Bible to the Book of Exodus, Abigail's favorite so far. Her father liked the Exodus best, too, as it mirrored his own wandering from England to the wilds of Massachusetts. Their mother's parents too had followed God's chosen leaders. Abigail had read the story of the Red Sea last week and wanted to know what miracle would befall Moses's followers next. She began to read the verses that recounted God's saving the Israelites from starvation in the desert.

When she had finished, William began the discussion. He turned to Will. "The people complained to Moses. Why?"

Will's cheeks were pink from flames crackling in the hearth. He knew the answer. "They were starving. They said they were so hungry they'd been better-off if they'd died in Egypt."

"Does that remind you of anyone today?"

Will thought but shook his head. "We aren't starving."

Abigail chimed in, "It's like Goody Livermore, isn't it? I mean, when anything goes wrong, she says she wishes she'd never left England. She blames it on her husband, says she never wanted to come."

"Oh. Yeah," Will agreed.

"Would you read that verse for us again? "William often made them repeat passages he wanted them to remember.

Abigail read: "Would we had died by the hand of the Lord in the land of Egypt, when we sat by the fleshpots and ate bread to the full. For you have brought us out into this wilderness to kill this whole assembly with hunger."

"What's a 'fleshpot?'" Rebecca asked.

"A pot of meat," William answered. "A stew."

Susanna lifted baby Samuel to wrap him more securely. "Can you remember your grandfather's story about coming to Plymouth?"

"Yes," Will replied. "He told us half of them starved."

"That's fifty men, women, and children, just like us." William wanted the reality to sink in.

"That's right," Susanna agreed. "The women had no food for children but the clams they gathered every day. Did they make a mistake to come?"

Abigail answered more like a teacher than a pupil. "It wasn't Moses who brought them to the wilderness. It was God. It's like us. God brought us here. If we complain …"

Joanna laughed, "Father scolds us!"

"And now you know why." While William approved of Joanna's quick wit, her levity undercut his serious mission. "You take the Lord's name in vain to complain."

William thought, *I know I am supposed to believe I left England because of God's will. Why don't I feel it? Has God abandoned me?* He too often felt the same way that Goody Livermore did. Self-doubt ate at his faith, and he couldn't shake the feeling that he belonged in Somerset, not Watertown. *The children will never realize our trial*, he thought.

He continued, "What does the Bible say? Did God teach them a lesson?"

Rebecca stirred. "God had to show them."

"What did God show them?"

"He showed them his glory. He told Moses he'd give them meat, and manna. Then he sent the pheasants and the manna. He proved he was God."

"He gave the women in Plymouth clams," Will exclaimed. The children laughed.

"Did they believe then?" William relentlessly drilled.

Rebecca spoke up. "No, because they ignored what he told them. He said He gave them the right amount of manna every day. They weren't supposed to save it until the next day, but they did it anyway."

"Oh right," said Will. "The food turned maggoty."

"Ugh!" Once, Rebecca had almost stepped on maggots infesting a dead squirrel on the path.

"Just like our food," Susanna said. "It spoils."

"What else did He teach them?" William asked.

"He taught them to gather twice as much food the day before the Sabbath," Joanna said.

"Why did He do that?" their mother asked.

"God didn't give them any food on Sunday," she said saucily. "That's God's day to rest. He said they must honor

His day."

"As we now do," Rebecca said. "We prepare our food for Sunday on Saturday, so we can rest." She knew this lesson from the past.

"Now let's look at the New Covenant," William said. Susanna had already opened to the New Testament, laying the red ribbon between pages at Matthew, Book 12. "What does Jesus say about keeping the Sabbath? Read Matthew 12 this week, and we'll talk about it on Wednesday."

"The parable of the sheep!" Will exclaimed. He knew Matthew well, and the grace of the New Testament.

They would study the bible again on Wednesday, the day that they attended Reverend Sherman's lecture.

William had no more questions to add. They heard a lone wolf howling, and the lamp sputtered. "It's time for bed."

William lifted sleeping Benjamin and carried him to the four-poster bed in the master bedroom, where Susanna laid the sleeping Samuel in his cradle. Joanna rose and gathered Will, Abigail, and Rebecca. Philip followed. They climbed the stairs to the chilled loft, finding their straw pallets in the dark from memory. Abigail then led their bedtime prayer, the one they'd all learned from their New England primer. They knelt by their beds, bowed their heads, closed their eyes, and hands clasped, prayed. "Now I lay me down to sleep, I pray the Lord my soul to keep. If I should die before I wake, I pray the Lord my soul to take."

The last coals on the hearth glowed a deep maroon. Susanna snuffed out the last candle before she joined William where he knelt by the bedside. Susanna had resisted saying the Lord's prayer when they'd first married. Her separatist Pilgrim parents had taught her that the Lord's Prayer and hymns were ostentatious, rote prayer that came between their personal connections with the Lord and His word. William had insisted despite her upbringing, and now, the pair said the Lord's prayer aloud before they slept, and Susanna sang the psalms in Sunday meetings.

Chapter Nine

A DAY OF REST

Watertown, September 1666

The next day, the Sherborn family dressed for church. Susanna had decided to spend this Sabbath in bed with newborn Samuel, as she felt it was too soon to walk the one-mile distance to the meetinghouse. William's heart was full as he watched Joanna step into her mother's shoes. Both Susanna and he had taken her for granted; Joanna took on her younger siblings daily, without reward, dressing, feeding, and shepherding them. Her appearance suffered as a result. The heavy eyebrows accentuated the masculine jawline and plain features. Joanna made no attempt to improve what nature had given her or to adorn herself. William made a mental note to find time to work with this daughter. Joanna combed and plaited her younger sister's hair, fitting the white linen cap over Rebecca's red-blond locks and turned to fuss with Abigail's shawl.

"Becky, don't forget your shawl. It's cold this morning." Joanna thought her sister so flighty that she'd forget her head if she wasn't reminded it was still attached.

Rebecca climbed to the loft and returned wrapped in a green shawl that complimented her red hair and freckled skin. She pirouetted in front of her disapproving sister and went to help Benjamin dress.

When the bustling family had completed donning their best, William heard the drum call from the distant meetinghouse. For a blind moment, he resented this summons, crudely adopted from the Native Americans. The church at the first praying town in Nonatum, across the St. Charles River, had given their former minister the idea of using a drum to call the parish. In his mind, William was hearing the tuned carillons of his birthplace. When the bells of St. Mary Magdalene had pealed, his heart had soared with the joyful outpouring volley of cascading notes. Taunton's carillons were the finest in England, fit for a King's ear. He quickly silenced his memory, realizing mutely that he had again offended his God. True love of God should be enough to call his attention and joyous participation in the Lord's Day. The other? Papist, the anti-Christ.

Focusing on last night's lesson, he realized he too shared suspicions with those biblical emigrants from Egypt. Who could ever leave the past behind, not second-guess their most passionate choices moving them to futures they might regret? Yet, once again he tried to slam shut the doors of nostalgia and doubt. *That way lies unhappiness.* He affirmed the path forward, granting that God had led him to Watertown. God has shown his favor in every way. *Is not my prosperity proof of it?* He silenced his doubt, giving thanks for his boisterously healthy family. *Ten born, all thriving*, he thought. *Thank the Lord.*

Father and flock filed from the house, following Hill Street over the hilltop and down to the meetinghouse. The overcast sky promised rain, but that would make their Sabbath more bearable. No one wanted to sit inside on bright days, when breezes stirred the trees. William smelled the Devil hunters' harvest before he saw the bounty nailed to the entry wall: three wolves' heads, a bear's head, and a rattlesnake skin. The town council had paid English sterling for each one: least for rattlesnake, most for bear heads. Young Will bragged that he'd be the next to kill a bear. He'd seen one lurking on the edge of their farm. Black bears were mostly opportunists who stole from the gardens and rustled poultry, but they could be dangerous and attack if provoked. The wolves threatened their cows, and foxes could decimate a hen house. Taming the Massachusetts wilderness was constant work for the community, which competed with wild animals for its repast.

A goodly communion gathered this morning; nearly all the members lined the yard. Reverend Sherman then threw open the doors and the parishioners streamed inside, men and boys over sixteen on the left; women and children on the right. The prominent families sat in their gallery pews near the pulpit.

William and his sons, John and Philip, made up the men in the family, but his sons were absent this day, John still in Groton, and Philip in Cambridge. William knew John wouldn't have come anyway. He'd never accepted the Puritan faith and attended sporadically only to please his parents and avoid the fines. William wondered how he'd sired a son who was an agnostic, like those Godless strangers who had shared the Mayflower with the Puritans. They thought only of profit. He grieved that John had not yet found his own soul; he knew a life without divine direction would be hard. John's children would suffer, too.

Joanna and the children kept their pew on the right. He would greet Mary later, on the way out. She usually sat in the gallery with her husband's family, the Browns.

Pastor Sherman nodded to the congregation, and they murmured and shifted in their seats until silence fell. They bowed their heads and clasped their hands in prayer. Then the reverend read the day's passage from the Bible. The congregation stood to sing a hymn. When Reverend Sherman turned the hourglass over, the congregation sat down. The sermon would end when the white sand had sifted through its waist, in two hours. It would end when he'd analyzed the words of God, found its lessons quoting liberally from the scripture, and applied it to their daily lives.

When the meeting broke at noon, the family went to the yard to break bread for their lunch. The threatening rain had spent itself in a brief shower, and they entered a fresh world. William approached the Reverend, who stood at the door to thank his parishioners.

"Reverend Sherman, I must speak to you."

The Reverend took him by the arm to pull him aside. The church goers took the clue and continued their way to their midday meals. "Of course. And congratulations on your new son."

Smiling, William thanked him, then, lowering his voice, he said with a frown: "My daughter repeated a story that Joanna Morton, our midwife, is a witch. She'd overheard it in school from a classmate."

Reverend Sherman returned William's concern, his forehead wrinkling. "Why? Did she point to some action?"

"She said Goody Morton poisoned Johnny Kemball. He died of scarlet fever, but now this rumor is afloat that her medicine poisoned him."

"Ah yes, the Kemball boy. We buried him a fortnight ago. I'm glad you brought this to my attention. We must root out lies."

"Clara Thompson is the child passing on the rumor. Perhaps the entire class has heard it now."

"I'm more concerned about the source, the Kemballs perhaps."

"Could you meet with us?"

"That's a good plan. I think I want to start with the school, deal with the children first, then speak with the families involved."

"Thank you." William felt relieved the Reverend felt it was urgent. "Joanna is no witch."

"Of course. I've always approved her midwifery with good conscience. A rumor like this, especially one from children, threatens the public good. We must see this as an opportunity. God is giving us this chance to amend our ways. Tomorrow, then." The two men shook hands, and William returned to his family for the cold lunch Susanna had packed. Soon, the parishioners shuffled back to the meetinghouse for the elder's talk. His commentary and the lively, open discussion following it, would take up the afternoon. They would end this day giving thanks for God's bounty.

....

Chapter Ten

FALSE WITNESSES

Watertown, Next Day, September 1666

On Monday, William, Joanna, Mary, and Reverend Sherman set out for the schoolhouse to stop the rumor. The two men led.

"Have you thought more about returning to England?" Reverend Sherman asked.

William did not answer right away. Their steps in dry leaves crackled in the air. He stopped walking and turned to the minister to begin his fully deliberated answer. "I have thought it through," he said, and then continued walking. "As you said, taking everyone with me would split the family. I can't do that. Also, I believe the Lord sent His message when Susanna faced death giving birth. I took it as His warning. By His grace we have Samuel, and Susanna lives. I promised Him that I'd not leave them."

"A wise decision. You've kept your promise to God. You would do well to keep your holy contract with our congregation, too."

"I will keep my covenant and end my life in Watertown, but the dreams keep coming. I conclude that God wants me to go alone and for a short visit. I don't know why, but I believe He wants me to follow His way, and He will tell me when the time is right."

"Perhaps." The Reverend paused, thinking. "I do not give weight to dreams, but the Bible contains so many references we shouldn't ignore them. After we spoke, I found a passage in the Book of Acts 2:17. How did it go? Something like 'And in the last days it shall be, God declares, that I will pour out my Spirit on all flesh. And your sons and your daughters shall prophesy, and your young men shall see visions, and your old men shall dream dreams.' I hope these are not the last days!"

"Your verse does herald doom."

"Not doom if it is reaping souls for heaven. What I take from this passage is visions, prophesy, and dreams are Godly. His Spirit. Not ours. I approve of your decision to undertake this voyage after Samuel reaches a reasonable age, and on your own. We have ghosts, but we should not feed them our offspring. You must keep your promises to the young and to God."

"I'll not ask for a letter of dismissal, then, but I'll be wanting to worship in Somerset while I'm gone."

"The parish will agree to a recommendation, if you promise to return, and to assure your return, I will write a recommendation."

When the party reached the schoolhouse, Richard Norcross welcomed them warmly. William was surprised at how quickly the Reverend taught children that rumors were 'false witness', and to bear false witness against their neighbor was to break God's important command. It also broke the Massachusetts Bay Colony law against the criminal offense of lying. He explained if any pupil fourteen or older continued to pass this rumor, the court would punish them according to the seriousness of their crime. He made his point frightening when he took Clara Thompson from class in front of her classmates.

At Clara Thompson's, her mother, shocked that her daughter had caused any problem in school, punished her immediately. She interrogated her daughter on her understanding of the eighth commandment in front of Reverend Sherman as much to show him that she had brought up her daughter in the faith as to punish her. The good Reverend wasn't satisfied with her demonstration, but then continued to test Clara's understanding to make sure she was on the right path.

During this interrogation, Clara confessed the source of the rumor had been her classmate, Joey Kemball. Reverend Sherman had been correct that the source of the rumor lay within the grieving family.

Their visit to the Kemballs revealed a cluttered and dark house. The grieving family was suffering, especially Goody Kemball, as her husband testified. Reverend Sherman heard both the mother and the son confess to falsely accusing Joanna Morton of witchcraft; the mother in anger and her son misunderstanding what he saw when his brother died.

William had watched his daughter Mary closely during the encounter, but beyond the tension she emitted, he could detect nothing untoward in her behavior. He did note that the atmosphere warmed from a dark chill to a comforting heat in the hour they were there, but that could have been the addition of four bodies to the small room where they gathered. It wouldn't do to read too much into the changes, but he did note that Joanna watched Mary intently. He wondered if she attributed the change to Mary's work or to more natural causes. In the end, he was satisfied that Reverend Sherman could not suspect her of working magic.

Chapter Eleven

WINTER'S DARK

Watertown, January 1667

Pearce was good to his word and left for Boston soon after the September council meeting. In Boston, he convinced the magistrates that the present surveyor had again incorrectly surveyed the land grants in Watertown. Boston ordered yet another survey to reassess the Watertown community's holdings, and Pearce announced it at the December meeting. William didn't agree with the colonists who received Pearce's orders with hostility; he would always want more land. After Pearce campaigned door-to-door to put his proposal through, that the land be sold to pay for the mill, more were convinced. Any decision would have to wait for the next meeting in the spring. However, more urgent problems overrode these protests.

Scarlet fever reared as Joanna Morton had predicted. The numbers of children attending the school dropped by half. More graves appeared in the churchyard. The townspeople passed no more rumors of witchcraft, despite the parishioners' suspicions that God was punishing them justly for their sins. Self-reflection yielded so many of these that parishioners had no doubts when Reverend Sherman reminded them in his sermons. If the pestilence was not enough, he told them God's wrath had wrought the great fire in London that followed the Black Death epidemic. These events had been prefigured by a solar eclipse which closely followed the Puritan ruler's death and the monarchy's restoration. God had spoken; no one doubted it.

The Boston Court acquitted Jonathan Phillips in October when evidence was presented in the form of two letters testifying to the man's innocence. In the first letter, three residents of Groton interviewed Goodman Ong, who might otherwise have to go to Boston as the chief witness. He was the workman that John heard say Phillips had molested Mary Daniels. The three citizens signed a letter documenting that Richard Ong had told them he had never seen Jonathan Phillips do 'anything of the kind.' He'd never said it to John or anyone else, nor had he witnessed the middle-aged Phillips molesting the girl.

That left the jury with the prospect that either John Ong was recanting his accusation or John Sherborn had made it up. However, the court could find no motive for either of the men to cause Jonathan Phillips a grievance, and the court did not charge either Goodman Ong or John Sherborn with lying, even after the second letter was read before the judge.

In the second case, Reverend John Sherman wrote a letter to Magistrate Danforth in Boston casting doubt on the words of John Sherborn. He wrote that creditable people said that John Sherborn 'carried on so at Groton in the short time he lived there that, if the character given of him be true, little credit is to be given to anything which hath no other and better evidence than his testimony.'

While the magistrates might have prosecuted John Sherborn for lying, a crime less serious than fornication, but one punishable with flogging and fines, another custom ended further inquiry. When the accused had status—Freeman Phillips was the son of a founder, their first minister—the court preferred acquittals to preserve public order. If such an affair disrupted the community, the woman would be reprimanded or punished to dismiss the case from the court as well as public memory.

Though John Sherborn's accusation held no credibility and was thought a lie, it led to no criminal charges in this case. Corporal Bond was the friend to get this word to William, who needed little more to condemn his son, even when Susanna pointed out Reverend Sherman's obvious bias when he wrote the letter. Neither Susanna nor William knew what Reverend Sherman's claim that John 'carried on so' in Groton referred to.

The years sixty-six and sixty-seven brought the harshest winter William could remember. After a cold and rainy October, November's daily snow kept the family housebound. Will and apprentice Jacob could work independently running the shop. Apart from checking their weavings, William was free for other chores. He had household improvement planned for the season—repairing the rail on the stairs to the loft, for one—but today, he refurbished their snowshoes. The bentwood hoops and rawhide straps were perishable. They'd not needed snowshoes last winter, which was mild. This year, though, drifts were already up to his knees. The blue-black clouded sky dropped two or three inches daily, and the sun never showed its face. *In England*, he thought, *we'd never see a winter such as this.*

The night before—to make life worse—a blizzard blew in from the coast; gusts of wind rattled shuttered windows, seeped through the clapboard, and whistled through trees surrounding the house. The snow didn't let up in the morning.

In the great room, Jo and her mother finished winding skeins of new-spun yarn as Rebecca darned socks and rocked the sleeping Samuel's cradle with her foot. She'd piled every sweater on the baby to keep him warm, and he looked like some burrowing animal with only his nose and mouth showing. Philip, unable to ride to Cambridge to work with Dr. Stone, pored over Thomas Thatcher's newly printed broadside. He huddled next to the one unshuttered window in the great room, which admitted light through veins of frost crackling the pane. The pamphlet was titled, *Brief Rules to Guide the Common People of New England: How to Order Themselves and Theirs in the Smallpox, or Measles*. The advice was Thatcher's response to the smallpox epidemic in Boston last year. Benjamin played beneath the table, where Abigail had made him a house, tenting a quilt over the boards.

William pushed past Abigail, who sat at the boards paring vegetables she'd pulled from the cellar for their meal. The sharp sweet smell of the chopped carrots, turnips, and cabbages stabbed the atmosphere of long confinement. He'd become used to the thick smells of body sweat, ash, burning timber, cooked food, and the homeliest of bodily emissions. Oddly, mixed with heat radiating from the hearth, the family sensed the atmosphere as warmth through their skin rather than stuffy odor. It spelled comfort, like warm wool worn by encircling arms.

He leaned over to grab the handle of a pot of boiling water from the fire. "Don't move. I just need the pot." He'd need to soak the rawhide straps to restring the last pair of snowshoes.

Abigail nodded, but before she could answer, a frustrated shriek issued from below the table. She bent and peeked under the drape. "Benjamin Sherborn, you give that back!" Ben was pounding her prized possession on the floor with a force that could break it. She didn't know how he'd smuggled it in without her seeing; the carved bear, a gift from her brother, John, was large. She tried to pull it from his hands, but he resisted.

"No," Ben yelled. "It's mine."

William did not usually intercede in fights. His wife took charge; because he was the parent to mete out punishment, his children were afraid of him. He demanded their obedience, and they complied or suffered his punishment. However, Ben had devilish traits, and Susanna had asked for help in correcting him; he was obligated. "Benjamin," he barked. "go sit in the corner." A stool sitting at the far corner of the great room, where it was coldest, was the first order of punishment severity for misbehaving Sherborn children, the equivalent of the stocks. If shunning didn't work, sanctions followed—withholding food and favors— with corporal punishment, a whipping, for the worst.

Benjamin hugged the figure to his chest, his possession complete. As Abigail wrenched it from him, William bent, grabbed him under his arms and lifted him kicking. Benjamin sat on the stool brooding at first, but soon was whimpering.

"Not a sound. The next words from your mouth? You say, 'I'm sorry' to your sister."

He returned to his task, knowing that Ben would hold out for an hour or more. Ben was his most stubborn child, with the traits of a natural-born bully. William could only pray Ben would see God's light in time. For now, though, his covenant with God made him responsible for any failings of his child. He must find the way to bring Ben to sanctity.

Only one of the bentwood hoops needed reinforcement, which he'd patched. By now, the wet deer hide was ready for stringing. The job was weaver's work; he strung the woof and wove in the warp to create the shoe's racket, letting the drying rawhide shrink, adding tension to keep the frame's shape. The trick was in making sure the long strips were uniformly wide and would not break.

Susanna left her wheel when she'd finished and joined him on the settee, securing her blanket-thick shawl over the shaggy sweater she wore. The clapboard house was drafty in high winds and even the improved central hearth was little defense in a storm. She studied his handiwork, "Good; I'd a hard time reaching the hens this morning. The snow's so deep already."

William grunted. "The almanac predicted snow. Looks like it was right." He pulled a steaming strip of rawhide from his pot, shaking it to cool it, and then squeezing the excess water out. "Last one. We'll have snowshoes now."

"Are you still planning on putting in the stair rail?"

"Plan to." The meaning of the word 'plan' that William shared with his wife was ironic. In the colonies, plans were long mental lists, which in large families, could change if not vanish in a puff of smoke with unexpected events: Benjamin breaking an arm, the cow's calving, disaster in the henhouse after a fox marauded. The best planned stores of food in the fall could run out before spring.

"I was thinking," she said, "I know it'll be more work ... but the baby... the boys ... could use a rail."

"I don't follow.

She signaled the rail by making a T with one hand flattened above the hand representing the post. "You have one rail for adults." She switched her hands to parallels. "Then, a rail below it, at the children's height."

William smiled. Her design was much as his mental image had been. He'd pictured a crossbar to stabilize the rail posts. But her request went further, and he liked her idea. "You mean, make the crossbar a handrail, too?"

"Yes, that's it. The crossbar. If it was their height ..."

Pounding on the front door interrupted her.

Will yelled from the workshop, "I'll go!"

"Fine," William said. *Who's out in this weather?* he thought. Too curious to sit still, he sped down the hall in time to see Will silhouetted in the door by swirling, blustery snow. Two men bent against the wind, and judging from the snow caking their faces, they'd come some distance.

Chapter Twelve

THE HEARTH

Watertown, Same Day, January 1667

Young Will opened the door, barely able to see the two men through the swirling snow. "Come in. Corporal Bond isn't it?"

"Aye," Bond gestured to his companion. "And Goodman Clinnery, to you." Corporal Bond thought children—and the slight boy was a child to him—should show respect for adults, even one such as Joseph Clinnery who wasn't a voting freeman. Bond pointed to his snowshoes. "Where do I put these?"

William, now at the door, pulled both men inside. "Quickly. Leave the storm where it belongs." He had to slam the door against the high wind.

Stamping their feet, the men hung their dripping snowshoes on the pegs Will pointed to, and then their capes, thick with packed snow. "It's beastly out!" Corporal Bond said. He bent, beating the ice from his beard.

Joseph Clinnery, his wool Monmouth pulled low on his forehead, had a round face with bright red cheeks. His bushy eyebrows, now caked with ice, stood straight up, which gave him the look of surprise, and he could barely move his stiff, swollen lips to speak his 'thanks.' He reached to shake William's hand. "I'm Joseph Clinnery."

William shook his hand, noting he'd seen him at the mills before. "What brought you out in this weather?" William exclaimed, his brow wrinkled with concern. *Bond lives miles away,* he thought. *I'll warrant it's an emergency, may be the roads.* Although another selectman had taken over his position as Highway Surveyor at the annual elections in December, he'd volunteer to help his former partner clear a road.

"I stayed at Joseph's when I couldn't get home last night." Corporal Bond nodded toward his companion. "This morning, the wind blew down a tree, took his roof, and toppled the chimney. Family's safe; they put out the chimney fire, but they need shelter. Tree's blocking the road, too. I thought of you immediately. Thank God you were close; we can take care of the tree."

William knew little of Joseph Clinnery, whose homestead was nearby, but bordered the west edge of his fields at the bottoms. Gravity in their town could start and end friendships; a near three-hundred-foot climb through forests challenged communion. He marveled the two men had made it up the steep hill on snowshoes in the storm. *The snow must be so deep it covers the tree fall*, he thought.

"Your family's welcome here; we can heat the south parlor for sleeping, but we'll need help for the tree." He turned to his son Will, who was sweeping snow to the door after knocking packed snow off their cloaks to keep them dry. "Will, you take the horse. Get Goodmen Livermore and Coolidge."

Susanna, who had heard the commotion, joined the men. "Yes, bring your family here. We have room."

Corporal Bond nodded to her, "Good day, Susanna." The two had a working acquaintance after William had paired with him to check roads last fall. She turned to find another layer of clothes for Will; he didn't have enough meat on his bones to keep him warm in this storm. The men needed a warm drink, too. They shouldn't have to ask.

"Take snowshoes, just in case." William handed Will a pair. "Avoid any drifts if you can. I wouldn't be surprised if we have another foot of snow on the ground, and it's blowing. The roads are treacherous. And tell them we'll need ropes and hitches for the tree."

"Can Jason come?"

"No. Jason needs to finish the cloth we set up; we have too many unfinished orders to take a break. Just bring the neighbors." William turned to the men. "We should leave soon, but you need to warm up first. Come." He led them to the Great room where Susanna had already poured steaming water into the largest tankard. She added a generous portion of rum and brown sugar and stirred before passing the vessel to the men.

"Susanna's toddy will warm you up."

William crossed the room and stood behind his son Philip, who bent focused on his book—his powers of concentration were a legend in the Sherborn family. "Philip! We're going to need your help."

Philip jumped in surprise and reluctantly closed his book. "What is it?"

"We need you," William repeated.

Once Philip had come to full attention, he quickly took in the scene. "Happy to help," he said, crossing the room to join the men at the hearth.

"Philip," Corporal Bond said. "Joseph Clinnery here is going to need your help to get his wife and babes out the house. Had a fire there." Corporal Bond held out the tankard to him. "Have a warmer before you go," he said.

"Thanks," Philip said, and sipped the warm sweet drink that set his stomach on fire.

William returned just in time to see Will stomping through the door, which whiffed in windblown snow before he closed it. Their coats, hats, mittens, and scarves hung on wall pegs in the rarely used room across from the workshop; high-topped boots stood in various attitudes beneath the bench. He sat down to lace up his boots, then tied on the snowshoes, admiring his recent handiwork. Snow would easily top his boots without snowshoes, but the webbing would keep him from sinking, at least enough to keep his feet dry.

The two men joined him, all of them donning long capes and tying on snowshoes. William gave them scarves to wrap around their faces for the trip to Joseph Clinnery's house. Susanna appeared with Joanna. "Jo," she said. "Build us a fire in here. We're going to have company. I'll see about some sleeping mats." She thrust a deerskin sack into William's hands. "You'll be needing to eat later," she said. William knew it was dried fare: nutmeats and fruit, maybe salted venison. He nodded his thanks and turned.

Stepping out the door, the wind caught William sharply, taking away his breath; with no sun visible in the sky and snow whirling thickly, he did not throw a shadow even though it was midday. He noticed Will leading the horse from the stable and mounting. He wouldn't bring help for an hour or more. Stepping with a thwomp, William sunk inches into the soft powdery snow under his body weight, even wearing snowshoes. He started slowly; his body had to become used to the high step and wide stride that tested the muscles in his legs. Soon, though, he could jog a bit, cutting a trail through the white expanse. Snowshoes had an advantage; he didn't have to follow a road and could cut direct across his land to Joseph Clinnery's house. The wooded slope to the bottom was steep, his only obstacle, but leaning backward, punching his heels into the snow, he rode the snow's downhill drift with each step. The four men descended quickly.

The house, a two-room finished home with an attached lean-to used for the kitchen, was still standing, but the top of the enormous maple had grazed one corner. The branches took out a corner of the roof, splintering walls, ripping out thatch, and toppling part of the wood and clay chimney. Fortunately, the windows were still intact. *Salvageable,* William thought. *A foot closer, the trunk would have smashed the house. There's Providence here.*

"Philip," William called out. "I want you to get the family and take them up to the house. Any injuries, you're the one to help."

Philip nodded, proud to accept this responsibility. He trotted through drifts and pounded on the door. "Goody Clinnery," he called.

The three men circled the tree, which stretched across Common Street and more than one hundred feet into

Goodman Clinnery's yard. Foot-high snow puffs already covered the branches, but they could still see the lay of it. Clearing this tree from the road would take days, even with a large party to help. The root wad was gargantuan and dwarfed the three men. The stout trunk had been putting on rings for several hundred years. What's more, the section of trunk with the largest and most numerous branches blocked the thoroughfare. *What a waste*, William thought. *Bark looks like sugar maple. Much maple syrup gone.*

Corporal Bond grunted. "We'll not be using Stone Street today!" William noted he used the old name for the street which had been changed ten years before. Now everyone knew it as Common Street.

"I think not," William agreed. "But we could start."

Bond shook his head. "I think a plan's in order. Way I see it, we have three goals here: the house, the road, the yard, in that order."

William hated to think what losing this route would do to outlying farms. Sleighs used the Road to the Pond because it connected with Common Street, which led to the Charles river and the center of town. "Agreed, shelter's first. With three parties, though, we could work them all."

"Until the storm lets up, we won't be able to do much." Bond stared up through snow that drifted in waves on the wind.

William, completely swayed by Bond's argument, fell in line. "If we cut the top section, we can haul it off the roof."

Joseph Clinnery, who had been silently listening to his neighbors decide his fate, had his own priorities. "We could rebuild the chimney, then."

William turned to him. "Don't see you can fix the thatch until spring."

"But if I seal one room and we have heat ..."

Bond pounded his palm with his fist. "Right. We could start that today."

"It's what I was hoping." Joseph turned and walked toward his house.

William nodded to Bond. "Tomorrow, the snow will end, and we can find others to start on clearing the road."

While the men were circling the house and calculating how they would reach the critical spot to begin sawing, Philip led Mary Clinnery and the children from the house. Philip carried the two-year-old piggyback and sacks of food and bedding in each hand. Mary led the six and eight-year-old on snowshoes, carrying another sack over her shoulder. The children wore their blankets. When Philip started up the incline, the laughing children after him, Mary stood with her hands on her hips staring up at the formidably steep slope. No help for it. She set out, wondering how long before her children had used up their good cheer and their play became a forced march. It was predictable.

By the time Will joined the work party, trailed by John Coolidge and John Livermore on horseback, the three men had identified the critical place to separate the treetop and had begun to remove branches. They worked until nightfall and then made their way up the slope to the Sherborn's house. The snow had stopped, and a yellow light framed the shuttered windows, casting their glow on the drifted snow, spelling warmth and shelter for eight more souls.

Chapter Thirteen

THE BALM FOR ENVY

Watertown, Same Day, 1667

Joanna had built a roaring fire in the parlor hearth, which radiated a cheery light in the otherwise gloomy room, its window being shuttered against the storm. Before Philip would surrender the shivering Clinnery family, he'd examined and treated Joseph junior's burns. Only then could Joanna offer them hot cider, dry wraps, and a seat by the fire. Philip's work done, he gave up on studying in the full house; with so many people, concentration was impossible. He joined Will and Jason in the workshop.

Rebecca and Abigail had never met the oldest Clinnery girl because Ruth attended a dame school; overcome with curiosity, they volunteered to help Joanna fix pallets of straw against the wall for beds.

Mary Clinnery was a slight, narrow-faced woman of poor complexion, and one might judge from her unkempt hair and soot smudges on her cheeks that she lacked all vanity. Susanna, however, suspected Mary was having a difficult early pregnancy, though she'd never say it—no one ever discussed the workings of a woman's body in public. Mary opened a sack, speaking to her daughter.

"Ruth," Mary said. "You can spread these blankets." She turned to Abigail. "I've brought food." She lifted another of the sacks. "Where do you want me to put it?"

"Come with me." Abigail led her neighbor to the great room, where the men were already eating their evening meal.

Susanna bent over the hearth, stirring a bubbling pot. "Ah, there you are Abigail!"

"Mother, Goody Clinnery has brought food with her. Where can we put it?"

"Please call me Mary. I'm not one to stand on formalities."

"Mary, then." Susanna wiped her hands on her apron and took the sack from her guest. Peering inside, she spied the frozen meat she'd brought. A frozen ham hock, a pot roast, a trout, and side of bacon would obviously need to be stored in the cache outside until they could thaw it. These treasures would certainly enliven their standard fare: stews made from game Joanna's hunts supplied.

"I thank you," she said.

"I have dry good as well. Rolled oats and barley."

"We'll be just fine. I'll help. We can put it with ours." The two women left to get the sack in the parlor.

Benjamin was still in disgrace, but too curious about the new kids; he saw his opportunity. He apologized loudly to his sister, and Abigail accepted; with her father's approval, she took him by the hand to join the other children. The Sherborn children adopted their neighbors easily, and once they'd thawed by the fireside, they ventured a game.

John Coolidge and John Livermore sat with Joseph Clinnery, Richard Bond and William at the table boards in the great room eating a savory game stew by the crackling fire. Susanna and Joanna heaped more wood on the fire.

"We've a good start on the tree," William agreed, nodding. He turned to his neighbors. "You stay here tonight."

John Livermore shook his head. "The snow makes it light as day. We'll be fine. The ride's not thirty minutes." Although he had no desire to brave the weather, he knew that his wife would worry when he didn't make it home. She was unhappy living in Watertown, having come from a large village in England; she couldn't get used to the wilderness.

"The snow's drifted now," William countered. "You won't know where your horse is stepping, even if you can see the surface. If it's crusted, worse yet. Your horse could break a leg. I wouldn't chance it if I were you."

John Coolidge was not as eager as his neighbor to leave, knowing from experience that drifted snow on back country roads was treacherous. "He's right. We'd do well to listen to William."

"No argument from me," Corporal Bond chimed in. "If it's no problem for the missus, I'll not be wanting to go back out tonight."

"It's no trouble," William laughed heartily. "What's a houseful of friends? What greater glory of God. Glad to have you."

"I've cleared the loft for you," Susanna said. "You'll join Philip and Will; the children will sleep in the parlor. You're always welcome here." She poured a pitcher of ale, passed it to the men, and removed the trenchers from the table boards.

"Good!" William said. "It's settled then?"

"Agreed," John Coolidge said, nodding.

"Will can see to your horses," Susanna said and left to get him. Will's love of horses and skill with them always made him the natural choice for any stable work.

The men grunted and, decision made, they relaxed into the long evening; they filled their tankards.

"I thank you for the help," Joseph said. "With six of us, it made short work of that tree."

"Tomorrow," Corporal Bond said, "we'll get a crew to clear the road."

"I'm volunteering to help you seal off the damaged room." John Coolidge, a joiner when he wasn't farming, brimmed with confidence. "We can strip branches and put them to work as logs for a wall, a regular palisade. You won't be worrying about wood for two winters!"

John Livermore took a swig from his tankard. "I've got time to spare. Count on me."

"What man has spare time in these parts?" William asked. "Did you take on another servant?"

"No," John Livermore answered. "I haven't told anyone yet. You're the first."

No one noticed Susanna return to fix their beds in the loft. Alerted to news, she hovered on the stairs in the shadows.

The men looked mystified because no one had heard anything. "What's the news, man?" Coolidge said.

"I'm going back to England," Livermore said.

"When?" Corporal Bond sputtered, wiping his beard. "Why?"

"Spring comes, I'll book passage back," Livermore replied. "The whole family."

Stunned by this announcement, William was instantly jealous of his neighbor's decision to leave. "Leave? Have you talked this over with Reverend Sherman? Are you sure?"

"Never surer," he said. "This winter's been the mallet drives the wedge. We can't endure the hardships here, not to mention the nightmares we'll all be scalped in our sleep. I don't need to tell you my wife has never been happy here."

"But your covenant with God? He has provided for us," William protested. "You're a freeman, selectman. You'll abandon ..."

John Coolidge interrupted him, "Let's speak truth. Is there a man hasn't thought it: sell here; buy in England?"

Corporal Bond wouldn't let John Livermore sidestep. "You didn't answer my question. Why now? The monarchy is back, and you think Puritans will keep their standing? Land be damned. What good, when you can't practice your faith? You're sailing into trouble."

Livermore reared, his arms braced against the boards, in mock resistance. "What, man, you think the persecution won't reach you here? You think you have it better? Way I see it, you've not only got the King, you've got the Indians, and don't forget: they're armed. It's no secret Metacom is dealing with the French and Dutch; he wants his land back. I fear the savages will overrun us."

Corporal Bond shook his head. "You heard rumors. I heard in Boston that Metacom and Ninegret had joined forces, but it wasn't so. Metacom was peaceable, turned over his guns while they checked out the rumors. They gave him back his guns."

"You can't compare England's rule with our colonies," William insisted. "There's an ocean between us and months follow any order from the King. *That's* something, but I take your point." He bent his head, stared unseeing at the table boards between his elbows, then he straightened and caught John Coolidge's eyes. "I *have* thought of going back. You're right." He turned to John Livermore. "But it's a mistake; trading financial gain for my commitment to God? The covenant bids me stay." William fell back on the argument he made to himself whenever he regretted not following the great reverse migration after Cromwell took office. Now the monarchy had been restored, he could congratulate himself that he'd resisted temptation ten years before.

Susanna lowered herself on a step, pulled her shrug around her shoulders against the chill. She'd never realized he thought seriously of returning to England; in fact, she'd not heard a word about it since they were young. She stared at the men, her brow furrowed.

"That Covenant's a thin promise and fading ink, for me," John Livermore said. "Reality is stark. God doesn't speak in words alone. What I tell is for your ears alone. I'm looking for a buyer."

Corporal Bond shook his head. "You're making a mistake, and the congregation will tell you the same."

William stared at his neighbor, not hearing Bond. "Your land adjoins mine. I'm your man."

"I figured either you or John would bid on it." Livermore turned to John Coolidge. "Did you want to bid; are you alright with William's bid?"

"I couldn't buy you out now, though I wish I could. William, it's yours," John Coolidge said.

Corporal Bond stared at the table, defeated now. "I'll not betray you."

"When the time comes. I'll keep your secret." William knew John Livermore wouldn't be leaving for months, and after their minister put his proposition before the congregation, John might not leave at all. The parish did not send deserters away with blessings and good wishes. Deserters were 'cast down' in Biblical terms; in fact, the church members were militant about it. John would ask the church for a letter of release, testifying to his good character; he'd need it for Puritans to accept him in any other parish. *We'll see*, William thought. *He's a long way to go.*

That night, after everyone had gone to bed, he was unable to sleep. He thought of what his friend was up against. One of the reasons he had decided against leaving home was that he'd split his family. What would Mary, John, and Philip suffer if he left the colonies? *Would they denounce me at meeting?* he wondered. He was sure John Livermore was making a mistake and thanked heaven that he hadn't done the same. *If my dreams are truly messages from God, I must wait for that day when I can go with grace. I cannot leave without their blessings.*

Chapter Fourteen

AMENDED TREATIES

Watertown, April 1671

In 1669, William bought twenty more acres from his friend, John Livermore, who did not leave for England because of opposition from the church. The parish had occasion to argue that they didn't want to make their church 'a place of imprisonment.' In the end, he resigned and chose to use the sale of his land to buy a larger house closer to town, and an elite group of women invited his wife Elizabeth to join them for weekly teas. The land William purchased was partly upland, but the larger portion was cleared meadow at the foot of the hill that ran toward Clear Pond. William could grow feed for his livestock, and the following year added a roan colt and another cow to his barn. John Livermore sweetened the sale of his land with a half dozen sheep.

Will Jr., who turned sixteen that year, could not be separated from the new colt, which he named Pilgrim. Eager to join his brother John in the Watertown infantry, Will joined the company on the drilling field only to be asked to leave. Captain Prentice had to talk fast to convince Will he belonged in the cavalry instead of the infantry for his love of and skill with horses. In the end, Will joined Captain Prentice's ranks, feeling as if God had tapped him on the shoulder when his father agreed to let him train Pilgrim for battle.

William's tenth child, Samuel, turned four in 1669, was hardy and healthy. William had seen his grandchildren Ruth and William Sherborn born, gratified that John had at last named a son William, after his father. Of course, he would always suspect John's motives. Mary bore more: Jonathan and Patience Brown. The news from Groton, from his daughter Suzanne, was the birth of yet two more grandsons, Joseph and Samuel Morse. Philip's wedding to Deborah Barstow had been a town event. Now a doctor, Philip had settled near Cambridge on land Deborah's uncle had given them. In all, William was a grandfather blessed with eleven grandchildren, but in truth, only Susanna kept count. He couldn't remember when he began to lose not only the number, but their names; Susanna had corrected him more than once. *What's more*, he scolded himself, *only four have married so far! Six more weddings, I'll have an excuse for forgetting their names.*

He had more to celebrate: the English victory over the Dutch, which resulted in renaming New Amsterdam to New York. The victory assured some security for Plymouth, and settlers could hang up their guns. William served two more terms as selectman on the Watertown council, as road surveyor and fence patrol.

Still, thoughts of returning to England rose again when his affairs turned for the worse. He had to attend the burial of Philip and Deborah's first child in October, and autumn brought divisions in the new town council, with lasting changes to the community.

The Watertown Council elected Deacon Thomas Hastings as clerk and moderator, and he sought to restore their moral responsibility to both man and God, which the clergy thought had eroded. As Deacon, Goodman Hastings had charge of collecting money from the congregation, paying the pastor, and distributing alms to the poor and sick, experience that he applied heavily as the council leader.

Captain Beers, who kept the ordinary in Watertown, joined Corporal Bond as a deputy to the Boston General Council. Though both deputies were military men, they had opposing views on matters involving Indians. To William, the newly elected selectmen too appeared to have come from a darker, harsher world than he had known. The thought nagged him the new administrators were Royalists, but he knew that was a stretch. The Massachusetts Bay colony continued to foster independence from the crown. They still were the only colony whose governing board and officers did not reside in London and met in Boston. However, Watertown's newly elected leaders exacted accountability with such rigor that William thought all humane leniency had disappeared. Divisions in the council officers had lasting changes for the community.

In Deacon Hastings first year, the council sanctioned seizing property to pay taxes and fines where the money was not forthcoming. Where selectmen formerly had acted as constables, assessors, or collectors, the council now paid hires to carry on these roles, and selectmen supervised them. The council paid these hires half the fines they collected, or the full fine for any stray animals they found. William thought these new measures invited the Devil into their midst. The more infractions the new hires found, the more money they made. *What's to stop them from making up the causes?* he thought. *Puts temptation in their way.* A staunch Puritan, he knew human nature to be mean and base without God's grace.

In the second year of Hastings service, the council voted to punish people who abused the small fines for wandering cattle, pigs, and sheep. Repeat offenses were fined again, and the fines doubled, then tripled for each offense.

School was free for local children, but the schoolmaster had always collected fees for students from other towns. Since he was one of the few preparing boys for higher schooling, as he taught Greek and Latin, Richard Norcross drew many boys from out of town. Now, the council demanded that he deduct these earnings from the thirty pounds he received from Watertown each year (for thirty years without a raise, it must be said). Students, too, were fined two shillings if they did not bring their cord of wood by November.

The town's poor were subject to unreasonable demands. The council continued to take collections to help those dependent on the community. They were few: an elderly man with no children, a widow, and a church member fallen into debt. However, William couldn't help wondering if Deacon Hasting's attitude toward the poor had been prejudiced by his wife's service to them. Deaconess Hastings had long led the women's auxiliary, who primarily worked with the poor; she distributed the funds that her husband collected from the congregation.

The pair had worked together well, but this year, the Deacon appointed someone to tell Ed Sanderson that he needed to put his older children into service, so they could learn a trade. When Sanderson resisted, the Watertown Council harshly insisted that if he didn't put his children into service—a girl of seven and a lad of eight—they would bring the matter to the Magistrate in Boston. Mary Ball, a widowed ward of the state, was asked to leave town on morality charges. The council barred John Chadwick from moving to Watertown when a rumor reached Hastings ears: the man was in debt and destitute. Charity vanished when he warned the man's brother, Charles Chadwick, and friend, John Stratton, that he would charge them damages if John Chadwick moved to Watertown. *How long has he harbored such dislike for the poor*, William thought? *Why didn't we see this?*

When William shuffled into the great room at Hasting's house for the April 1671 council meeting, he was panting. He stopped to shake hands with the town clerk, his host Thomas Hastings. Crossing the room, he joined John Coolidge, who sat next to his brother Nathaniel.

"John, Nate," he nodded, taking a seat next to them. He saw Ed Sanderson attending the meeting, no doubt to respond to the threats imposed on putting his children in service. William nodded to greet him, though he could hardly look him in the eyes. Years ago, when Ed Sanderson had sold his house on the hill to raise money to pay his debts, William had bought it. The man had never recovered, and he fell into permanent poverty. The family now depended on the Watertown citizen's charity and had for several years. William would have gladly taken Goodman Sanderson's daughter into service to learn spinning. She was near Ben's age, and though she'd not be productive for a few years, she might moderate Benjamin's ways. However, the man's pride made it impossible, and William deferred to Goodman Sanderson's need for dignity. Still, he felt he owed Sanderson something. He was so pleased with his property on the hill that he'd willingly paid him twenty bushels of Indian corn more than they'd bargained for when Sanderson disputed the title to the house.

Slowly the room filled: Corporal Bond, Captain Beers, James Pearce, his son-in-law Jonathan Brown who had newly joined, and Richard Norcross, among others: the Foxes, Trimble, and Hannigan. Goodman Perry was absent. They took seats or stood against the back wall.

With no preparation, Deacon Hastings sounded the gavel on his tabletop. "Order, order." When the murmuring died down, he announced: "We have a new matter needs settling today. The Natick praying Indians want to fish at the weir in the Charles River. They are willing to pay us for rights."

"Natick!" James Pearce thought the idea was preposterous. "It's miles upstream."

"I must remind you," Deacon Hastings responded, "the land south of the Charles River once was the Massachusett tribe's town—Nonatum. Back in the day when Reverend Elliott preached there, the Speen family—we don't know their Indian name—owned Nonatum and the fishing weir. Must be twenty years ago."

James Pearce would not let it go. "They have no rights."

Deacon Hastings nodded. "That's right. Dedham town granted them land upstream, west of Newton, on the other side of the bend in the Charles River. Reverend Elliot convinced Sachem Waban and everyone in Nonatum— they were all Christians—to move to the land deeded at the end of the Natick trail. Elliot pointed out they'd be the first praying town in Massachusetts Bay Colony."

William leaned toward John Coolidge as Hastings went on. "Hmph, there're two tribes live along that trail who aren't Christian. What about them?"

Hastings continued, "I don't know whether Speen still owns the Nonatum land or the weir. It appears they abandoned the weir then. I'll put it to discussion."

Richard Norcross sat forward. "Not exactly abandoned. The Massachusetts still fish side-by-side with us. Isn't that enough for them?"

James Pearce was not appeased. "A few do, I'll grant, but I think they mean to camp here."

"I see," Richard Norcross replied. "You're saying they want the rights, so the tribe can camp at the weir. They want no trouble."

Thomas Hastings nodded. "Yes, our weir is as far as the flood tides come. They fished for alewife in the spring same as us. The flood tides stop here, so they get no spring runs; Natick's too far upstream."

Captain Beers said, "Must be thirty miles upstream! They have no claim on the weir now!"

"You'd think so," Thomas Hastings replied. "But the Charles River doubles back north, and the bend puts Natick town ten miles from the weir, as the arrow flies."

Corporal Bond cleared his throat. "Magistrates in Boston just settled a case with the Natick Indians, a land dispute. The Dedham council's been pasturing livestock in their plantations; it ruined their crops. Might just be a case of needing more food sources. Too long to walk, but camping would work."

"I'm presuming that's the case." Thomas Hastings was not unaware of the Dedham conflict with the Natick Indians. Dedham and Natick were separated only by the headwaters of the Charles River. "The camp would be on the south bank, probably on the smelt pond that runs into the Charles. They'll take their privacy."

Jonathan Brown stood up. "It worries me. They are not neighbors I would choose, even the best of them. Watertown has long had the advantage that no Indians live near, thanks to Reverend Elliot."

The room rustled as men nodded, agreeing. All would recognize Jonathan Brown was speaking from his heart. They had not forgotten the man nearly lost his daughter (and William's granddaughter) to Indians. Of course, the Indians were absolved. They had returned the four-year-old Lydia to the Browns when they'd found her wandering in the woods. But the panic Jonathan had felt after a day and night searching, when he first sighted the half-naked Indian and his squaw hand in dirty hand with his child? The stories he'd heard about children abducted in nearby towns? These were nightmares no one could easily dispel.

"Not good neighbors," others murmured. The words 'drunk,' and 'petty thieves' could be distinguished in the chorus.

"What are the choices?" William asked.

"Watertown could buy the rights to the weir from them," Thomas Hastings explained. "We have never formally paid for the land or rights. We could clear Speen's title to the Nonatum land and the weir."

"We already have rights." Corporal Bond interrupted.

"I don't think so. We have title only by the weir being on the King's land. We can make it official if we buy the rights from the natives. There'll be no question then."

"I like the idea, but it isn't easy as that."

"No exaggeration there," Captain Beers pitched in. "Indians are backward, but that doesn't mean they aren't cunning. I went to Boston last week, and hear the Wampanoag are at it again."

"What did you hear?" John Coolidge spoke up. Everyone quieted, listening for his answer.

"Few weeks ago, Governor Prence in Plymouth heard intelligence the Wampanoag were preparing war … repairing guns, sharpening hatchets, assembling and the like. Behaving badly …."

"Was it preparation for war or hunting parties?" Richard Norcross asked.

"Well, that's what Prence wondered. So, he called King Philip to meet him." Captain Beers scoffed: "That didn't go so well."

"Why?"

Corporal Bond headed off the conversation. "The sachem had the gall to demand Governor Prence leave hostages before he'd meet with him. I understand Metacom finds it hard to trust Prence; his brother died after just such a meeting. But his suspicions make negotiations impossible. Sachem Metacom would go only after two of the Governor's men volunteered to be hostages. Then, Metacom saw that the governor responded—naturally, I say—by showing up with his fully-armed military guard! Metacom canceled, gathered his own forces round."

Captain Beers commented, "Right. Way I see it, the Governor wanted to talk, but how, when Philip's got an armed guard with him?"

Challenged, Bond began to argue. "No trust on *either* side. The army mediated a face-off between the two in Taunton."

Captain Beers couldn't resist. "Taunton! King Philip came with his troop in full war dress, body paint, headdress, guns, all. So much for our treaty."

"And so did Governor Prence. The way I take it, Metacom's telling the Governor he's his own man. He's standing up to him."

"That isn't how I heard it," Captain Beers said. "The Governor made Philip go over the treaty again and demanded he surrender his guns."

"Hmph. He did, in exchange for a new treaty. The Governor agreed that Boston would mediate any conflicts between him and Metacom now."

"You believe Philip will give up his guns?" Captain Beers challenged.

"He did! The treaty's good. He explained himself, too. He was preparing defense against the Narragansetts, not an attack on Plymouth. The Narragansetts were enemies back when Metacom's father was sachem."

"I thought they were allies now," Jonathan Brown said.

"Right," Captain Beers agreed. "His brother's widow lives with the Narragansetts; Weetamoo, she's a sachem in her own right. Sounds like an alliance to me. King Philip did turn in their guns at the meeting. But you think the rest of his tribe will? Would we give up ours?"

"They've changed their way of hunting. They need them now." Corporal Bond was losing the energy to defend Metacom against his opponent.

Captain Beers hammered in his viewpoint. "I say, never trust an Indian!"

"We'd have a hard time with a camp across the river," Nathaniel Coolidge said. "I don't like the idea."

His brother nodded. "I agree. Can we take a vote on this? I think we should buy the fishing rights outright."

All but four of the council members voted to buy exclusive fishing rights from the Massachusetts, that included a one hundred fifty-acre lot surrounding the smelt pond that connected with the Charles River. Nathaniel put together the contract and settled on a price. Selectmen Beers, Bond, and Hastings were appointed to negotiate with Sachem Waban.

When the meeting came around to Ed Sanderson, he finally agreed to put his grammar-school-age children in service, thus avoiding the magistrate's bench in Boston.

Chapter Fifteen

UNCIVIL JUSTICE

Watertown, October 1671

The changes wore William down, and the news about Indian affairs was alarming. To keep abreast of developments, Watertown freemen had recourse to news from either of the Watertown deputies to the General Boston Court, Captain Beers or Corporal Bond. Captain Beers was most popular because he ran a public ordinary (a pub). Men easily stopped at the tavern on Bank Lane, close to the Charles River, to light up a pipe over a tankard of ale. William, homebody that he was, had never developed that habit, though his son John had been Beers' apprentice and often stopped at the inn. Another reason William found Corporal Bond a better source for news was Beers himself. The captain was the cause of the estrangement between himself and his son. Not only did John idolize this aging warrior, he internalized Beers' acid hatred of natives from the age of ten, and William couldn't tolerate listening to him.

More sensibly, William cultivated a friendship with Corporal Bond, who showed not only tolerance of, but preference for men beneath his station. He was not an ambitious man, as his military rank testified. He'd never be a social climber even though he was genuinely unaware that his birthright would always distinguish him from the masses he served. William had first come to know Bond when his neighbor John Coolidge had encouraged him to partner with Bond as Road Surveyor five years ago. Though his first impression had been poor, William had to admit that he'd been mistaken about the man's character; his wealth had never corrupted him. Corporal Bond showed humility and compassion. Since then, William had more than once mentally thanked John Coolidge for the wisdom that directed him to work with this man.

William found that Corporal Bond was informal and spontaneous, and he and Susanna tried to make as many of these occasions as they could. They invited him to stop by whenever he was in the neighborhood and pulled out all their hospitality when he did. It soon became a habit.

'I was just riding by and thought I'd stop in,' he'd say, walking in without knocking. Susanna and William would put down whatever they were working on and sit for a spell, in the yard in warm weather, by the fire in the cold. Sometimes, Susanna would direct him to the fields or barn to find William, and the whole work party would return to the house, the men drinking ale into the night.

It was nearly the end of September when Corporal Bond stopped by one afternoon to pull William out of his workshop. The two men found Susanna in the great room preserving fruit and asked for ale. The children were out for a change.

"Come and sit with us," Corporal Bond said.

"I will." Susanna brought tankards of ale to the table, setting one before each man. She loved these unannounced visits from their confirmed courier.

"What's the news?" William asked.

"You're right to ask. It's a damn cockup— I can't make out where we go from here. Excuse my swearing, Susanna."

Susanna slid a platter of bread and cheese across the boards. "Don't stop because of me."

William gestured to Bond, handing him the cheese knife. "Must be serious. You don't usually swear."

"Not in present company," Bond said. "Usually."

"But this is different?"

"You can judge for yourselves. Maybe two weeks ago, Governor Prence decided Metacom was breaking the treaty; he only gave up ninety guns, no more."

Susanna returned with her own drink, pressed apple cider, and sat down.

"So, he called in Metacom, threatened force if he didn't comply. Nothing happened. No Metacom. Then, Prence," he spit out the name, "sent out an alarm to Boston and Rhode Island too. The courier arrived in Boston with a message that Plymouth was equipping their troops and advising everyone to bring guns to church because Philip hadn't complied."

"Without any provocation other than not showing up?" William asked.

"Yeah. Thing is, when Philip heard that Prence had asked about the guns and threatened force, he rode to Boston, to take advantage of his new treaty, you know, the one he'd signed in Taunton. He wanted arbitration, as promised."

"That's his due," William said.

"Right. Well, Metacom arrived the same day as the warning letter and talked to our Governor Winslow."

"What did Winslow do?" Susanna asked.

"For one thing, he listened. The way my friend tells the story—he was there—Metacom hadn't turned in his guns for a reason. He believed the English wouldn't give them back. He'd heard from the Assowomsett and Middleboro Indians the English took their guns to force compliance and then gave out the guns to settlers. What's more, they threatened the Saconet Indians with war if they didn't submit themselves by treaty."

"Sounds like he has reason to not comply," William said.

"No one would. So, Metacom explained to Governor Winslow the treaties of his father, brother, and him were of friendship, not subjection. He knew the praying Indians were subject to Boston, but they had magistrates to represent them in courts. Never the Wampanoag. Metacom even challenged the governor to find one place in the treaties that said they were subject to Governor Prence or the Plymouth Colony."

Susanna, whose parents had come on the Mayflower and lived in the Plymouth Colony when Massasoit drew up the original treaty, agreed. "Massasoit wanted to be our ally, and twice we fought on each other's behalf. We fought the Narragansetts together. He was never subject to us!"

"So, what did Governor Winslow do?"

"Word is he sent a letter to Governor Prence warning him he's inviting war and told him he should avoid it."

"At least Winslow was honoring the Taunton treaty."

"Not quite," Corporal Bond said, shaking his head. He held up his tankard for a refill, and Susanna passed him the pitcher. "True, he warned Governor Prence, but Winslow told Metacom he'd read the treaties but didn't think he could change Prence's mind."

"No clout."

"That wasn't the end of the trouble. The next week, the three governors held a joint meeting with Metacom, and Governor Prence aired his accusations to all."

"Three on one. Hardly fair if you ask me," William said.

"The worst was, Governor Winslow, who made out he was sympathetic to Metacom, joined the others to charge him. Prence had a list. He started with Metacom refusing to give up his arms."

"We know why he didn't comply there," Susanna said.

"Then he said Metacom had been insolent and refused to meet with them when they wanted. Not finished, Prence said he was harboring our enemies, was uncivil to his neighbors, and misrepresented himself to the Boston magistrates."

"Welcome to England," William said wryly.

Corporal Bond commented on the last charge. "The Taunton treaty named Boston as arbitrator between Metacom and Plymouth. Metacom asks Boston to mediate his appeal and they hold that up as an offense? And they expect peace?"

He'd found the most flagrant fault, but Susanna and William held that King Philip had defended himself well to the charge of incivility. Metacom's neighbors thought he should do whatever they demanded. How was he 'uncivil' if he challenged the justness of their request?

"He can't win," William said, "even if he's right."

"I fear," Susanna said, "Governor Prence will make enemies of our friends."

William felt defeated, the promise of their city on the hill, upholding God's laws, had failed. Corruption would creep in to spite their dreams and efforts.

Chapter Sixteen

THE GOOD SHEPHERD

Watertown, December 1671

One December day in 1671 William returned from town to find the workshop was empty; Will and Jason had gone out. The house, too, was unusually quiet. Curious, he pushed his way past the stack of bolts at his workshop door to the back of the house. His wife sat on the settee, her skirt crushed by their sixteen-year-old daughter, Rebecca, who clung to her in tears. Susanna's face was set in a frown with creases between her brows; she looked worn out, more tired than he'd seen her in a long time and angry, too. When she heard him enter, she stared intently into his eyes. It was their unspoken signal of imminent crisis; he must drop everything. This was important.

"What is it?" William asked. "Where are the children?"

"I've sent them out," Susanna said. She held the corner of her apron up to dab at the tears, which darkened the faint freckles on her daughter's cheeks. Her skin had paled from the reflection of her green dress, destroying the natural beauty of her complexion. "Stop crying, my dear," she said to Rebecca.

"I'm sorry. There's no other way to begin. Rebecca's with child." Shrinking from her father's gaze, Rebecca erupted in another flow of tears. "Hush, hush now," Susanna insisted.

Flabbergasted, William sank into a chair. *How? When?* Their lives were so regimented, sunup to sundown, he could not immediately see how. When they weren't at work, they were at church, or in Rebecca's case, at school.

"Samuel Church has gotten her with child!" Susanna said.

Astounded, he thought, *Sam Church? He's twice her age!* The Sherborns would never have associated with him; everyone knew Sam Church to be intemperate and quarrelsome. The magistrates had locked this drunken bachelor in the stocks twice. *This cannot be.*

"Did she make this up?" William asked. "It's preposterous."

"I fear not," she answered.

"But where did she meet him?"

"Have you forgotten? Rebecca attends school with the Clinnery girl, Ruth, now."

Rebecca had met Ruth Clinnery the night of the blizzard, when a tree fell on the Clinnery's house, and the two had become fast friends the weeks the Clinnerys stayed. The friendship changed Rebecca's life. Rebecca had never been a good student; she was flighty and imaginative, unable to focus on her lessons. She'd struggled to keep up with others in Richard Norcross's school. When her new friend spoke so glowingly of her Dame School, Rebecca had begged her mother to let her visit, and afterwards, Rebecca fought both her parents to stay.

William nearly refused his daughter on religious grounds; the Watertown Council had reprimanded and fined Goody Cooke for teaching separatist doctrines. But Susanna had prevailed. "I grew up in Plymouth. My parents were separatists. What's wrong with that?" He had no defense and let his daughter change schools. Rebecca thrived in her new environment; she'd loved tailoring from the moment Goody Rachel Cooke put a needle in her hand, and she'd quickly risen to be the top performer in her school.

Susanna turned to Rebecca, who had mopped her tears with her sleeve and gained back some composure. "Tell your father how you met him."

Rebecca never looked up once as she told her tale. "At Dame School, at Goody Cooke's house. I met him there.

He had lunch with us, every day. He was nice, father. He gave me a silver thimble, to remember him."

"And you accepted it? T'was a bribe, not a gift!"

Susanna nodded her agreement. "Samuel works with Goody Cooke's husband; he's been helping him build."

He's a sawyer, is he not?"

"That's right." Rebecca stared at each parent in turn as they decided her fate.

"At least he has a trade."

"Are you thinking of letting this match go forward? With his reputation?"

"It's an alternative, isn't it?" William turned to Rebecca. "Have you told anyone at all that you are expecting?"

"Just you and mother."

"Not Ruth? Your sister? This Samuel?" he spat out.

"No one," Rebecca shook her head.

"Don't think of it," Susanna said to William. "You can't hide a pregnancy; it's not a secret she can keep. Even if she marries him, she will pay for this."

Susanna turned to her daughter. "You foolish, foolish girl! Even if a man tells you he loves you, he may lie, and if we force a marriage, you cannot avoid punishment for conceiving out of wedlock. We must post bans, and then wait for the wedding. A baby born too soon? Everyone will know your sin. You will disgrace your family, and the magistrates will put both of you in stocks for fornication. Oh, that I live to see the day a Sherborn girl sits in stocks!"

"I'll not know if a wedding is possible until I speak to him; his character is wanting. Nor will he care about punishment. Such insolence! The stocks are nothing for him."

Susanna shook her head. "I'm with you. We still have a way out. We could send her away until the baby is born. She could stay with Suzanne in Groton."

"I'll not be part of such hypocrisy. Rebecca must face what she has done before God and man; she has a conscience and knows her sin. I'll not have her lose her soul as well as her good name."

"I am to blame, not Samuel!" Rebecca stood and faced them with her head up and eyes blazing. "I have promised to marry Samuel. He's not a drinker like some say. That was a long time ago."

"He does come to Sunday meetings now," Susanna said.

"Aye, for two months. Two months he is seducing my daughter! Am I to trust any man who does not come to me with his intents, a scoundrel who extracts a promise from a child who knows nothing of men's ways?" Temperate of nature, and slow to anger, William felt overwhelmed with rage he'd seldom felt. "I cannot trust the man."

"For Rebecca's sake," Susanna said, "can you put aside virtue? I know the church rejects ambition as a motive to join our church. I know proving God's grace is the only reason to accept one in our fold. I understand the parable of wolves in sheep's clothing. But even if Samuel's motive is to gain the object of his affections instead of God's grace, can we dismiss that lightly? Might not that be a good sign, for Rebecca?"

"My dear, to save the family, I fear we will need to bow to necessity; Rebecca has made her bed to suit herself. I must talk with Samuel Church before I can say more."

Susanna pulled Rebecca close when she began to sob. William left the house, saddling up Old Gray to ride to Goody Cooke's, where he'd find Samuel Church at work. The December air lanced his lungs as he lifted the saddle over his horse's back and pulled in the cinch. His mind raced through what was becoming a litany of grievances for his children. First, John had embarrassed them all when he slandered the Phillips boy; then, Joanna's uncomely behavior was attracting gossip; and now, Rebecca was guilty of fornication with a man of bad repute. He talked to his God on the ride, grieved for the loss of his children, the sheep he'd failed to protect.

Chapter Seventeen

MAN TO MAN

Watertown, December 1671

Goody Cooke didn't live far, and soon he was at her door. She pointed out to the back when he asked to see Samuel Church, and William found him at the bottom of the sawpit. Samuel worked under the 'dogs,' those planks that hold the log above the sawpit. He worked at the bottom end of the saw that chewed the tree trunk stretched across the dogs. William noticed Samuel's partner, the 'top' dog, a younger man with a shock of hair covering his eyes. He had to lean over the shadowy pit to make out Samuel Church, who stood barefoot in the oozing mud at the bottom, soiled up to his knees. Samuel had tucked his hair into a grey wool monmouth to keep out the sawdust and stripped down to rolled-up trousers and a dirty unbleached shirt. Even in the cold, sweat beaded on his forehead. William, who usually admired the grime of men hard at work, detested Samuel's appearance. *What did Rebecca see in him?* he thought.

"I'm William Sherborn. We need to talk," he said, "in private." The top sawyer nodded and left for the house.

Samuel Church climbed the ladder from the pit, grabbing the jacket hanging from the dog. He pulled it on before he bent to introduce himself. "I'm Sam Church," he said, extending his hand.

William didn't take his hand. He took a threatening stance, instead, and growled, "I know who you are."

"It's Rebecca!" Samuel Church exclaimed. "She told you?"

"Told me what?" William hissed. It couldn't be worse for Samuel Church. *He didn't have the courage to tell me himself?* he thought. *He let Rebecca tell me?*

"I told her not to say anything." Samuel's forehead wrinkled, his head bent as he avoided William's eyes. "She shouldn't have. I don't know what you must think of me."

William softened. At least he's not stupid. That's something.

"We want to marry." Samuel glanced up sideways; he had adopted the ways of many tall men who posed threats by their height alone.

"She's just turned sixteen; she's not a wed-able woman until she's eighteen. That's two years from now! Are you willing to wait?" He probed to find out if he knew Rebecca was pregnant.

"Mister Sherborn, I see no reason to wait. We love each other." He broke off, grunting as he tore off his hat, again staring at his feet. Thick brown hair, peppered with gray, tumbled to his shoulders.

"You are twice her age. That's the most obvious reason to us; *you* have no time to wait."

"I am older, I'll admit. But understand that I resisted my love for her until I could no longer put it off. When she said she felt the same, even with our difference in age, well, I was lost."

"That's even more obvious."

"What do you mean? We've been proper ... we've never ..."

"Don't make it difficult by lying, too," William interrupted. "We know because Rebecca is with child."

"With child? How? We only ..." Samuel looked shocked.

"In the usual way," William relented more. His test had removed another horrible motive. Samuel had not agreed to marry Rebecca because she was pregnant. Nor had he deliberately impregnated her to get his way. He would deal with the lie later. The Puritan church was much harder on liars than it was on coupling out of wedlock. "You'll pay for this sin in the eyes of God and man. You can't escape God's eyes even if you can avoid the rest. You want to marry, but are you prepared to be a father?"

William ended by giving his permission to Samuel Church, his first anger receding with a hiss, like surf that flowed back to the sea. Later that night, he spoke with Susanna. "I've been thinking that Samuel's reputation is so marred that even marriage will cause a public scandal. That's punishment enough. It's best the pair marry and move to Groton as soon as possible. They will have a fresh start, and no one will know Rebecca got pregnant out of wedlock. Perhaps John will let them lease his land there. Samuel will have no want of work in Groton, if we can believe what John tells us. Suzanne can help Rebecca grow up; I cannot imagine her with a dependent child!"

"Thank you," Susanna breathed a sigh of relief.

William posted the bans on the church door immediately, and the family came together in a flurry to prepare a hasty January wedding.

Chapter Eighteen

SPRING WON'T WAIT

Watertown, May 1672

Though Susanna and William had invited all their friends, few attended Rebecca's wedding. After noticing the bans at their Sunday afternoon prophesies, the congregation avoided the subject as though embarrassed. It was obvious they didn't approve of Rebecca's poor choice and the erring parents who backed it with a public wedding. They not only shunned Samuel Church now; they avoided Rebecca as well.

Sherborn family friends who were suspicious the sudden wedding signaled wrongdoing wanted to avoid confrontation; partly, the weather stopped guests from attending. Reverend Sherman was late getting to their house in the snowstorm. Thus, the wedding dinner was a small intimate group consisting of Samuel Church's brother and father, the Sherborns, and Rebecca's closest friend, Ruth Clinnery. William had refused to invite Goody Cooke, who he was sure had been aware of the dalliance between his daughter and Sam Church. He would always hold her as responsible.

Richard Norcross had turned down the wedding invitation, but a long-term friend of the family, it was not to express his disapproval. His wife had become ill, and not three weeks after the wedding, despite the excellent care of midwife Joanna Morton and Doctor Philip Sherborn, she had died of a necrotic infection. Master Norcross closed the school for two weeks after his wife died. Susanna enlisted Mary and Joanna to escort her to his house on several occasions; she brought pots of savory stew and Johnnycakes for the family, and comfort for her bereaved friend. The community stepped in to help the mourning father care for the children who remained at home, and matchmakers began speculating on a suitable wife for the widower.

Still, February light sent sap running in the maples, and colonists were already tapping the sugar flows to make syrup. At the month's end, when the schoolmaster again started up school, the thaw began; icecycles dripped, then disappeared from the eaves and sills. March came with some bluster and snow, but the days lengthened; winter was gone.

When it was time, the Sherborns said good-bye to Samuel and Rebecca Church, who had agreed to William's suggestion that they move to Groton. They were homesteading on John's land grant. Sam made enough in wages and trading—sawyers were even more in demand than weavers—to pay a carpenter to raise a one-story house. William and Will helped Sam Church load household furnishings in his cart, and he and Rebecca chucked the mule, riding off on the narrow, rutted road. It would take three days to reach their new home if it snowed.

In early March, William noted blossoming skunk cabbage in the marsh paralleled the news from Boston. The first purple spades melted the ice and snow around them as they pushed up from the muddy marshes and scented the air with the smell of rotting meat. They were the reason colonists often talked of 'stinking swamps.' These deep-rooted plants grew thickly throughout Massachusetts, wherever standing water pooled. While Corporal Bond had bad news from Boston—in March, England had, for a third time, declared war on the Dutch—he upheld it would not embroil the colonies this time. In the second war with Holland, Britain had won the Dutch colony and renamed it New York. The third war would stay in Europe. This confidence grew stronger when the French allied with the English in the battle the following month. Most predicted a short conflict. With no new reports of conflicts between Sachem Metacom and Governor Prence, the colonists breathed easier. Seemingly, the Indian chief wanted only to sell all of his land, which the colonists—few suspecting the chief's rash behavior or his arms purchases—were too happy to buy.

By April, snows turned to rain, and the first spring wild flowers nosed up from the thick moldy loam of the forests. Joanna, who had a hunter's keen eye, was the first to spy the snowdrops. She knelt in a patch of snow by the green starbursts studded with drops of white petals, calling out, 'they're blooming.' William joined the rest, who couldn't resist taking time to see them. This European transplant was a gift; Goodwife Clinnery had tied a few snowdrop bulbs and bluebell seed boles in the corner of a handkerchief when she'd come from England. She'd rediscovered them with joy, tucked in a forgotten corner of her sack, and planted them in her yard. Miraculously, they'd thrived in their new land. When she brought specimens to Susanna, she'd assured her 'these are but a poor gift to repay you for your kindness, but I'd like you to have them'. William had responded by saying they were as precious as gems. He'd joyfully walked the paths of Somerset's Exmoor forest each spring in his youth and welcomed these reminders from his home.

So eager for air and color, his offspring couldn't refrain from their own joyful searches. In time, their viewing became walks on carpets of the native pink spring beauties, and later, the mayflower shrubs. At the wood's edge, they could see the bluebells twinkling amid the first green buds of the brush. Wood poppies and mayapples raised beaks like birds from nests of wet leaf mold, then opened to green domes. The returning robins and cardinals gave sound to the sweet winds.

In May, when the Charles' flood tides rolled in waves all the way to Watertown, callers rode out to announce the alewife were running. William knew John and Will must already be fishing alewives at the weir. They filled their sacks using nets, but the swarms that swam upstream on the spring tides to spawn were so thick, they could pluck them out by hand. After beheading the spawn, Susanna fried them to a buttery brown, and the family savored the roe inside and crunched the crisp, chip-like tails. Jo filled a crock with brine, testing the salt content with a raw egg. When it floated, she added the alewives to the brine, weighing them down with a stone. Smoked, the brined fish would provide months of snacks or seasoning for chowder.

Touched by this spring renewal, William woke from another Somerset dream. This one he couldn't ignore. In the dream, he'd leaped from the ground effortlessly, swung with the ease of a spider on its web, to stand on a wooden beam, high above St. Mary's church pews. He stood next to the shadowy form of a giant golden angel, who bent down to speak to him. 'You must make a leap of faith,' the Angel said before he burst into a wall of flame. William thought he was to jump into it. He woke with a gasp.

The morning spring rain brought a heavy mist that blanketed the fields in a magical light. The returning migrants fluttered up from the fields and twittered sweetly to their nesting mates. He couldn't keep his mind off the trip he had so long postponed. It seemed spring warmed his blood, and the longing rose like the sap running in the trees, imbuing the winter feelings of fatigue and defeat with energy. *It is time,* he thought, and the plan for his voyage coalesced in a covert silence.

....

Chapter Nineteen

TAKING COMMAND

Watertown, June 1672

In June, he announced to Susanna that he was going to Boston to buy passage on a packet to England. "I plan to sail in August and return in April or May, weather willing."

Susanna nearly dropped the spindle she was winding. She'd heard nothing of his wish to go back since that terrible winter years ago. She'd thought he'd forgotten. "I know you wanted to go before, but for years you've not said so. Can you tell me why? And six months? So long?"

"I'm fifty and have little time left for such a vigorous trip. And it is my conviction that God has called me to England before I die, though I confess I don't know why. My dreams always take me back to Somerset."

She set down her work and pointed to a nearby stool. "Please sit. You are making me nervous. William, you will abandon me for six months: this house, the farm, at harvest? You know that we must prepare for the winter. What are you thinking? I can't manage on my own."

The stool screeched across the floor as William drew it close to sit. "I'm not abandoning you. I will hire more help, and we have David in the fields. You do well to let him lead. What's more, Will's old enough; he's already half running my weaving. He's talented and has your head for business."

"He's but eighteen; he's not reached his majority. And Benjamin! A child! What are you thinking? The children increase my work, even when they try to be helpful."

"I was eighteen when I came to Watertown; he's old enough."

"They're boys. The rest have their families; John has a newborn and Philip, a pregnant wife. I cannot bother them to come here to make repairs or rescue a sheep."

"Don't forget Jacob; he can weave when you need Will to help with the farm. Preserving the harvest is no problem with Joanna and Will pitching in. Joanna is nearly as capable as any man. She is a grand hunter, winter or summer."

"Aye, Joanna is my rock, but not for long; she is twenty and already some say an 'old maid.' She should be meeting her future husband, not playing nanny for a brood of brothers and sisters, and not providing game for our table. We use her ill. You should be arranging an engagement for her. If she gets older, she will find no one who will take her."

"May be, like Rebecca, she can find her mate on her own," William was starting to get angry. "She's too particular. I see in her no inclination to marry anyone at all."

"Don't let me start on that; she's your daughter. Don't tell me you haven't encouraged her to hunt and overlook her boyish behavior. Admit it. You have Abigail, too. She'll start her menses soon and needs a father's guidance. You don't want her to be boy crazy the way Rebecca was. You abandon us all! You have made me a common scold, and now must I sit in the stocks, too?"

"I understand my decision is a hardship for you, but I've thought it through carefully and spoken with Reverend Sherman about it many times. I wanted to take you and the family to England with me, but he pointed out it would only divide us. Our married children could not come. Then, you've never experienced such a trip, and I fear, at our age ..." William stood and began to pace, gesturing widely. "So, I let go of the notion that I'd take you to England with me. I've postponed this trip for five years and cannot any longer. You must have faith that God has his reasons and that He will provide for us."

"You never said a word about taking us to England. How could you keep this from me?" She shook her head and sank back on her chair, expectantly leaning forward, elbows on knees, hands folded as if in prayer. She couldn't look at him.

"Reverend Sherman talked me out of it, and I saw no reason to upset you with an event that would never come to be."

"Well, I'm gratified that you didn't forget us."

"Not ever," William avowed. "You are my life."

"I'll accept your decision, as is my place, though I cannot without complaint. You must understand that I fear you may never return. It's a nightmare to think of the ocean swallowing you up like a misbegotten Jonah."

"Possible; we are mortal all. I can offer you only this comfort—I will draw every breath in my body with the purpose God sends me. You are that purpose." He dropped to the stool and took her hands in his.

She smiled, but her face fell as she took his hands. "I know that you love me, but I ask that you state your love in more practicable terms." When he drew back—he thought she'd insist that he stay—she explained earnestly. "What will I do if you leave me suddenly? Aye, and with six children to care for? I am a woman and can own no property in my name! You have no will. Might you arrange it before you leave us?"

William was speechless. In his prime, death had never crossed his mind. "You imagine my death before I die." He turned from her, frowning.

"I am but a practical woman; I can do no other way. You *know* me."

William softened, allowing her to pull him towards her. "Aye. I'll not fault you for your good head!"

"My place is not to guess what may come, but to know what I must do whatever comes. Please understand. You would put my mind at rest."

"I'll think about it. I'll need witnesses to write a will."

"Thank God," Susanna whispered. "When will you go to Boston?"

"As I said, the end of July. I'll take Will to return with the horses. I want to stop and visit with Philip and Deborah, too."

"Will you tell the parish?" Susanna asked.

"I'll have to; I'll need a letter of recommendation if I am to continue my covenant while I am gone, and I'll need your testimony if I am to win their blessings. Will you grant me your blessing?"

"Always, husband. I am resigned. I'll see to outfitting you for the trip. You will need new clothes more to the English fashion. Oh, where is Rebecca when I need her? She would know."

The next day, William rode to John Coolidge's house. The stocky man was cleaning the barn with his son.

"John," William greeted him. "I need to ask you a favor."

John stopped, leaning the fork against the barn wall and stamping the hay from his feet. "What brings you?"

"I need to write my will but need witnesses. I could use your help with the inventory, too. I can pay you."

"I'm happy to help, but now? Are you ill?"

"No. I'm well enough. Susanna is asking me to write it. She says if I die without a will, she'll be destitute."

"That's not true. Your estate would fall to the colony, and the magistrates would parcel it to your wife and children. English law gives the land to the oldest son, and the widow has the use of the house and land while she lives."

William stepped back. His oldest boy, John, was a sliver in his heart. John rejected the church and because of it could in no way stand as a respectable member in Watertown; could he trust him should he inherit the house and lands? Clearly, he would need to look into the laws.

"I'll let you know when."

"Why does she see a need?"

"You'll know soon enough, but I'd rather not say now." William frowned. He didn't want to tell his friend yet about the trip. He intended to ask the congregation for approval but facing close friends with the news was a different matter. John Livermore had unfortunately let out his secret to friends, and the news leaked. Not only the church confronted John Livermore but the Watertown Council. He'd not been able to leave for England without ruining his social standing.

John looked at him askance, wondering what secret William harbored. "You probably do want to have a will, because you'll be of a different mind where you want your money to go. I can't see you turning over the farm to John. Meanwhile, rest your mind the law will take care of Susanna. She needn't worry."

William thanked him and rode home, thinking of how he might divide his property. The more he thought, the more complexity he found. *Six hogs, eight pigs, ten sheep and nine lambs! There's the bull and four cows. Two calves, too. Two oxen. How to divide them? The farm needs the oxen, and weaving needs the sheep. Susanne must feed the children. The farm in Stonybrook, and Will's horse, Pilgrim? It's not his. I own all four horses. What would happen should John—the least deserving—inherit all?* This last thought tightened his stomach and speeded his heart. Although he'd decided to put off writing his will, he had nevertheless begun to realize it might be urgent. Susanna was right.

Chapter Twenty

LEAVING HOME

Watertown, July 1672

Elder Chadwick had taken his post near the lectern. He began the community announcements with William's business.

"William Sherborn," he began, "is traveling to England, and asks the congregation for a letter recommending his character to those of the faith in his home, Somerset."

The request inspired a wave of murmuring as parishioners turned to their neighbors to exclaim their surprise. John Coolidge, stunned by the announcement, looked as though William had just betrayed him. John Livermore shook his head in disbelief. That William had not confided in them, his best friends, was an affront. Other parishioners could not believe William would ask; they thought he'd be the last one to abandon the colonies. He was reliable, a homebody, not an adventurer. Soon, calls were heard above the clamor.

"What grounds?" called one. "The grounds?" said another. "What of your family?"

The Elder Chadwick called the meeting to order. "I think it best if William Sherborn explains his request. Goodman Sherborn, what say you?"

William stood, nervously fiddling with his hat, which he'd removed out of respect. "Good day," he mumbled.

"Speak up," one shouted. "We can't hear you," shouted another.

Unaccustomed to speaking in groups, he had to overcome his panic. He took a deep breath. "I ask for your blessing because I am answering God's call. For many years now, God has sent me dreams about returning to my birthplace, Stogumber, but I confess, I do not know why or what God has planned for me. I have had these dreams for five or more years but have not heeded the Lord's words. I'm sorry I can say no more to give reasons, but last week, God's angel appeared to me and told me that I must 'take a leap of faith.' The feeling I must leave now is so strong I can no longer put off the voyage. I can only assure you that I am as mystified as you may be."

"He speaks the truth," John Livermore said, grudgingly. His own trip had been waylaid by the congregation because they felt that he was abandoning his covenant for personal profit. "He confessed his dreams of returning when I prepared to leave myself."

Reverend Sherman added, "William has confided these dreams to me for more than six years now and fought his wish to return so he could perform his duties to his family and our community. His service as selectman and as father to his family are exemplary. Thus, I am led to support his request."

"But what about your family? Will you take them?" John Coolidge now knew why he had asked him about writing a will. Still smarting that William had not trusted him with his plan, he demanded that William account for himself.

"That's right," someone else pitched in. "What does your wife say about it?"

Susanna stood. Facing William, holding his attention with her eyes, she testified, "I've known his desire for more than five years." She recalled his confession to his neighbors the night of the blizzard. "He has stayed his desire for so long, I couldn't ever assume he abandons me. He leaves only when the colony is at peace and we are well-set. I can in no way refuse him, as I too believe that God is asking him to make this voyage. I give him my blessing and my prayers for a safe return."

William added, "I plan to return in six months and have arranged for my family's well-being while I am gone."

The discussion between individuals rose in a peak. John Sherman weighed in, speaking for the Watertown Council: 'William has no duty outstanding this year. I see no reason to object." Joseph Clinnery called, "Young Will needs help while you're gone, he can call on me." Fox added, "You don't need to worry about the Indians for now. Seems a good time to go if you ask me." Corporal Bond agreed. "For now." Another wave of discussion followed while the congregants agreed the time was good; the colonies were secure. Elder Chadwick again called them to order. "What is your decision?" he asked.

"We give our blessings," John Coolidge said, "because he agrees to return. We cannot do without his continuance."

The Reverend John Sherman, who sat among the attendees for the prophesying, stood. "I will draft the letter of recognition for the congregation."

Once the congregation had reached its consensus, the afternoon prophesying continued. The day's philosophy mulled on laws: some were natural, or, God-given, and some, civil, or, man-made, the family-society. The Puritan way was to follow the natural laws; where civil laws took a different direction, reform was necessary. They discussed the rights and duties of the righteous ruler, using Nehemiah and his acts for a model of good government, which Jesus in turn supported in his sermons.

In the month that followed, Susanna made ready for William's journey, hiring Goody Cook to make a new suit of clothes that would serve in England. She listed the orders of each child in the family for gifts from England. William wondered how his children even knew the existence of some of the items they wanted. Even Samuel, his youngest, had asked for a toy he'd seen another child play with. The girls wanted fine cotton fabric, lace collars, or ribbons. Suzanne had written from Groton that she'd like a copy of Milton's *Paradise Regained*, which though published a year earlier and available in Boston shops, was too expensive a buy in the colonies. She wanted the gift for her husband, Joseph, who wrote poetry himself. She asked for the latest book on midwifery for herself. Rebecca wanted imported fabrics. Mary ordered her first china teacup and saucer. Susanna, ever practical, wanted a new, larger crock for fermenting, or a kettle to replace the battered old one she'd had since they wed and a lace collar. Once she'd outfitted William with a new suit of clothes, she oversaw packing toiletries for him: soap, beard trimmer, and vinegar for lotion.

William found his old ship's trunk, which he now used to collect mementos, having emptied it after his first trip aboard a packet. He spilled the contents on the floor, finding at the bottom a dog-eared and yellowed catalog he'd used to outfit himself in England. He chuckled at his find, reminiscing on the items that he'd crossed out. The ship's company aimed the lists at supplying whole families, but he had come to Watertown a single man.

Although the catalog warned him he would find no fairs or markets in the colonies, he'd thought that without a wife and children, he'd not need any household items or hardware for building carts and houses. He'd cut back on his food stores as well. Stupidly. He'd brought only his looms, spinning wheels, bales of wool, a few tools no man could live without, a pot to eat from, a wooden plate, a spoon, and a knife. He did bring the recommended clothes: one suit each of canvas, frieze, and cloth, four pairs of shoes, a pair of boots, three shirts, and a Monmouth cap. He also brought a canvas mat, rugs, and blankets for his bedding. The catalog had recommended armor, with a long piece, sword, bandoleer, and ammunition, and he had reluctantly packed everything but the armor. He understood he needed the guns and swords for hunting and self-defense but considered the armor was for soldiers, not weavers. Short of food, lacking fundamentals to build any lodging, only the kindness of the Puritan family who boarded him kept him alive the first year.

He sat before the trunk with the same list, realizing it was nearly useless for his return voyage. This time, too, he began by cutting out items he wouldn't need. However, he paid closer attention to food and drinks, medicines, and bedding for the trip. Passage in a ship's hold might be more comfortable with preparation for privacy and consideration of seasickness. He knew how important dry clothes and bedding were to voyagers. Last, he didn't neglect to pack a small hand loom and distal, so he could fill the weeks of idle hours with industry. *Idle hands were the Devil's playground*, he thought.

More than once, William thought *I must write my will*, but tapping the idea brought such a flood of complications that he always abandoned it. Then, he would berate himself for once again avoiding his obligations to his family. He never once found the real reason, either, though he had a litany of shortcomings he asked forgiveness for in prayer.

Susanna set Will to the task of making sure his father had proper supplies for the voyage. Will calculated the food stores his father would need on the trip. That was the easy part. Step two was the difficult part. He had to pack the food on their conveyances, in this case, two riding horses and a pack horse. He would have to adjust the amounts to the space allowed.

The two would ride to Boston, stopping in Cambridge to stay with Philip and Deborah. Will would return from Boston with the two horses when they'd unloaded William's supplies for the trip on the ship's wharf.

Despite the long weeks of preparation, William was not ready. As the day neared, he seemed dazed, unable to think through the simplest list of tasks he must complete. Now that he was to realize his dream, every bone in his body resisted. Instead of efficiently checking the lists against his cargo, he lost himself in memories of his first voyage. Suddenly prone to 'wool gathering' he found he couldn't finish the simplest chore but was sidetracked until he worked three tasks, finishing none. On the night before he left, he felt a strong need to speak to Susanna, but could say nothing. The silence wrapped them, binding their arms to their sides, and they miserably lay sleepless, unable to communicate.

In the hour he was to leave, he lost himself in admiration of Will's horse as he watched Will lead Pilgrim into the yard. William knew his son doted on Pilgrim; *this is his horse*, he thought. *I must give him Pilgrim when I write my will.* With the horses packed and Will already mounted, he finally had to confront his last good-bye.

He turned to Susanna, and overcome, hugged her, and unable to blink back his tears, cried. She too wept; they had not been parted for thirty years. When the moment had come, their goodbyes whispered, they separated, and William mounted his horse. Susanna stood in the yard watching until the two had passed from sight.

....

Chapter Twenty-one

GIDDY WOMEN

Cambridge, July 1672

Now that William's son, Philip, had become a country doctor, William rarely saw him. Philip's reputation had grown once he'd left his apprenticeship in Boston, and he was often in demand. Then, Deborah's uncle gave the newlyweds land in Cambridge, close to Cambridge Road, but distance compounded the problem. So, he had not seen his son since the burial of their firstborn child. Philip and Deborah lost the little girl from summer diarrhea, or what Philip called 'cholera infantum,' only a week following her birth. The whole family had attended Little Deborah's burial to watch the tiny coffin lowered into the ground.

Deborah had been inconsolable; no one could comfort her. The English in William's life had been reticent to show emotions, and he thought Deborah's unabashed grief, expressed by wailing and heart-wrenching sobs, not only unhinged her but also showed her as faithless. Could she find no comfort in knowing that God had taken her baby as His own? There was no blame, though his Puritan daughter-in-law must feel punished. Since he'd seen her rarely—and most memorably at her wedding and the burial—the two impressions made her behavior on the latter occasion, even more extreme. For that reason, he'd put off visiting the pair. He approached their house with apprehension, not knowing if he'd be welcome. Philip had passed word through John on a visit to patients in Watertown that Deborah was again with child, and William hoped she had resolved her grief.

The house they built on the gifted land was a starter home: one story, with a gabled attic, set back from the road by a steep grassy slope framed by forest. William chuckled when he saw the thickly wooded lot. *Never look a gift horse in the mouth*, he thought. *They'll have a hard time clearing this acre; probably swamp in the back.*

Philip's reputation as a healer had spread; most of those he treated had relief from their ailments, to his credit. William had always known that his son would succeed because of his manner with patients; he had a soothing voice and even as a boy, listened intently, drawing out those he talked with. William knew this quiet man, who spoke little until it was necessary, was thinking all the while he listened. He'd once told Susanna that he could see the wheels turning in Philip's head. His intelligence, however, had its drawbacks. William had sometimes felt inadequate around his son; they'd never been close.

William dismounted and wrapped the reins of his mount around the hitching post in the yard. Will followed suit. The serving girl curtsied to the men, her blond curls bouncing with the slight dip. Only ten, she giggled when she greeted them. "Master's gone, but Mistriss is here. Wait here. I'll get her." She smiled broadly, clearly excited by the prospect of having visitors, and fluttered down a hall.

William glimpsed a formal parlor through a door on the left; a band of sunlight spilled from the open curtains to cross a large circle rug woven from rags. A high-backed settee faced the hearth, where it caught the most warmth. In minutes, the maid returned. "What's your name?" William asked.

"I'm Sophy. Mistress excuses herself. She can't come to meet you, but she'll see you in the great room. You're family, and she says that's okay because they don't mind the mess."

William laughed, "Well said." She led them down a hall to the center of the house. Will followed, ducking his head as they crossed the threshold to the common room.

William's first sight of Deborah eased his apprehension: her cheeks glowed ruddy from sitting near the fire, and her bearing was hearty. She smiled and gestured from her chair, pointing as she lifted her feet from the footstool. "Philip will have me off my feet! Please, sit. I'm sorry I couldn't come to greet you, but I dare not leave my chair without him scolding me. Isn't that so, Sophy?"

William graciously answered her invitation by taking the chair across from her, and Will sat on the wooden settee. The low cooking fire in the hearth made the room warm and stuffy, and William loosened the scarf tied around his neck and threw off his jerkin. Sophy fussed with Deborah's cushions. "That's right, Mistress. You're to mind the baby."

Deborah laughed. "She's my jailer, you know. Philip will have her tattling on me! He will take no chance that we lose this one."

Here, her voice dropped, and the catch in her throat caught William's attention. *She's still grieving*, he thought.

"I'm so glad to have visitors; Sophy and I don't get out." She caught Sophy's hand. "Sophy, will you get us some ale? And perhaps biscuits?"

"Yes, ma'am." Soon she busied herself at the hearth, ladling ale into mugs, arranging biscuits from a basket on a wooden platter.

Nervously, Deborah chattered on. "Philip and I were just talking about how we miss family, and here you are! To what do we owe this visit? Some special news? Is everyone well?"

"Everyone's well. I must apologize for not visiting sooner. Since you moved to Cambridge, we fret that we have so little time."

"You must have so much news. Are the children well? Do you hear from Suzanne and Rebecca? Philip will be home soon. He'd never forgive himself if he missed your visit. You mustn't rush off!"

Will sat forward and broke into the conversation. "We hope we'll not inconvenience you, but we'd like to stay overnight."

"Oh wonderful. That's the best news. Are you on your way somewhere? To Boston, perhaps?"

William said, "To England."

Deborah laughed. "You are joking with me, surely. You will stay overnight on your way to England? Oh, that *is* a story!"

"But it's true. You've not heard because my decision was sudden. I am leaving from Boston for England in three days."

"England! Oh, my parents would love to go with you! I never hear the end of praising England." Deborah gestured to Sophy, who stood nearby with a tray. Sophy set the biscuits down on a side table and handed mugs to her guests, extending a mug to her mistress as well.

"I can only have juice. No ale and biscuits for me, now. Philip says it's not fit fare for baby. I do so wish Philip were less strict. Do you go alone? You are not thinking of leaving forever?"

"Yes and no," William chuckled. "I go alone and will return in spring, when the winds turn the ships home."

Sophy turned to her mistress and whispered something in her ear. "Yes, Sophy." Deborah raised her head. "Sophy says that you have animals with loads tied outside. You are welcome to use the barn. I'm sorry I can't show you, but perhaps one barn is like another."

"Yes. Will, I think that's your job. When you have rested, would you?"

Will drank deeply from his mug, wiping his mouth on his sleeve when he was through. "I'll do it now." He rose and strode out the door, happy to flee from the overheated room and, he thought, giddy woman.

"Sophy, we'll be two more for dinner, and you'll need to fix the loft for our guests. You had better start now."

Sophy's joy at having visitors was short-lived. Her shoulders slumped as though she longed to resist her mistress's commands but dared not. It was the closest she came to an insolent answer. "Go on," Deborah continued, "no backtalk now."

William frowned, unable to stop from judging Sophy's behavior. Deborah had clearly coddled her serving girl and no doubt believed she was exercising kindness instead of tolerating bad behavior. What is more, she did no favors for her charge; Sophy was too young to know the results of expressed attitudes. Nevertheless, he couldn't help being even more critical with Deborah. Surely these light housekeeping tasks would not disrupt Deborah's pregnancy. Of course, his experience was only with his own Susanna, and heaven knew that she could withstand any hardship. He watched Sophy set up the table boards near an open window in the corner of the room where they would benefit from a breeze.

"Phillip is gone so much, and I get no visitors. Because I can't go out, I don't know what I would do without Sophy. She is a child still, but uncommonly bright. I must only tamp down her love of play. I've never seen such a glutton for pastimes as my Sophy."

William nodded. "I've had experience with my apprentices. You are right. Getting their attention works best if we can make a game of it. But children her age must learn duty. Don't you think?"

Deborah brushed her hair from her forehead with the back of her hand, a gesture that became more frequent the more animated her speech. She changed the subject, which was upsetting her. "I cannot imagine a voyage to England. I was born here, but I've heard my parents speak of it; mainly, I remember them complaining that equipping their voyage was costly."

"Very costly. The fare is the main difficulty. Well, you can see that indentured servants pay for one crossing with three to seven years of work. Supplying food and water costs nearly as much as the passage; of course, those returning to England have little cargo unless we are trading goods."

"Will you take items for sale?"

"Mine is not such a venture. I'm not going for business. I am answering a holy call."

"A holy call!"

"I don't know how else to describe it. God is asking me to return."

"Ah, voices. I have heard God speaking to me but am never sure it's God. I mean, the Devil is more likely, don't you think? You are sure?"

"Whoever believes he speaks to God may be mistaken. To even think I am worthy for God's word, I am in danger of the sin of pride. That's why I speak to Reverend Sherman about such matters. I have no explanation of why I must go other than recurring dreams; I believe God sends them to me."

Deborah smoothed her skirts. "I don't dream, or at least, I never remember them. Philip said you came from Somerset? What town?"

"I was born in Stogumber, in the Upper tone valley near the Exmoor forests on the coast. I'll visit my brother and sisters and look to my parents' graves; beyond that, I must see what God has in store."

Voices at the front door interrupted them—Will was speaking with his brother, Philip, who had just returned to find him unpacking the horses in the barn.

Chapter Twenty-two

PSYCHIC VS PSYCHE

Cambridge, Same Day, 1672

The brothers entered the common room still talking eagerly. A foot taller, Will dwarfed his older brother, a sturdy man of medium height. William noted that Philip's prominent blue eyes—made so by the thick, dark eyebrows—lit up when he saw Deborah. *He's besotted with her,* William thought. Will stood while his brother bent to kiss Deborah on the cheek, then took his former seat on the settee.

"You have minded the baby?" Philip asked Deborah. "It's so important that you preserve your strength *now*. The baby will be stronger."

Deborah flashed a curt smile and murmured, "Yes, of course."

Philip turned to his father. "I'm so surprised you have come. If I'd known, I'd have been here to greet you properly. Will said you plan to stay the night, but he would tell me no more. What brings this happy occasion?"

William, always in awe of his son's social skills, smiled humbly. "I'm leaving for England the day after tomorrow. I thought we'd take this time to see if I can bring something back for you. And to let you know, of course."

"England! This is a shock."

Deborah nodded her agreement, plumping the skirts that were now too warm. "That's why I thought you were jesting," she said to William.

"I didn't want you to find out by rumor. I'm not abandoning the family but am answering a spiritual call. I'll be back."

"Will you make a pilgrimage then?"

"Not unless you can count your grandparents' graves in the Stogumber churchyard a sacred site. I know I'll visit your uncle John and my sisters." William shrugged. "Beyond that, I'll ask God for direction."

"I'm astounded."

Sophy, who had prepared their meal, called them to the table, and the four took their seats on the benches. William appreciated the cool evening breeze from the open window, where the sound of wind through leaves gave a sensation the world was rhythmically breathing, a pleasant accompaniment to their conversation. William took up the tankard of ale and washed down a mouthful of rich stew, tasting of rabbit. After exchanging news of the family in Watertown, Deborah abruptly changed the subject. "Philip was in Groton last winter. Did Suzanne tell you?"

"Yes, we heard in a letter. Suzanne didn't give us details; in fact, she seemed reticent to talk about it at all. She did say that Philip had accompanied Dr. Knox on a strange visit. A girl was bewitched?"

"Ah, Elizabeth Knapp!" Philip exclaimed. "She has changed what I thought I knew, what I learned—forever. She is my muse!"

"Reverend Sherman spoke of her to our congregation. Wasn't she Reverend Willard's servant girl? Only fifteen? Some believed she was the Devil's minion."

"Sixteen," he corrected. "I've come to reject those opinions as folklore; even Reverend Willard, though he is more reserved in his verdict than I, did not believe her to be a witch. He's written a most astounding detailed report of her behavior and sent it to Reverend Cotton in Boston to review. A most extraordinary case."

"How so?"

Deborah smiled impishly, and insinuated, "Philip tells me that you don't believe in witches, either. He said you wouldn't let anyone read the witch hunter's bible."

"Deborah! I'd rather you didn't sabotage me so blatantly." He smiled fondly but turned with a sheepish frown to his father. "She's speaking of Hopkin's book. She knows I read it against your orders."

"You are your own man, now. I can no longer act to guide you as a father must. What did you think of it?"

"I found the inquiry diabolical, and I can see why you forbade us to read it. Dr. Knox and I had both read the book, so he asked me to back him when Reverend Willard called him to Groton. God was calling me to see firsthand a girl who was suffering many of the behaviors that Hopkins describes in his book."

William noticed that Deborah's face fell when Philip spoke of this time, as though she'd taken off a mask. *She must have felt abandoned when he'd left for days*, he thought, *and her baby barely a week in the ground*. He grunted a reluctant approval when Philip immediately leaned across the table and took her hand. *Is he apologizing?* The couple held one another's eyes before Philip could continue.

"I confess that when we lost Little Deborah, I couldn't bear to think about her; I was numb. Her death sorely tried my faith, especially my belief in Divine Providence. So, I couldn't resist that opportunity to escape."

William nodded. "That's understandable."

"Dr. Knox—Richard and I both apprenticed with Dr. Stone—well, we arrived on a Sunday, and after Reverend Willard's sermon, examined Elizabeth in his home. He told us 'she'd confessed the Devil was causing the trouble, and she wanted Reverend Rowlandson from Lancaster to pray with her.' He came, but despite the prayers and her sincere contrition—he said she'd even confessed to murderous thoughts—her fits continued."

"Were her fits like those Hopkins described?"

"Somewhat. Sometimes it took two or three people to restrain her, but such fits are not unheard of in medical practice. Dr. Knox decided, and I agreed, the fits had natural causes. Elizabeth was so contrite that we couldn't assume she was pretending her distress. Indeed, it bewildered her."

"Perhaps her stories about the Devil were attempts to explain events she could find no explanation for?"

"That's what I thought; she was clearly unbalanced. The Devil, the way she told it, was offering her relief from her work at the Willard's house: money, clothes, ease. The Devil's offerings made clear what Elizabeth's needs were. I took it as reason enough to send her home, where she might recover."

"Did you cure her?" Will asked.

"On the contrary. Elizabeth followed a strict course of purging, as we prescribed, and she thought herself cured because the symptoms eased. She told the pastor 'I'm free of the Devil; I no longer see him.' Clearly, staying at home relieved her symptoms; she must have hated her work. You can imagine how demeaning it was for a hired servant to work where children her own age come for school. However, Reverend Willard told us that, despite being home, she still showed the symptoms of fits; though they had lessened in severity to the point she wasn't aware of them. She stayed home, but in a month, all the fits came back stronger than before: she barked like a dog and projected the Devil's voice without moving her tongue or lips. The Reverend called us back to follow up. These new symptoms convinced Dr. Knox the source of her fits *was* diabolical. He found no other way to explain it. And no physician will treat such afflictions, which we leave to the clergy and magistrates."

"What changed your mind? You said you no longer believe in witchcraft?"

"I faced the knowledge that either God was afflicting her with a disease of which I was ignorant, or she had, as she confessed, made a pact with the Devil. Elizabeth must hang as a witch if her confession was true. But Reverend Willard defended her, and his reasoning made more sense to me."

"That doesn't explain how you changed."

"My thought differed from Willard's but came to a similar conclusion. Elizabeth's reason told her that God couldn't possibly be both her creator and cause her affliction unless he was punishing her. We learn it from childhood on. But confession and contrition for every possible sin, even the wish to murder someone, or *herself*, brought her no relief. Sanely enough, she must assume that an external force was cause, not God's punishment. Evil. A Devil to mirror the supreme maker's power. Reverend Willard let me read his report on our second visit, and the details showed, clearly, Elizabeth's account for herself swung between these two extremes. She was either a contrite and piteous human, sincerely begging God for salvation, or she took on the Devil's voice and bearing, letting evil thoughts take control. She cursed Reverend Willard, planned to kill him in his sleep, accused neighbors falsely. She could not settle the truth, nor could Reverend Willard. Either way, her afflictions continued. No one knew how to stop them."

Sophy lit candles for the table, which flickered in the gloom. William had to accept what his son was saying, though he couldn't understand from his own experience what he meant. His most intimate relation—whether passion, grief, or joy—was to God; all stemmed from His Providence. He knew of no individual agency, and Philip's explanation was out of his reach. William keenly felt estranged from his son, as though he'd sired a creature outside his ken.

"At the same time," Philip continued, "I sank into cruel grief for little Deborah, though I'd fought it so long. I can't tell you how foul and dark my vision was then, so severe the pain, I could denounce my faith." He patted Deborah's hand. "This dark place, the Evil, I describe as the absence of God, of light, of life; and facing that void was more terrifying than an imagined Devil. That changed me."

William couldn't imagine what that might feel like, not knowing God was ever-present. Even when he had doubt, God wasn't absent.

"Elizabeth Knapp was cured in the end; all of her symptoms disappeared."

"We cannot lose faith in God. Surely he came to her rescue."

Philip nodded. "Perhaps. However, I come to a different conclusion. I sense a new medicine is needed, but I can't grasp yet how God makes ourselves agents of our own afflictions."

Deborah, who'd sipped her apple juice and dutifully nibbled at what Philip had prescribed for her, added: "Philip says I'm his first patient."

Philip laughed. "In some ways, that's true. I have asked Deborah to follow my experiment. I believe that her emotional health is as important as her physical health. So, I want her to rest, to ease any nervous condition that might affect her or the baby."

"You see, I am a prisoner." She giggled like her ten-year-old servant and took his hand across the table. William was struck by a sense of dissonance when she squeezed Philip's hand, when a grimace crossed her lips. *Was it shadows?* He thought.

"An agreeable one," Philip said.

The balance of the evening passed with gossip on the affairs of old friends and the family in the guttering candle light. Sophy had prepared places for them in the loft, where she'd thrown windows open to catch the cooling night air. They fell asleep with the sounds of their animals shifting in the barn, a lone wolf's howl, and a chorus of frogs from a nearby marsh. Early the next morning, William and Will climbed down the ladder to join Philip and Deborah for the morning meal.

Then Philip led his father and brother to the stable to saddle and bridle the horses. Trunks, caskets, and bundles heaped at the side of the stable carried the supplies that William needed on his voyage to England.

William followed Philip, uneasily feeling short of breath and heavy, as though someone sat on his chest. He credited it to his feelings. *A heartache,* he thought. I never knew it would be so hard to leave them, even a short while.

Philip led the old mare out of the stall and began to load the cargo. "You've packed enough ale to open an ordinary. Even more oatmeal."

"There's no fresh water on board the ship, and I may run out before the trip's end. Remember, we're on the ocean six weeks or more, God willing good or bad weather. Porridge and salt fish are staples, and I'll be buying just as much hardtack in Boston."

Will chuckled. "I calculated he'd be drinking a quart a day and eating a pound of fish. I don't think there'll be much waste here. I measured it all."

"You always were our mathematician," Philip said. "Father could look for a long time to find someone who can match what you do."

"Aye," William said. "I cannot agree more. And he does it in his head!"

"I can't imagine a sea crossing. Do you remember your voyage here?"

"It's unforgettable," William said, bending to lift yet another cask of ale. "I was lucky by comparison with some I've heard of because we only had one storm on our crossing; the sickness you never forget! For the rest, I remember cramped and stinking, except when we took to the deck. But we did see phosphorescence one night, God's gift."

"I remember Grandfather's stories, but you never talked about it."

"His story is of God's trial. He told the truth of every man's voyage, the trial and God's grace. I could add nothing."

"It makes me wonder why you would want to go now," Philip said.

"Do you remember your home in Watertown now that you have settled here?"

"I do," Philip replied. "I can never forget the marsh at the meadow's edge. John and I played there; I can still smell it."

Will howled. "You were monsters. You caught frogs, so you could throw them on the water to see their stomachs puff up; they died on their backs."

Philip's face fell. "We did. It was a wonder to us. We didn't think it was slaughter."

"Enough! Children have the conscience of wild beasts. I mean to say, your longing for that lost time will never leave you, and I only wish I could share my homeland with you."

The men continued strapping the bundles to the horses. William led Old Gray from a stall and slid the saddle blanket backward for the horse's comfort. He'd taught Will to pay attention to a horse's hair, to make sure he'd seat the blanket in the same direction the hair grew. Perhaps that had led to Will's love of horses, this small consideration. When William lifted the saddle from the sawhorse, he thought it had metamorphosed; it was heavier than he remembered. When he girded himself to throw it over his horse's back, he suddenly felt a severe chest pain that took his breath away. He stopped mid-motion, lost his balance, and toppled to the ground beneath the saddle's weight. He gasped, then curled around the pain in his chest, coughing with a strangled gurgle, and lost consciousness of everything except an angel that bent over him, reassuring him that he was alright.

Chapter Twenty-Three

CONVALESCENT

Cambridge, Next Day, July 1672

"Father!" Philip shouted, rushing to his side; he knelt beside the prone man and lifted the saddle from him, feeling his heart, which still labored in his chest.

"What's wrong?" Will followed Philip's lead to his father's side; he took the saddle from his brother and set it down, watching his brother apply his skills.

Philip patted shoulders, hips, and legs for broken bones or dislocations. Noting the uneven, thin pulse and the vomit now crusting his unconscious father's lips, and the weakness of his limbs when he bent them, he suspected his father was the victim of stroke.

"Apoplexy," Philip said. "He's alive, but in shock. He needs water. Go get Sophy. Bring water and a blanket." Philip straightened his father's legs and loosened the neckcloth. He threw a saddle blanket over him to shield him from shock. "Father, can you hear me?"

William drew his energy from the shadowy world that swirled around him. He heard the voices of his sons, excited, rushing about. The shadow coalesced when the angel bent low, his face near his own. He could hear from a great distance, 'can you hear me?' Gradually the shadows cleared, and the angel's face morphed into Philip's. He opened his eyes to find his son leaning over him. Awake now, he let Philip help him to a sitting position.

"Aye, I can hear you," he said. "What happened?"

"You fainted." Philip unbuttoned the top of his shirt. "What do you remember last?"

"I was saddling the horse. Fainted?"

Despite his father's obvious confusion, Philip was relieved that he could answer this question. At least his father suffered no mental damage from his stroke. "Quiet now." Philip held a cup of water to his lips. "Drink now. We need your help. Can you stand up?"

The water slid down William's throat. He'd not realized he was thirsty, but the water disappeared before he could swallow, as though his throat absorbed it before it flowed to his stomach. He nodded. "I can stand."

Philip nodded grimly; he'd already checked his father's legs and knew he had no strength. He pointed at the door. "Sophy, you get the door; we're going to carry him."

William tried with all his strength to stand, but to his wonder, could no longer move his legs. Fear seized him. When Philip and Will lifted him, his feet dragged uselessly on the ground. In this confusing state, William tried to feel his feet and then his hands. Nothing was responding to his will.

Once the sons, with Sophy's help, had stripped William down to his nightshirt and laid him in the bed, they let him drift in and out of sleep. After Philip had applied leeches to relieve the blood pressure, Philip sat by his side through a long night. By morning, William had recovered the use of his limbs, and waking from a sound sleep, struggled to sit up and leave the bed. Philip woke in time to help him stand, unsteady, but able to move to the chamber pot.

"I'm better," William said. "Frightening, but God is with me. I must leave soon if I am to reach Boston."

"You are not going to Boston," Philip said. "Imagine if you faint on the ship to England. No doctor there. No one. Do you wish to leave your family and be cast overboard, food for sharks? Are you mad?"

"What are you telling me?" William said. "I'm well enough now. Look. I'm walking."

"How does it feel?" Philip asked.

William caught his meaning. In truth, he felt terrible. His chest was sore, as though someone had bruised him with a fist, and he was slightly nauseous from the ache of breathing. While he was standing, he couldn't ignore feeling weak, so weak he could barely grip the chair rail for better balance. His hands were like jelly, his legs without the strength to carry him.

"You need to recover," Philip said. "It'll be weeks before you can go."

"I can rest on the ship," William argued.

"You're not going to Boston, not for a long time," Philip said. "We need to get you back home, but you are in no condition to ride. I can borrow a cart from my neighbor. You need to recover."

"But I'll recover?" William said. "You were sounding the death knell."

"I cannot guarantee what God has in store now," Philip said. "I must be honest. Some survive many years. Others don't. Most have repeat attacks. With consequences."

William was stunned with the news. *Now*, he thought. *I am to die now? Here?* Death had never been in his plans until Susanna had brought up the idea he might perish at sea. *In Watertown? It's too soon, not nice enough*, he bargained. *What of God's plans? Of England?*

Philip found a cart, and the sons helped their father board it, where he sat in a semi-prone position for the eight-mile journey home.

William's convalescence did not go smoothly; Philip and Will were able to help him to his bed, but the effort of the long ride and walk to his room weakened him further. He suffered another small stroke and this time, fell into a coma for an entire day. Philip did not leave his side afterwards but sent Will back to notify Dr. Stone and Dr. Knox in Cambridge, who would see to the needs of patients he could not attend to now. Susanna felt relief when William woke again and spoke to her with a sound mind, though not sound body. He pronounced words with a distinct slur.

That day, when Philip had finished bleeding William, he skillfully pressed his fingernail under each of the black leeches and flipped them into a container held to catch them. Once he'd removed them, Philip drew his mother from the sickroom. The paraphernalia for bleeding littered the table boards: the crock of living leeches, a spatula for removing them, the salve to stop the bleeding. Philip picked up a cloth and dried his hands, then pushed aside the tools to clear a space for her. Philip held her hands. "Mother, please sit down."

He began to clean the leeches, immersing them in clear water before he dropped them into the well of living leeches he cultivated for his practice.

Susanna sank onto the bench. Philip continued, "This second heart attack is a bad sign. He's so weak now. I have bled him. He's responded. His blood pressure is down. But his heart is weak, irregular. I fear the worst."

Tears welled up in her eyes, and she swallowed hard, tightening her grip on his hands. "Do I understand what you are saying? How serious? Will he live?"

Philip held tight to her. "It's not likely."

"How long does he have?"

"A day, a week, a month, I cannot tell when, but it's certain he hasn't long. He needs to get his affairs in order."

Susanna wrung her hands, blinking back tears. "I spoke to him about a will before he left for England, but I don't know if he wrote it; I don't want to nag him."

"I'll talk to him today," Philip promised. "He still thinks that he'll recover."

"I hate this; please don't destroy his will to live."

Philip released her hands and stood. "It's not in his nature; you'll see."

Later that day, Philip met with his father and gave him the news. William was curiously not surprised; he had woken from the long coma in confusion. Having never been so ill, not in his lifetime, as the fog cleared, he realized that his state might signal his end. At first, he felt an intense sadness that he would have to leave his family behind, life as he knew it. It was some time before his faith rose to give him comfort for this grief. At first, he thought the angel in his dreams, who urged him to take a leap of faith, had mocked him; he could see that he had seriously misinterpreted this message. But that changed with his son's talk.

Chapter Twenty-Four

A WILL TO LIVE

Watertown, July 1672

"You were lucky, father." Philip snapped the bedding tight. "Remember how you couldn't walk after the attack? You recovered the use of your legs; others who suffer attacks like you did are paralyzed or they can no longer speak. God has spared you."

William hadn't thought himself lucky, but as Philip told him the fates of others, he conceded that he had some measure of good fortune, small measure.

"You can still get your affairs in order," Philip said. "I don't know how long you have, but you are still of sound mind and able to walk."

The thought struck William: *I haven't yet made the will Susanna asked me to write.* He felt overwhelmed. He bent forward. "Your mother asked me to write a will before I left, but I put it off. I'm in my right mind, as you say, but so exhausted."

"We are all here to help you; you don't have to do anything. Just tell us what you want; we'll do it."

William thought, *I'm not dead yet! I can make my will.* The more Philip talked, the more gratitude he felt: God had held him in his hands. He'd not let him fall as others had. "I've already talked to John Coolidge about an inventory; he will help. If you'd start it ... and I'd like John Livermore to witness the will, too. They should be paid for their troubles."

"I'll see to it," Philip said.

"And Susanna must be my executor," William said.

"No one better," Philip agreed.

By August third, still on his sickbed, William made his will.

His two witnesses, Goodmen Coolidge and Livermore, read the inventory. William had not realized how much land and wealth he'd amassed until he heard it listed. Amazed at the bounty, he began to understand Susanna's apprehension; most of his wealth was land. She couldn't inherit any of it in her name, nor could she buy and sell any property. How would he insure that she had full charge of both house and land, her living? How could he make sure she could keep the family together until their majority?

Aided by his witnesses and the town clerk, he made out the will in such a way as to guarantee her continuance in the house. To do so, he needed to will the property to his sons, with clauses that she would have full use until she married, or they matured, whichever came first. He willed the house to the youngest boys, Benjamin and Samuel, who would not come of age for ten or more years. Dividing the house and lands between them, neither could force Susanna to leave when they could claim it.

William knew no one would object to awarding Will his looms and all weaving accouterments, and he'd already mentally awarded him the red roan gelding. Will doted on Pilgrim. He then divided Stonybrook farm and the attached meadows into two parcels, half for Will, half for Philip. That left only his son John unaccounted.

He was so conflicted over rewarding John that he sought the advice of Susanna, who favored the young man despite all his failings. John had steadfastly rejected membership in the church and thus, was forever barred from the Watertown council and freeman's status. Showing their respect to William, the council had hired John to manage the mill, but William envied Goodman Fox, who brought his son to council, a boon that he'd never have. Then too, John had become estranged once he'd joined Captain Beer's company; he was so vilely prejudiced against Indians it defied all reason. He no longer fit into the progressive family's fold.

"John is not going to change," Susanna appealed, "but he's still your son. Don't disinherit him. Even if you cannot in full heart give him the measure of his brothers, give him something. Perhaps that will cause him to reflect on his portion; it may yet do him some good."

With her advice, William decided to give John the cash equivalent of what he'd given his brothers in land. However, he'd receive the money only after his mother died, and then, only a quarter of the total dispersed over four years.

"It's fitting," Susanna chuckled. "He will inherit his money from me, after I die. The girls? You will give them something?"

William smiled. "I knew you'd be asking. Yes, but only the married girls. Joanna and Abigail are still in their minority. They'll marry in time."

"You cannot know what a woman needs," Susanna said. "For a man, it's like staring at the moon; you see only one side. I am concerned about my part. May I read it?"

William pushed his will across the table. "Of course," he said. "The magistrate assured me that your will is the present standard to protect widows."

Susanna paged through the will to find the passages on her inheritance. "The will states that I will have use of the house and land until Benjamin and Samuel are twenty-one or I marry, whichever happens first."

"The magistrate explained that's how I insure the house and land remain in the Sherborn family," William said. "The land goes to the boys."

"That is well and good if I find another such as you to marry," Susanna said. "But I must remind you that widows do not fare well alone. A woman *must* remarry, and choices are few."

William adjusted his pillows and wriggled to get more comfortable. He was clearly agitated by the prospect. "I hadn't thought much about it," he said. "You're saying a widower may not have the means I have?" William immediately thought of the only recent widower that he knew, Susanna's friend, Richard Norcross. He was a trustworthy man, who made but thirty pounds a year as schoolmaster. He knew because he voted on the man's salary each year at council meetings. Suddenly realizing that Richard Norcross could be a candidate to succeed him, he thought, *What if?* But he couldn't bear to think it.

"That is precisely what I'm saying," Susanna said. "So, I must sacrifice my present life to seek protection in a new marriage. It's complicated because I have children, your children. It's likely a man my age will have children too, and he is doubling his responsibilities."

William could stand it no longer. "A man like Richard Norcross, you mean?"

Susanna stopped, stunned as she caught his drift. "William!" she exclaimed. "You cannot be thinking that I've set my cap on him! He's a long-time friend, like a brother to me. The thought repels me. And you, you know as everyone does, he's courting Goody Adams, a widow. We hope that he will post the bans soon."

William bowed his head, ashamed that he'd entertained the thought even a moment. "Forgive me," William said. "But the magistrate explained the clause is to protect a widow from men taking advantage of her wealth."

"Do you think I need such protection?" Susanna said, laughing.

William blushed. "You would put most men's scheming to shame! It's why I've asked you to be executor. John Coolidge and Sam Livermore will help you. I've asked that you pay them."

"Then, can we change this clause, just slightly?" Susanna asked. He could not deter her. "You give me the use of the house and land until the boys are of age or I marry. Just put a period after 'the boys are of age,' and strike out 'if I marry.' Then, whether I marry or not, the children may continue to live at home, and Sherborns will always own the land."

Of course, William thought, and picked up the pen to add the period. However, he didn't cross out 'if she marry.' Instead he added to the phrase 'if she marry,' that he would pay her four pound each year out of his house and lands. He paused, then added a semicolon and the phrase, 'if she marry not, I give them to her during her life.' *They'll not be confused about that*, he thought triumphantly. William fell back on his pillow. "I fear I have not much longer. Philip said that after two attacks such as I suffered, a third may be fatal. I want to say good-bye to the girls, Suzanne and Rebecca. See my grandchildren."

"I'll send Will to Groton to get them." Susanna massaged his hand. "You must take care to rest. It may be several days before …"

"I'll not go before I see them to say good-bye properly."

When he began coughing, Susanna rose to get Philip, who'd waited in the common room.

"Philip, your father and I are ready to sign the will. Could you send someone to get our witnesses? I'm going to get Will. He can ride to Groton to bring back the girls."

"I will."

Susanna caught his arm as he passed. "And thank you. I was so worried."

She headed for the workroom to tell Will, and Philip joined his father in the sickroom.

John Livermore and John Coolidge, the joiner, later signed the will and named Susanna the executor. They called in Deacon Thomas Hastings, the town clerk, to record and file it. William steeled himself, let God's strength string out his shallow breaths until his children gathered around.

Chapter Twenty-Five

A LEAP OF FAITH

Groton, August 1672

Will could not spare Pilgrim, but rode him all day and night, stopping often for rests on the narrow road to Groton. He could not afford the usual two days. Fortunately, the trail followed a mainly flat route through thick woods, interspersed with open meadows, crossed by fordable creeks. Water levels were low in August. He would need to give the horse a day to recover but wouldn't push him on the way back to Watertown. His father wanted to see his grandchildren; that meant they would be hauling a cart. Another two days! He only hoped his father could last that long; Philip had stressed the urgency of his case.

It took Will some time to find Suzanne's house, which he had never visited. She lived close to the Nashua River, at the west edge of town. Thick forests surrounded a roomy yard with what looked like a vegetable garden along one side Will remembered Suzanne had always cultivated her own medicinal herbs in Watertown. An expanse of marshy meadow flanked the other. He dismounted and called her name at the door.

"Come in," Suzanne called back, appearing at the door seconds later. "Will! I can't believe you're here." Suzanne had not seen him since the death of Philip and Deborah's daughter, and Will had never visited her in Groton. Her baby, only six months old and still nursing, voiced a welcoming screech. Suzanne had strapped baby Mary to her back with a shawl, papoose style, and the infant peered over her shoulder.

Will was a foot taller than his sister and bent to catch her eyes. "I have no good news," he said. "It's father."

"Father! What?" she stammered. The last time she'd seen him her father was a healthy man nearing fifty.

"He's gravely ill," he explained. "Philip says it's apoplexy. He believes he hasn't much time left before he passes. Father wants to say his goodbyes and has asked that you come."

Suzanne, a practicing midwife used to emergencies, took the news in stride. "Is he still of sound mind?"

"Yes. He can talk and reason. Philip says he was lucky."

"Indeed. Then we must leave immediately. His condition could change quickly. Have you told Rebecca yet?"

"No, it took some time to find *you*. I don't know where she lives."

"We'll go now." She turned and walked swiftly to the great room. "Martha," she called. "I will leave now. You have charge of the children. I should be back within the hour, though."

Will heard the unseen helper answer, "Don't worry. I'll be here."

Suzanne bustled back. Will had nearly forgotten how Suzanne could always enlist support for her proposals. Staring at her now, as though to renew his acquaintance, he concluded she had the look of a leader. Her brown hair was pulled back tightly, revealing a high forehead and cheekbones, broadly set eyes. Is it her face? Her bearing? he wondered.

"Rebecca's house isn't far; we can walk. You know they lease John's land?"

"I recall that was the plan when they married."

Suzanne led him out the door. Despite painful stiffness at the beginning, after the long ride, Will was grateful for the walk.

"Don't be shocked at their home. They're still building and have barely settled in."

A mile up the road, they arrived at a small one-story, two-room hut. Although the chimney was intact, the thatch showed bare rafters at one end, and Sam Church had covered the four windows with oiled paper. They found the very gravid Rebecca working in a small garden that flanked the right.

Rebecca stood up, her hands holding up her belly to ease the catch in her back that made her wince. She glanced from her sister to her brother. "This can't be good."

Suzanne nodded, her mouth wryly down turned. "Rebecca, it's father. He's mortally ill."

Will could see why Suzanne had not sent for Rebecca; his sister was huge with child. *She won't be going anywhere*, he thought. He took her hand. "Father asked to see you."

"Then, we must go at once." Rebecca's first impulse was ever heedless of obstacle or danger.

Suzanne posed, hands on hips. "Rebecca, I know that you want to come, but I won't advise it. In fact, as your midwife, I forbid it."

"It'll be four more weeks!" Rebecca argued. "I'll be fine."

"No, you will not be fine. Seven months or eight months doesn't matter."

Will nodded. "I agree with Suzanne. She knows best."

"But if you're gone, who delivers my baby?" Rebecca brushed the dirt off her apron and led them to the house.

"I'll be back within a week, and I'll ask Martha to check on you."

Will followed his sisters into the house. He stood in shock at Rebecca's living condition. Cats leaped from the table, scattering for shelter, terrified of the intruders. He could see food from their last meals crusted the wooden tableware left on the table boards. His first impression from the clothing scattered on the floor was that someone had undressed as he crossed the room, discarding clothes as he went. His second impression included bird droppings in the corner where the thatch gaped, showing the sky. The air was musty with mold. Through the open door to the next room, he saw their bedding, a pile of straw and tumbled rugs in one corner. Even though his sister had been flighty, her habits when she worked with Goody Cooke were meticulous. She'd never been disorderly; in fact, her fault was too much concern with outward appearances, pride. He backed up Suzanne's advice, though he could see why Rebecca might want to join them. "Father's health is grave. God willing, we'll get there in time, but we'll travel through the night. We can't stop to rest."

Rebecca sat down, motioning for them to sit. "I don't care. Suzanne, you can't leave me, not now," she pleaded. "Better you deliver me in Watertown, anyway. If father dies, there's the burial. I'll want to be there to bury Father."

Suzanne frowned, but had to admit that her sister had a point. If he died, she might stay two weeks or more. "We'll be taking the cart, but the roads are bad. I don't want to deliver a baby before its time, and in the woods."

"You said I'm in perfect health. Nothing will happen."

Suzanne knew that despite her obvious depression, Rebecca was physically in top shape, even though not an optimal age. Grudgingly she gave in. "Alright. You have my permission. Will Sam come?"

"I don't think so. He has no love for father."

"And he won't be angry?"

Rebecca stared at her feet, her jaw set. She couldn't meet her sister's probing eyes. "I'll leave him word I'm coming with you."

Will knew he was witnessing some secret pact between his sisters. Unspoken words echoed in the room. He watched her bundle her belongings in a shawl.

Rebecca returned to the house with them. By evening, they had gathered Joseph Morse and Samuel Church from field and sawpit and packed the cart with supplies for the journey. Though the sisters had been apprehensive about Sam Church's reaction to Rebecca leaving, he had taken the news in stride. As Will saw it, Sam was happy to see her go, which made him wonder even more about his sisters' unspoken understanding. Suzanne arranged for Martha, her helper, to feed the chickens and goats while they were gone to Watertown. They left their dog, Tippy, to protect her, though her family lived not far away and visited often. Suzanne and Joseph had adopted Martha as family, and by turns, Martha's family had adopted them. Though it was unusual to treat servants with such familiarity, Suzanne's profession demanded frequent and sometimes overnight visits to her clients. Her oldest daughter, only nine, was still too young to take responsibility for her siblings.

Susanna, Hester, Joseph, and Samuel, children ranging from nine to two years in age, rode in the cart with their mother and Aunt Becky. Suzanne, in retrospect, was happy that she'd relented and let Rebecca join them. She was an invaluable help keeping the children from fighting or leaping off the cart. Six-month-old Mary was cradled in the shawl Suzanne wrapped across her back. A simple twist of her shawl allowed her to position Mary for nursing easily; she considered her arrangement an improvement on both the English and Indian ways women carried children. Joseph joined Will on horseback, and together, the family made their way to Watertown in the creaking cart.

When they arrived from Groton, the Morse's four children were swallowed by the Sherborn cousins, absorbed in recalibrating their loyalties and identities. Residents in the sleeping rooms had nearly doubled on their coming. Suzanne and Rebecca, now reunited with their mother and siblings, glowed as they bustled through the common room, helping to prepare meals in an atmosphere that belied the occasion—a man dying on his sickbed.

By the time his daughters arrived from Groton, William had come to realize that the angel in his dream had asked for this last leap of faith, his belief in a life everlasting, when the chosen would rest in his eternal care. During these last days, though, William suffered from a deep exhaustion. He drifted in and out of a restless sleep, with barely the energy to speak to his children who visited in his last few days.

Susanna carefully regulated the visits with his grandchildren as he slid in and out of consciousness. William wanted to tell them, each one, not to grieve for him when he was gone; the Lord was taking him home. They must have faith and love God. However, his mind wandered, and he ended saying whatever he thought, not profound or moving words. He had no wisdom for them, only chatty small talk.

Suzanne stood with her children clustered around her. Little Susanna dared to hold his hand when her mother nodded approval. Suzanne smiled, sniffing back the tears that rolled down her cheeks. Her children stared wide-eyed, not knowing what to make of their grandfather's labored breathing and pale face. "Say good-bye to your grandfather now. You may kiss him."

One by one her children kissed him. William closed his eyes and sighed, "Thank you." As the children filed out of his room, he raised his head to watch them go before he relaxed, staring up at Suzanne, who carried baby Mary. "I know that you named this one after your sister Mary." He lifted a finger from the bed to indicate baby Mary's head where she nestled in Suzanne's arms. "Tell Mary. She needs you more than you can know."

Suzanne nodded. "Yes, Father. I will." She bent to kiss him and, realizing he had spent all his energy, left the room.

William's heart was heavy when Ruth and John herded Little Johnnie and Ruth, and his namesake William into his room. He nodded at little Willy and smiled. To John, he said, "you may yet find your way to The Lord." He had nothing else to say.

When Rebecca had come, he could only express his sorrow that he'd made her go away. "Forgive me," he'd whispered again and again.

Of course, he didn't need a final farewell to his daughter Mary, who visited his bedside daily from the moment he fell sick, but the day before he died, he silently mouthed "I love you."

Eleven days after he'd made out his will, William no longer knew if he dreamed or woke. When he felt God was near, it was only with great sadness because he sensed he was a broken vessel that had leaked any good he might have done or been. He couldn't raise himself to that exulted belief that God had chosen him. A feverish conscience had stolen his days and turned his eyes toward night. Then, in the middle of his repentance, a numbing sucked at him, a heavy pull, like an ocean surf at high tide that swept from his feet to his shoulders. With one last effort, he plunged through the gel-like atmosphere into pure light, undifferentiated light, no shadow anywhere. Before he lost consciousness, a divine love poured through his veins, a streaming bliss. And he was gone.

Chapter Twenty-Six

THE GATHERING CLOUDS

Watertown, August 14, 1672

Though the church had no bell, Reverend Sherman insisted on carrying out the English custom announcing the death that morning, August fourteenth. The drum rattled one strike for the death of a man, and fifty strikes for his age. Thus, the neighbors who knew of his illness understood that William had passed. There'd be no work this day. The women gathered at the Sherborn house to care for the bereaved. The men brought food, which the women prepared while others performed barnyard chores or scrubbed. Mary Clinnery arrived first; she carried black crepe to cover the mirrors and pictures and tie the shutters closed. Nearest neighbors, John Livermore and John Coolidge, volunteered to dig his grave; their wives took charge of the now twelve children resident—seven more when Jonathan and Mary Brown arrived with theirs in tow. Joseph Clinnery had already built William's coffin, and it remained for Corporal Bond to transport it from Clinnery's farm.

When Biddy Payne and Martha Godfrey trudged up Hill Street with breakfast, they explained to Joanna that they would be taking over. Bereaved for the first time in her young life, Joanna looked dazed; she backed off. She turned to join her sister, Suzanne, who sat nursing her six-month-old daughter, and Mary, who was helping her son Abraham take his first steps. They were of little help to the women preparing the viewing room. Biddy and Martha sat the children on the table benches, lining them up like birds on two fences. "Eat, eat," Biddy Payne insisted, "You must be strong now because the Devil's out and about." Martha winced at her neighbor's suspicious prattle; she had reproved her more than once for talking that way to children. Their eyes wide with wonder at the hushed crew that swarmed the house, they ate without noticing Biddy's talk. They'd never seen so many people collect except for school or the meetinghouse. Then, Goody Payne shooed them out to the yard to play.

Struck by a summer sun, the younger set bounded up in a flaming delirium. Racing one another to the field's edge, they yelled for no reason, actions meaning no more than the whistle of a boiling teapot. For the Groton contingent, their grandfather was an idea; they knew him by name only. For the Watertown cousins, only William's children saw him daily; Mary Brown's and John Sherborn's children less so.

The older children were more sedate, all of them girls, and they made their way across the yard to huddle away from their younger siblings, whispering their secrets and repressing occasional sniggers and giggles. The oldest girls, ten and eight, respectively, and nine-year-old Susanna Morse, were exclusive. They rejected Hester, Susanna's younger sister, who had the misfortune of being old enough, but never her sister's equal.

Their aunt Abigail Sherborn, who at fifteen was the equivocal adult in this tribe, saw them isolate poor Hester and intervened. "Let's all play a game."

"What game?" The oldest cousin asked, testily.

Abigail could see that, clearly, her niece took after her mother, Mary, when it came to judgment. She would have to find allies who wanted to play because Lydia, the same as her mother, would only conform to consensus. "Have you ever played 'Old Woman All Skin and Bone'?" Abigail asked.

"No! Never!" Lydia Brown pronounced. She would end it there, but her sister became curious.

Her sister dared to speak out, "I'd like to play."

"Oh yes," Susanna Morse chimed in. "Mother taught us that. Oh, let's."

Since Abigail had learned the game about the same time as her sister Suzanne did, she was certain she could enlist the Groton kids. Suzanne had taught them to play. If they decided to play, Lydia would join in. She gestured to the three girls to follow and joined Hester across the field.

Hester Morse, shunned by her older sister, had joined the little ones in the yard. Williams four grandsons—all five and six-year olds—roughhoused with their Groton cousin. Ruth Sherborn, John's daughter, already showing motherly traits at four years, played with the youngest two boys and two girls.

"Hester, come on," Abigail said. "We're going to play a game: Old Woman All Skin and Bone."

"Yes, oh fun," said Hester Morse. "We always play it."

Ironically, the Groton children had learned a game that originated in their grandfather's birthplace, Stogumber, England. Though they had not known their grandfather, their mother Suzanne had taught all the Groton children how to play. The traditional graveyard game was a grisly "tag," where each had their turn at playing the dead woman, the grave digger, or the terrified living; it occupied them for hours.

Chapter Twenty-Seven

WHITE GLOVES

Watertown, Same Day, 1672

Goodmen Coolidge and Livermore dug the grave in the graveyard on Main Street, and afterward, rode up Hill Street to the meetinghouse, where Reverend Sherman stored a bier and pall for everyone's use. Though Puritan ministers shunned any ceremony as Popish as a funeral, their Reverend always attended processions to the graveside to pay respects to the departed. In the meetinghouse yard, the two men waited for Corporal Bond, sprawling on the ground to rest, their horses grazing nearby.

"You remember when I was going to go back to England?" John Livermore said.

"I do." John Coolidge picked up a stone and practiced juggling it hand to hand.

"Well, when William got the church's blessing, I was jealous."

"You still wanted to go back?"

"Never stopped. And here's William. Letter of approval. He's all packed. He's on his way, and the Lord takes him."

"Still …going home," Coolidge said.

"Right. I hear what you say. Maybe that's the only home we'll ever know."

"If you're right, it's not a place I want to visit soon."

"You know? I get that about you," Livermore said, chuckling. "You've never wasted a minute on going back to England."

Just then, Bond arrived with the cart. Livermore tipped his hat in greeting, and Coolidge threw away the stone he'd been juggling.

"I see you made quick work of the grave." Corporal Bond stepped down from the cart, reins in hand.

"Didn't want to be digging in this heat," Coolidge said. "I'm glad this is the last of lifting."

"Right. Let's get going. I still must pick up the coffin at Joe Clinnery's, and I'd like to get back soon. Susanna is likely ready for us to move William to his coffin."

Without a word, the two men loaded the bier in Bond's cart.

"You have the pall, too?" Corporal Bond asked.

"Right here," John Livermore said, patting the heavy velvet, tasseled drape, folded and tied to the bier.

"Good," Corporal Bond said. He chucked the reins, clucking to his horse. "See you soon."

At the house, neighbors worked with purpose. "Have you found a winding sheet?" Martha asked Mary Clinnery.

"I haven't," she said. "But Young Will should know where William kept his stock." William wove winding sheets to specification for the community, and thus kept some aside.

Rebecca, who'd overheard the women, said, "I know where they are. I'll go."

Mary Clinnery entered the bedchamber, where Mary, Susanna, and Philip kept watch. "Susanna, we need to clean him for the viewing," she said, carefully avoiding the word 'body' out of sympathy for her neighbor.

It was a signal to Philip and Mary to pry Susanna's hands from William's and lead her to the great room. Even bowed down with the shock that her husband had passed on, Susanna's nature rose to the occasion. She'd helped dress the bodies of neighbors, and she would not shirk her duty now. She walked to William's workshop, where Will and Jacob foundered like boys lost at sea. They moved listlessly around the loom, trying to warp a cloth.

"Will," Susanna said, "you and Jacob do not need to work today, although God knows, there's plenty needs to be done. I saw Rebecca looking for winding sheets. Do you know where your father kept them? We'll want the best one. Help Rebecca, then eat and take a walk if you can. We'll be preparing all day. Tomorrow we'll have the viewing and funeral. There'll be a dinner afterwards."

"Can I see father?" Will asked. "Before?"

"There's nothing to see now," Susanna said. "He looks no different from the last time you saw him, and don't you want to remember him alive? Wait until he's laid out."

Will slouched out, followed by the timid Jacob. They found Rebecca already at the storeroom. Together, they picked out a fine woolen shroud of winter white that met the Church of England burial rules, the one that wasn't too Popish for Puritans to use.

Rebecca rubbed the cloth between her fingers, then crushed it in her palm and released it. The winkles fell out immediately. "This is fine cloth," she exclaimed. "A waste to bury it."

The comment arrested Will, and he glanced at Jacob. "I think he was saving it," he said. "He started this sheet when Sam was born; he made it for one of us."

Rebecca hugged it to her chest and said, "Strange! We're still here, but he'll have the benefit of a beautiful shroud."

"Only thing 'strange' is the way you put it," Will said, his voice flat. "Benefit?" He shook his head, always critical of his sister's giddy ways. He wondered if she thought about anything before she blurted it out.

They made their way to the great room, where breakfast still warmed, a pan of scrambled eggs and ham. Biddy Payne had outdone herself. Then Rebecca joined Susanna, who rummaged in his England trunk for his new suit. Susanna wanted him to wear it for the viewing. Then they'd remove it and wrap him in the winding sheet for burial. She'd give Philip the suit afterwards because he was the same size.

Rebecca admired it. "Mother," she said, "this is the latest fashion! Did you have this made?" She rubbed her cheek on the sleeve before she arranged it on an armchair.

"I made it. Are you the only seamstress knows what's current?"

"You never cared before." Rebecca's voice trailed off.

Susanna smiled. "I'm lost without you here! So, I did the next best thing. I consulted with Goody Rachel Cooke. I have missed you so, Becky!" Rebecca hugged her mother.

Mary Clinnery and Martha Godfrey had already stripped William's body, wadding the soiled linen that he'd worn at the last; they would burn it. They'd heated water to clean him to aid in their labor. Susanna joined them, taking special care as she wiped his face and trimmed his beard. Martha held his head, so Susanna could wash his hair.

"I cut his hair just before he left for England; it just needs a bit of trim." Susanna combed the wet hair back, trimming the edges, then dried it with a towel.

"For a man his age, he looks so healthy," Martha said.

Mary agreed, then stopped when she saw Susanna's face.

Tears welled. *He's still young to me*, Susanna thought, blinking them back. A Puritan woman did not demonstrate grief, and in some ways, she felt that her farewell when he'd left for England was more final than his death. What's more, she'd had two weeks to prepare for this parting. She credited the sense of being wrapped in cotton to the Lord's shield; He would not ask her to bear a load too heavy.

Once he was clean, they removed the soiled bedding and rolled him onto clean sheets. Overcome suddenly, Susanna had to leave the room, but Joanna stepped in to help them dress her father, lifting, tugging, and smoothing, combing and perfuming. At noon, the coffin and bier arrived, and men moved his body into the coffin, where the women arranged him, smoothing his clothes and folding his arms. Martha brought a sprig of fern to tuck in his hands, which held a small bible. It was symbolic of his life everlasting.

"I wish we could have blue bells or snowdrops," Ruth said. "When I gave him some of mine—I brought them from England—he loved them."

"He did," Joanna said. "They reminded him of home."

When they'd finished, apart from his pale color, he looked as if he slept, his face relaxed, without expression, sweet.

Reverend Sherman had introduced the underbearers, sons of the men who would hold the four corners of the pall covering the coffin. When Will volunteered to carry his father, they had turned him down.

"You are family," Susanna said. "You'll walk with us."

"Least we can do for your family and for William, too," Reverend Sherman said. "He's shouldered a coffin more than once for this town." The Reverend had to find two sets of men to carry the bier, because the distance exceeded a mile. Luckily, the procession would wind mostly downhill.

The men moved the coffin once women had arranged the bier in the parlor. Mary found candles and fastened them to the bier for the viewing.

"Will you send out funeral gloves?" Mary Clinnery asked. Funeral gloves were sent to everyone as an invitation to burials. Guests were expected to wear the white gloves to the graveside. No one knew why, though Susanna's friend, the schoolmaster, had thought it was a gesture of comfort. By wearing the same white gloves the coffin bearers wore, mourners were symbolically carrying it too. The explanation seemed farfetched to Susanna, who always saw the practical side. More likely, she thought, it had something to do with handling bodies. Diseased bodies. The custom was to assure those attending the burial they'd not catch the disease.

Susanna stared at her blankly for a moment, caught off-guard. She had many pairs from other funerals she'd attended. "Yes, I'd forgotten." She felt dismay. *I'm already forgetting the basics*, she thought. She pushed aside the idea that followed, *'How will I live without him?'* A gulf of absence materialized and faded as quickly as the pang that caught her breath.

"You don't need to worry. Reverend Sherman will have as many as you need. He attends funerals so regularly, he has a store; I bought fifty from him last year for my sister's funeral. Shall I ask him?"

"Yes, I'd appreciate it." Given William's work as a selectman, and his standing in the community, she realized that fifty would not be enough. She did not want to insult anyone.

"Good. Corporal Bond will be taking the cart to town to buy spirits for the wake, and I can ride with him. We can deliver them to the parish this afternoon."

"An afternoon! Fifty houses? How can you?"

"We made a delivery tree for my sister. We'll leave them with church members who can deliver them to close neighbors. You must rest now. Have you eaten? Can I get you something? It's important that you have something to eat."

"I'm not hungry," Susanna said, sitting down suddenly on the empty bed, folding her arms tightly around her midriff.

"Then lie down. Rest. I'll bet you've not slept in days."

Susanna nodded and curled on her side at the edge of the bed, avoiding the hollow where he'd lain.

Susanna woke when it was dark to hear insects calling. Even through the barricaded shutters, she could hear a strident trill. She rose and fumbled her way to the bedroom door. She could see the hearth where red coals still glowed. She lit a candle, crossing to the back door to see. When she opened the back door, a wall of sound met her. It was solid, stopped her in her tracks. Every cicada, cricket, katydid, grasshopper, locust, wasp, beetle—June beetle, Bess beetle, long leg beetle, click beetle, dor beetle, dung beetle— lacewing, book lice, sounded their taps, hisses, screeches, squeaks, croaks, strumming, pops, and taps. Did the frogs join in? She couldn't distinguish them from the rest. The souls of everyone who'd died to this moment had waked and called her. She froze with fear at this deathwatch thought; her heart pounded. At first, she sensed the diabolical, but standing there in the cool night air, she woke to the sure knowledge that only the living spoke. All were struggling out of their wombs, eggs, cocoons, shells, with this feverish and senseless life. And what a call to life! Every flying, creeping, hopping, crawling, swimming thing shouted this grandest of hallelujahs to their maker, to life itself.

She stood transfixed, let the sound engulf her, let the vibration enter her trembling body through her parched skin, let it travel through veins and nerves. It tore open the numbing cocoon in which she was wrapped. She sank to the door sill, cradled her head in her arms, and joined the living; Susanna wailed.

Chapter Twenty-Eight

GRAVE THOUGHTS

Watertown, Next Day, August 1672

William woke. *I'm still here*, he thought. He stood behind his wife on the porch stoop, bent down, and placed his hands on her shoulders. Her cry had pierced his heart, and he felt only the longing to comfort her, to tell her he'd not gone, but he couldn't penetrate the veil that separated them now. Life, death. He could see her; why couldn't she see him? *She cannot*, he thought. *She'd be afraid.* William didn't abandon his post when she'd spent her grief; he stayed the night next to his coffin where she sat in her vigil.

At the viewing the next day, he stayed in the parlor, a witness to the family and friends who mourned him. He felt he had an unfair advantage over them, a bit like a voyeur who couldn't help practicing a vice he knew to be addictive. At some point, he noted that his daughter Mary sat across the room, her arms folded around his son Samuel, who stood at her knee. He could hear them plainly.

Samuel stared at William where he hovered. "Mary is father going home now?"

Mary turned to follow his gaze. "What do you mean, 'go home?' Has he not gone?" She wanted to know what the word 'home' meant to her little brother.

"No. He's here. I can see him. Mother said he went home to Heaven."

They had fixed their eyes on him. William was shocked. *Samuel? He too?* He had never imagined that two of his children might share the second sight. Samuel was six now, and he'd never seen it.

Mary sighed. This sweet boy shared her vision. "Hush now. You and I, we are going to keep a secret. No one knows our father is here with us."

Samuel turned to face her, his face puckering. "But I can see him!"

Mary arranged his collar, lovingly brushing lint from his shoulders. "Yes. And so can I. But no one else can. They will think you're lying, even when you're not. You and I, we have a special sight."

He squirmed around to look again. "Can I talk to him?"

"Yes, but not out loud. What did you want to ask him?"

"I want to know if he's going to heaven."

Mary squeezed his arm. "Samuel, he may not know; only God knows where he is to go. We who have faith must trust father will go to heaven. Why don't you say good-bye, instead, for he most certainly will leave us."

Good-bye, father, Samuel said silently.

Mary closed her eyes. *Father, I'll stand by Samuel; I promise to keep him safe.*

William heard them and willed the words he spoke to his children. *Tell your mother I've found bliss.*

He could see the tears well in Mary's eyes and spill down her cheeks, but she smiled nonetheless. Samuel looked away, nestling his head into her shoulder. "I heard him."

"What did he say?"

"He wanted me to tell mother something. What's bliss?"

Mary couldn't stop the fresh flow of tears that welled from her eyes. "Bliss is home, Samuel. It's home."

She answered her father. *I'll tell her. I will. I will never forget you.* When she turned her eyes away and dabbed at her tears, William knew he'd faded from their sight.

He'd attended funerals, and his was plainly no different. Parting was painful for families and friends, but all good Puritans were to celebrate when death restored loved ones to their heavenly home. He felt no sadness, only a great longing to console them, as in life. Tall candles flickered on the bier where William's friends would fasten their farewells. He followed Joseph Morse past the coffin and watched him attach the small slip of paper. William read:

> *In his prime struck down,*
> *Though his virtue known*
> *Take care of your soul.*
> *We know not when we go.*

The sentiment is good, William thought, though the rhymes aren't exact. It was typical of funeral rhymes that reminded the living that death is certain. He read another, thinking the hand was most likely a woman's hand. No one ever signed their names.

> *He asked for strength for the journey,*
> *But the journey gave him the strength*
> *To meet his maker in golden eternity*
> *For he's riding his bier the length.*

Yet other sentiments lamented death without ever mentioning coffins, skulls, or bones. He guessed that this rhyme had appeared on many biers; it suited every funeral occasion.

> *I feel as though time is slipping away*
> *And more is gone each passing day.*

Yet another verse caught his attention. At least he knew this one was written for him alone. He wondered who.

> *His true home is with God*
> *His bones to England go not.*

The most typical sentiment urged them to pay attention to their own mortality.

Oh, dear sinners awake
Our good path not forsake
For our end is ever near
Most certain never fear

William awarded the unknown writer of a brief two-liner first place. He could read no more.

A good man and steady
For heaven is most ready.

The visitors stood for minutes, silent, before they turned and made their way to the table boards, which bent with the weight of jugs. Punch laced with rum, whiskey, and barrels of ale invited all to partake. Pouring the drink of their choice, they made their way to the yard to talk.

For all their gravity, burials also provided one of the few opportunities that townspeople could put down their work and socialize to such an extent. These events also had the advantage of alcoholic beverages. Everyone imbibed and once inhibitions had been loosened, the conversation flowed freely. It was no wonder that no one wished to be excluded.

William lingered near his closest friend, John, who worried about his barley crops; a late summer drought threatened a good harvest. The selectmen gathered in a circle discussing the business of the day. Captain Beers and Deacon Hastings were deep in conversation about allotting money for ammunition. Captain Beers insisted that King Philip was selling land to raise money for arms. 'Why wouldn't he? If he can win a war, he'll get his land back.' The Deacon wouldn't listen.

Not yet, William thought. *Governor Prence put a moratorium on selling Indian land. But next year Philip will declare war.* He could see the future as clearly as he could see the bier on which he laid. When Governor Prence died, Josiah Winslow would end the moratorium on land sales.

William heard them from afar, accepting this distance as he would an ocean separating him from these shores. He'd never worry about Indians again. *Reports of Indian unrest never end, and they will have cause to regret their bad treatment,* he thought.

Joanna Morton held sway with a group of women, where she recruited helpers for the next new mother. Men and women separated in socializing as they had in the church pews. He wondered why; it seemed so unnecessary from his vantage point.

The visitation ended when the greater part of the townspeople had gathered. The women prepared the winding sheet, tucking it firmly around the body. Susanna could not bear to watch them lower the lid on the coffin and pound it in place, but Mary came to her aid. Holding her mother close, she whispered her message from her father. Susanna began to cry, then composed herself. It gave her the strength for this last journey to his grave, which was held in silence. The pallbearers led, holding the tasseled corners of the heavy velvet pall that covered the box and hid the underbearers, the six men who carried its full weight. *Define silence,* William thought. He heard villagers whispering, their feet shuffling in the dirt, their clothes rustling, the rhythmic thump of the box carried on shoulders. The rope creaked when they lowered the coffin in the grave. He was stricken at the clatter of dirt on the lid of his hollow coffin, sounding all the louder in the hushed crowd. He felt it! *It's time to go,* he thought. Enough of life, which felt oddly discomfiting now. He prepared his path to the light and claimed the bliss.

Susanna and her family led the procession to her house on the hill for the wake. People talked freely now, and while respectful, one could hear the relief in their voices, and later, laughter, a natural happening where people gather. Eating and drinking consumed them, affirmed life still to live, the time yet to come.

The Family Trees of
William, the Patriarch

John Sherborn
B. 1593 in
Stoghumber,
Somerset, England
D. 1639 in
Stoghumber
Somerset, England

Mary Granger
B. 1594 in
Stoghumber,
Somerset, England
D. 1650 in
Stoghumber
Somerset, England

Susanna Sherborn
B. 1643 in
Watertown,
Massachusetts,
D. 1716 in
Marlborough,
Massachusetts

Mary Sherborn
B. 1645 in
Watertown,
Massachusetts
D. 1732 in
Waltham,
Massachusetts

John Sherborn
B. 1647 in
Watertown,
Massachusetts
D. 1675
Charlestown,
Massachusetts

William Sherborn
B. 1653 in
Watertown,
Massachusetts
D. 1732 in
Watertown,
Massachusetts

Rebecca Sherborn
B. 1655 in
Watertown,
Massachusetts
D. 1689 in
Boston,
Massachusetts

Abigail Sherborn
B. 1657 in
Watertown,
Massachusetts
D. 1694
Groton,
Massachusetts

William, the Patriarch
and Susanna's Family

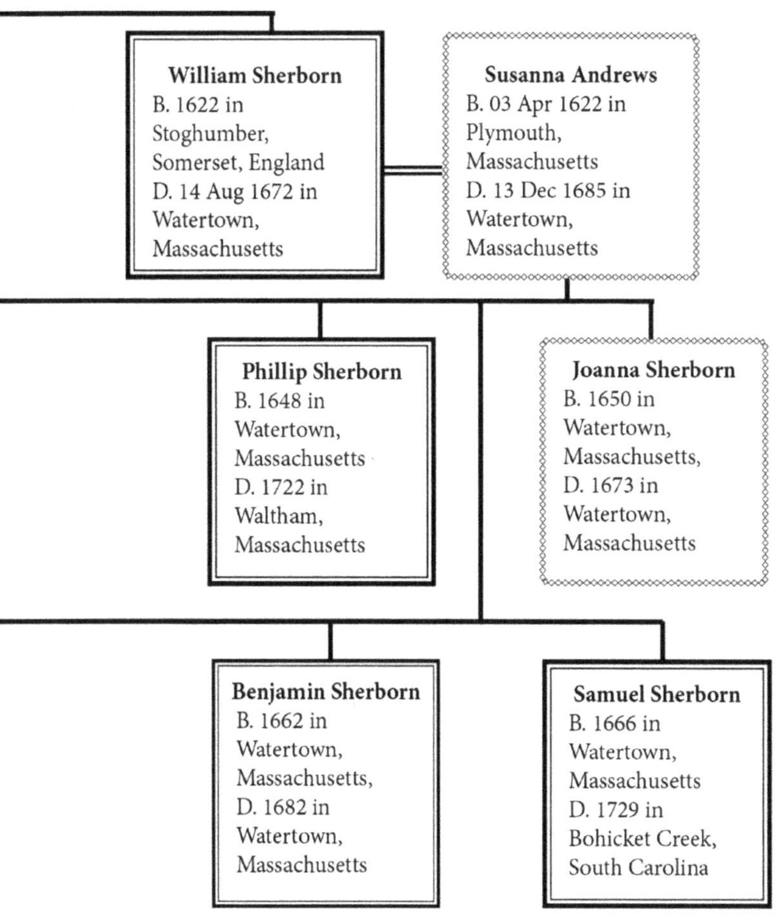

The Susanna and Joseph Morse Family - 1

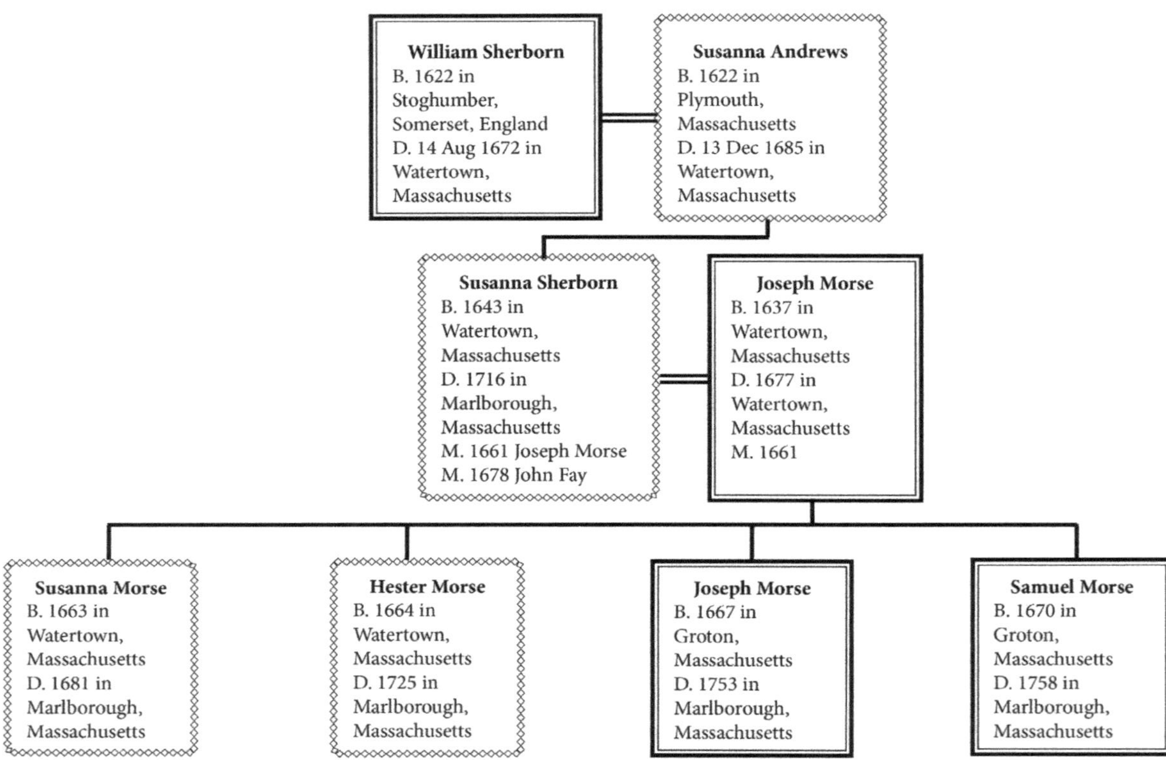

The Susanna and Joseph Morse Family - 2

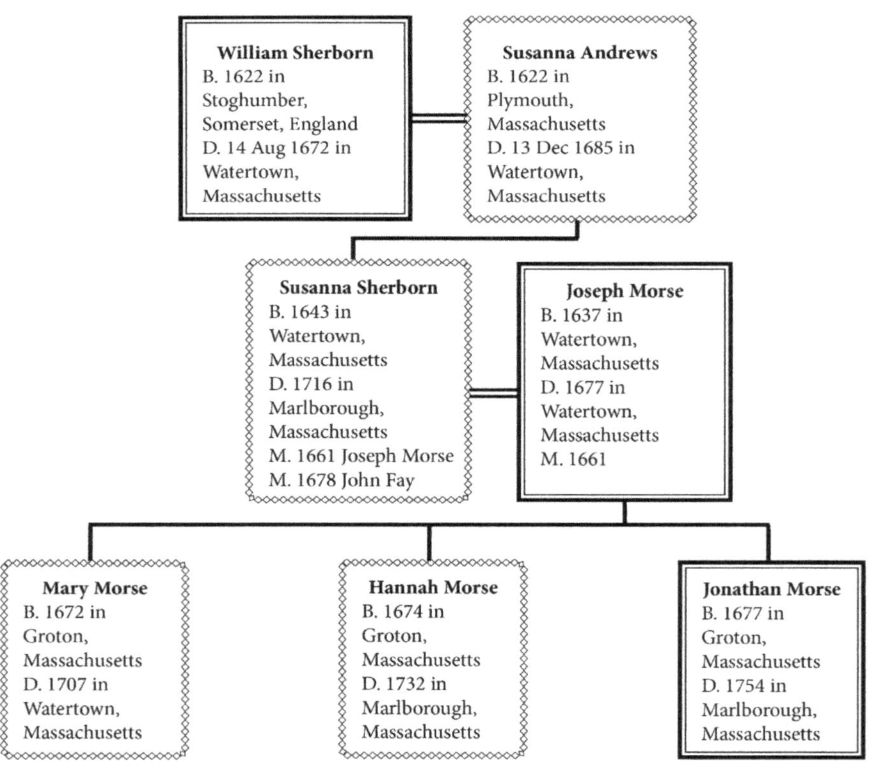

The Susanna and John Fay Family - 1

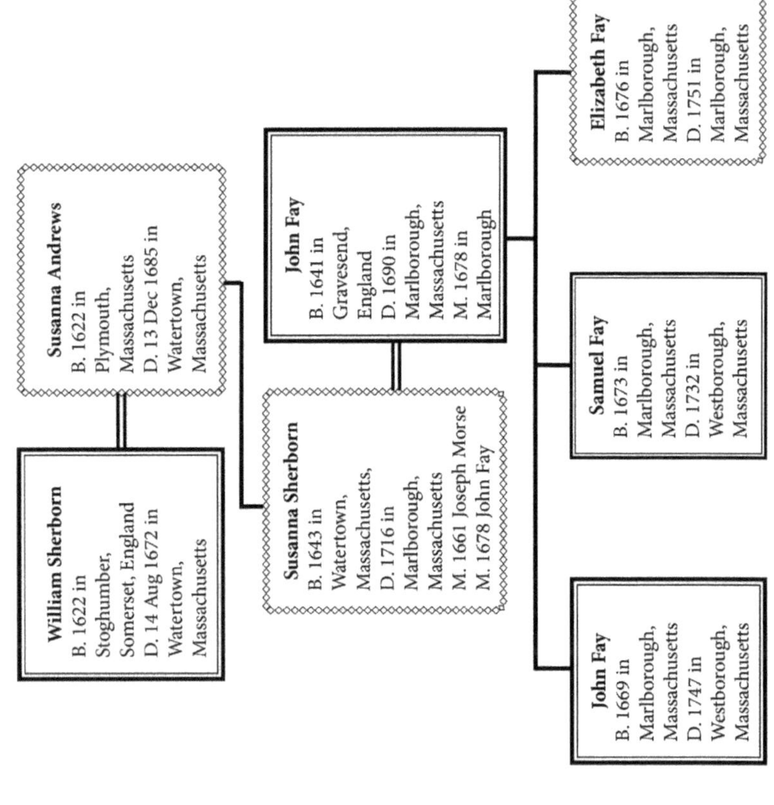

The Susanna and John Fay Family - 2

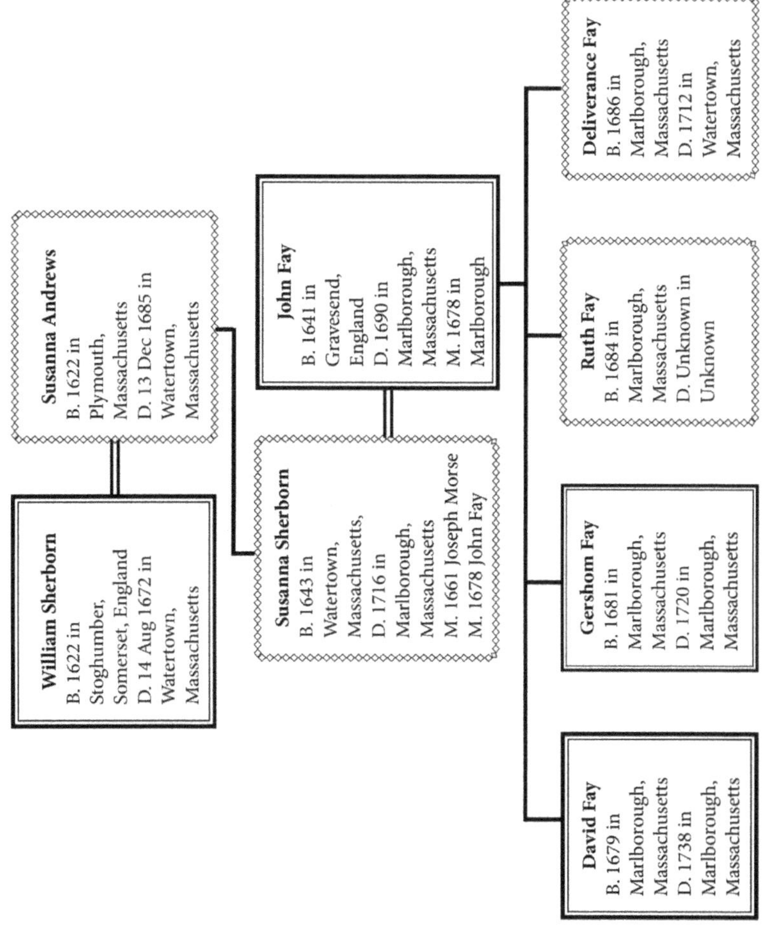

The Mary and Jonathan Brown Family - 1

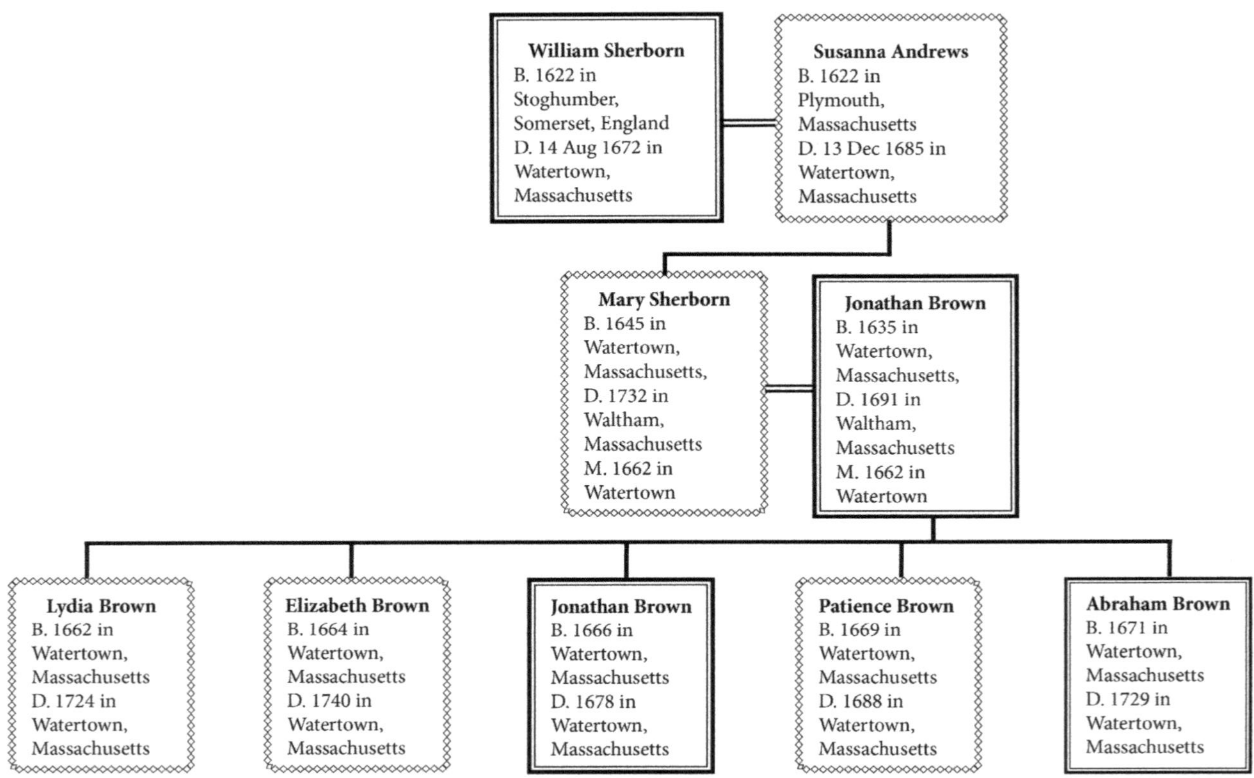

The Mary and Jonathan Brown Family - 2

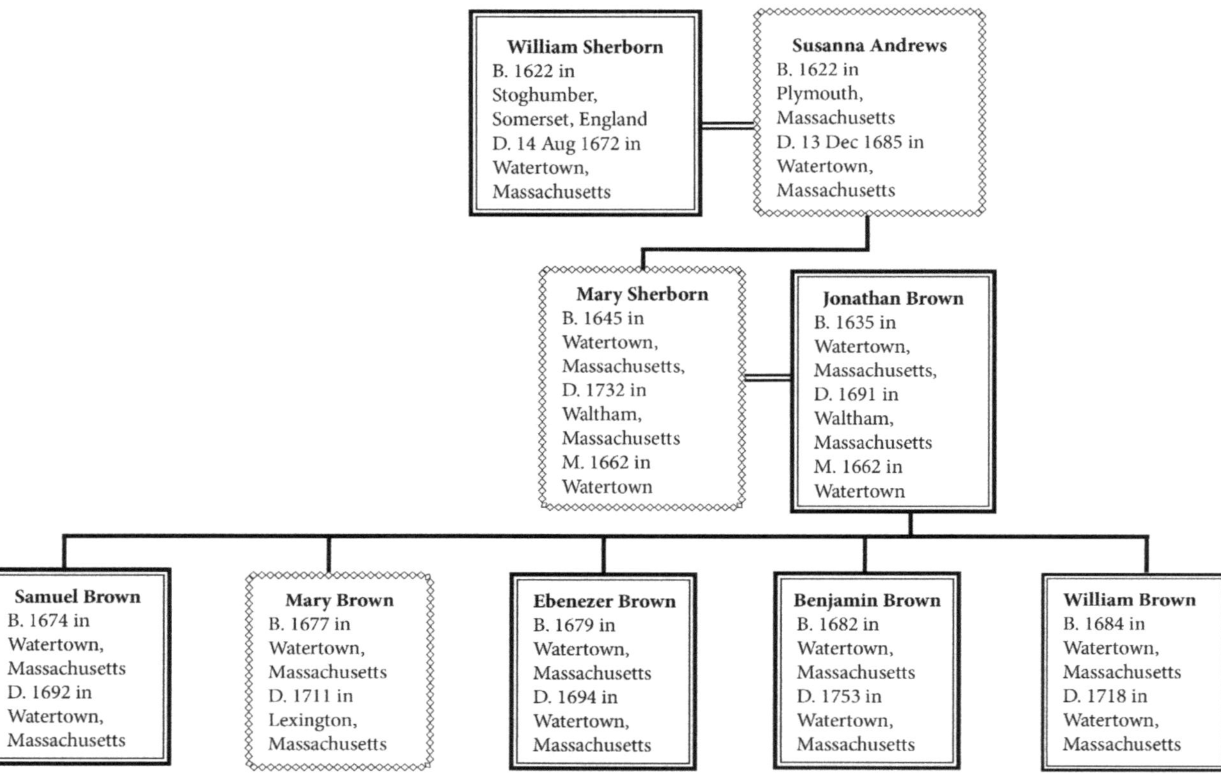

The John and Ruth Sherborn Family

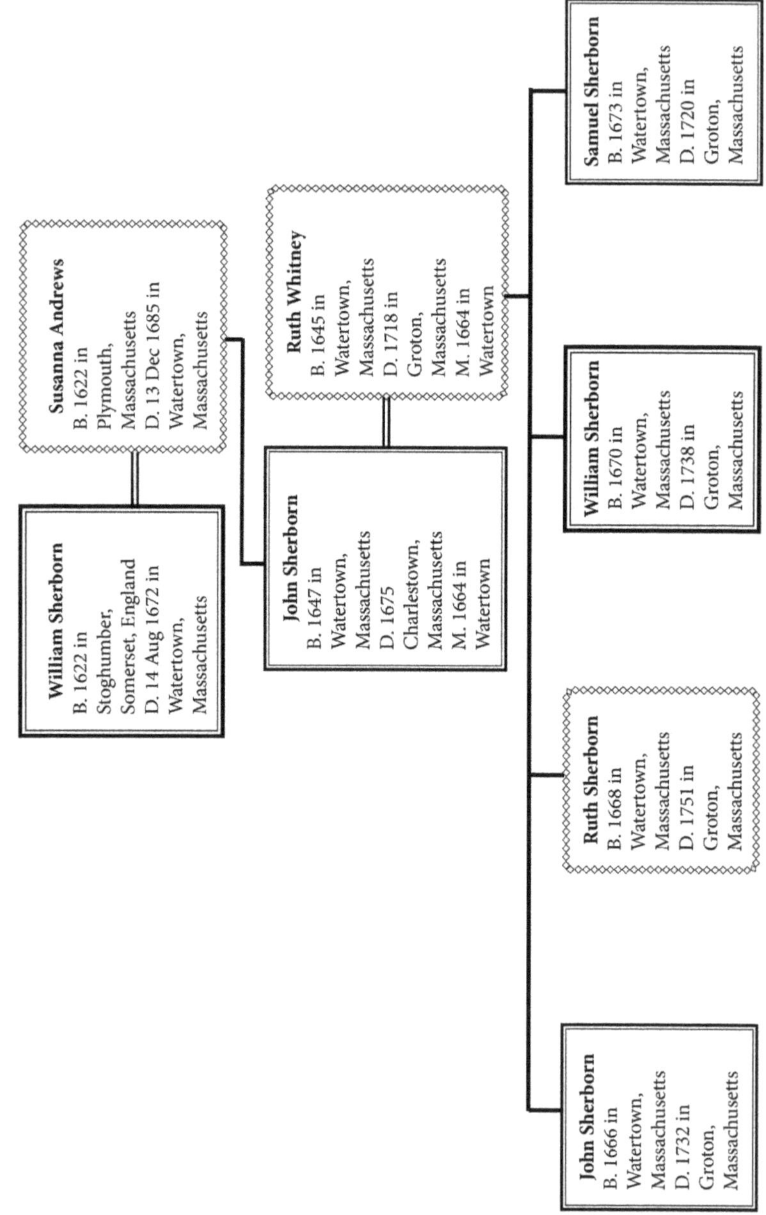

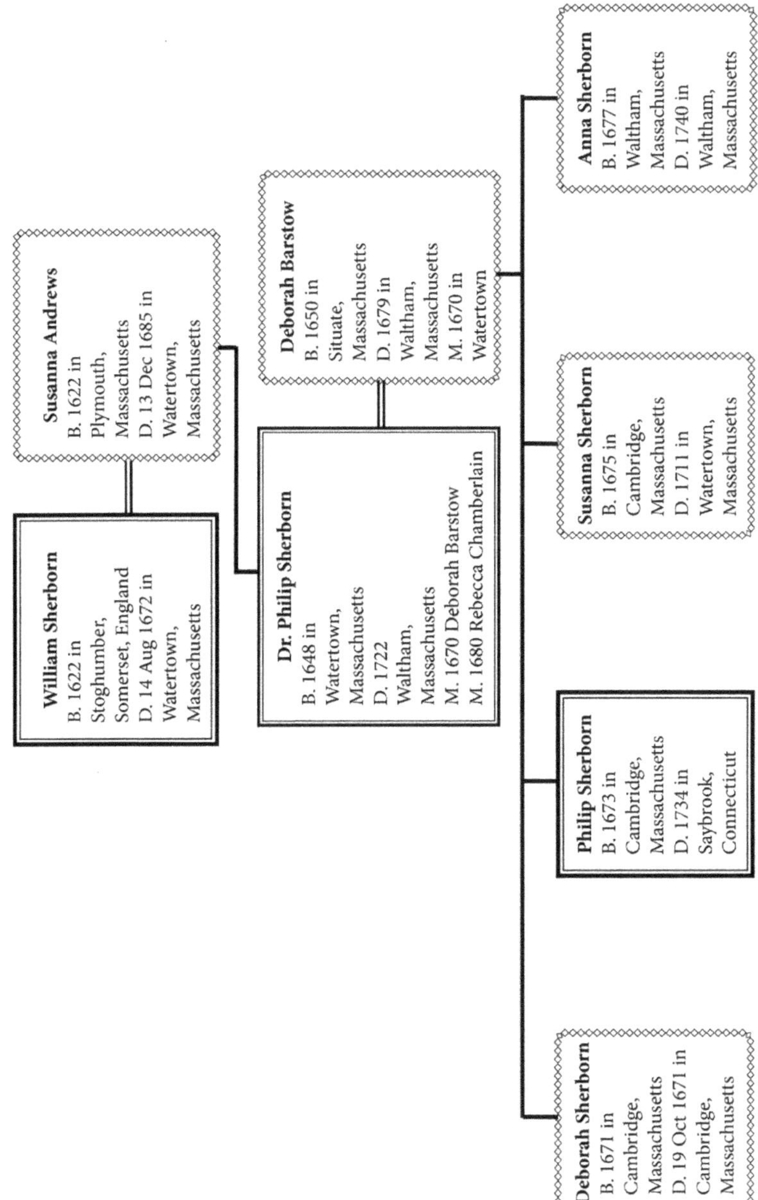
The Philip and Deborah Sherborn Family

William Sherborn
B. 1622 in
Stoghumber,
Somerset, England
D. 14 Aug 1672 in
Watertown,
Massachusetts

Susanna Andrews
B. 1622 in
Plymouth,
Massachusetts
D. 13 Dec 1685 in
Watertown,
Massachusetts

Dr. Philip Sherborn
B. 1648 in
Watertown,
Massachusetts
D. 1722
Waltham,
Massachusetts
M. 1670 Deborah Barstow
M. 1680 Rebecca Chamberlain

Deborah Barstow
B. 1650 in
Situate,
Massachusetts
D. 1679 in
Waltham,
Massachusetts
M. 1670 in
Watertown

Anna Sherborn
B. 1677 in
Waltham,
Massachusetts
D. 1740 in
Waltham,
Massachusetts

Susanna Sherborn
B. 1675 in
Cambridge,
Massachusetts
D. 1711 in
Watertown,
Massachusetts

Philip Sherborn
B. 1673 in
Cambridge,
Massachusetts
D. 1734 in
Saybrook,
Connecticut

Deborah Sherborn
B. 1671 in
Cambridge,
Massachusetts
D. 19 Oct 1671 in
Cambridge,
Massachusetts

The Philip and Rebecca Sherborn Family - 1

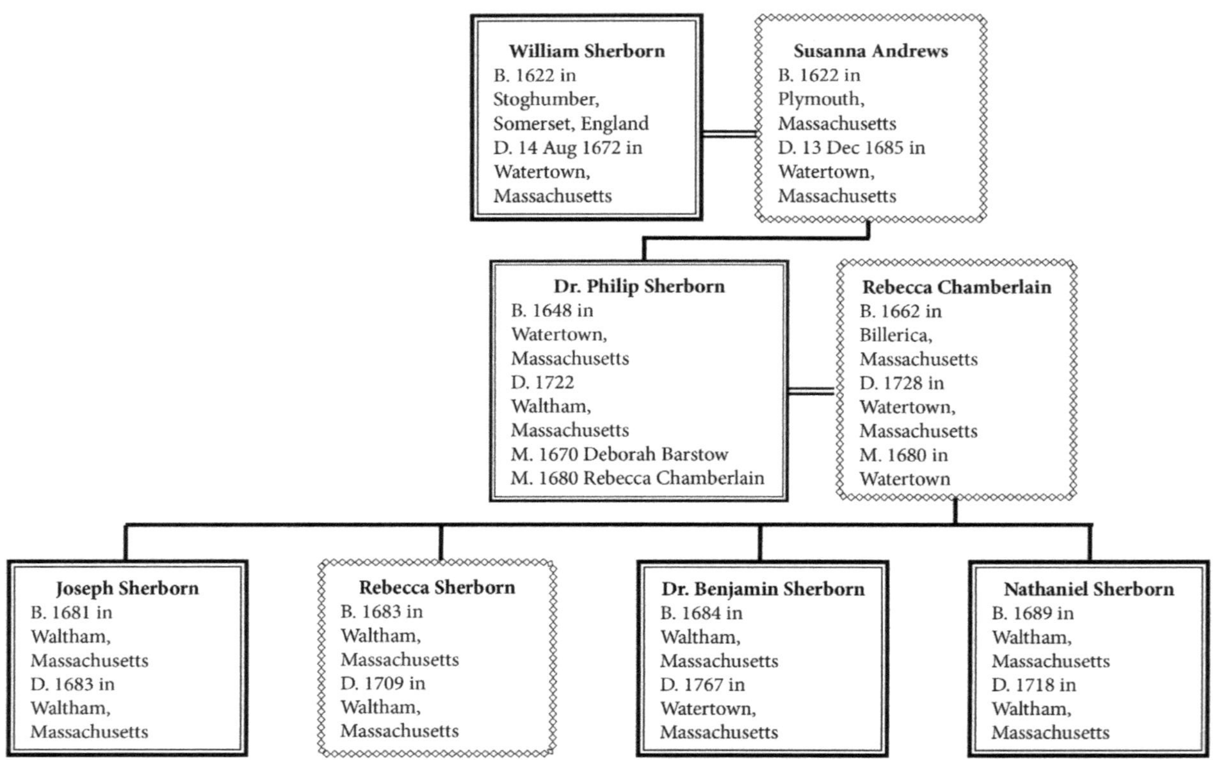

The Philip and Rebecca Sherborn Family - 2

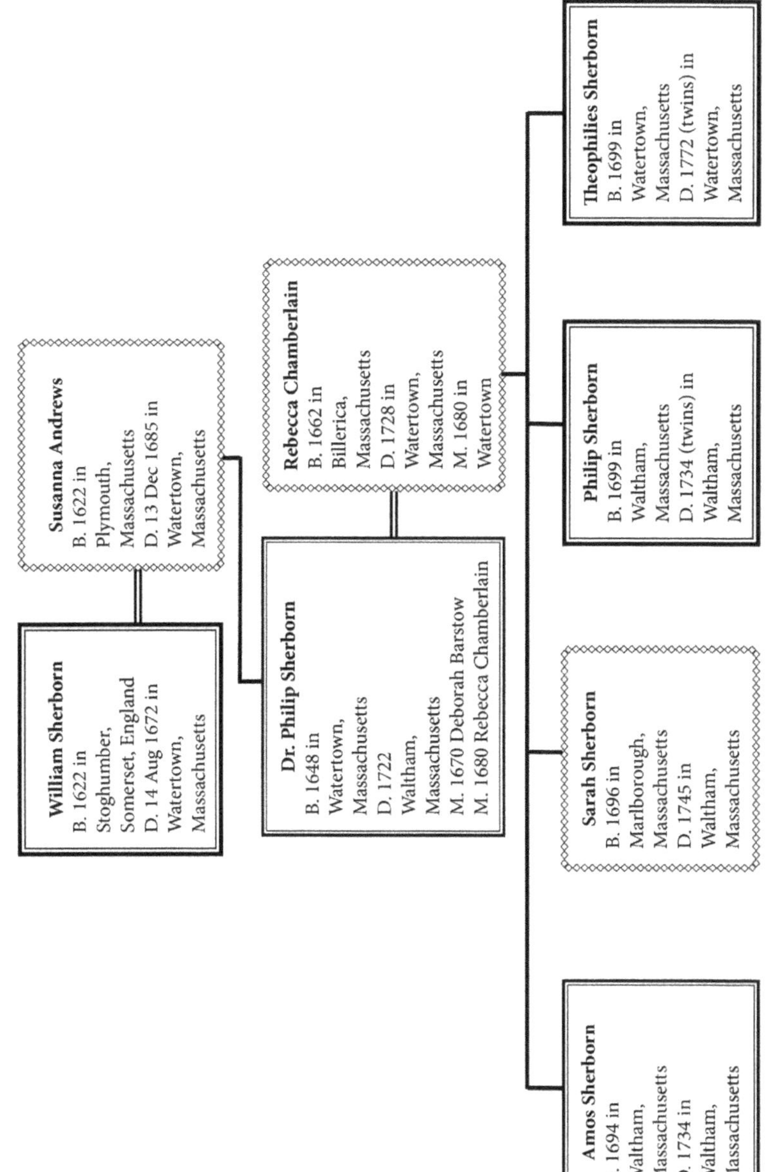

Joanna Sherborn's Family Tree

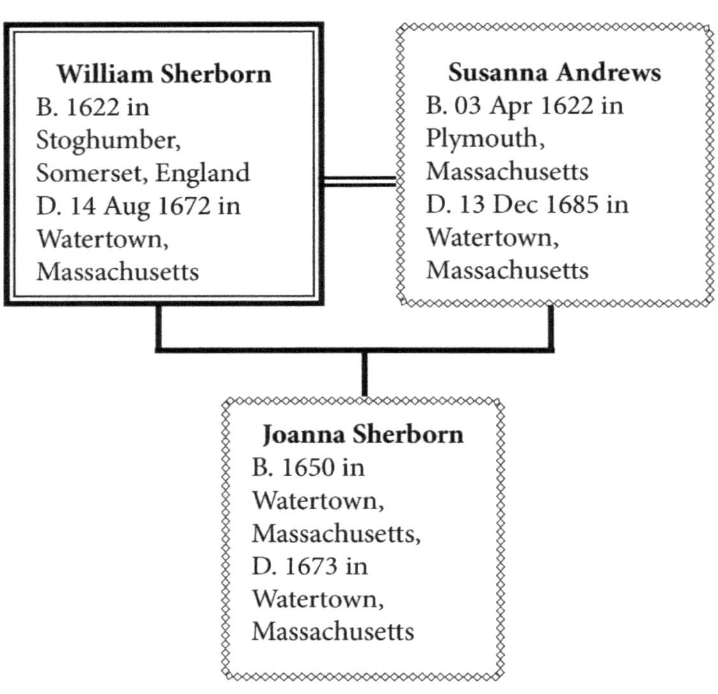

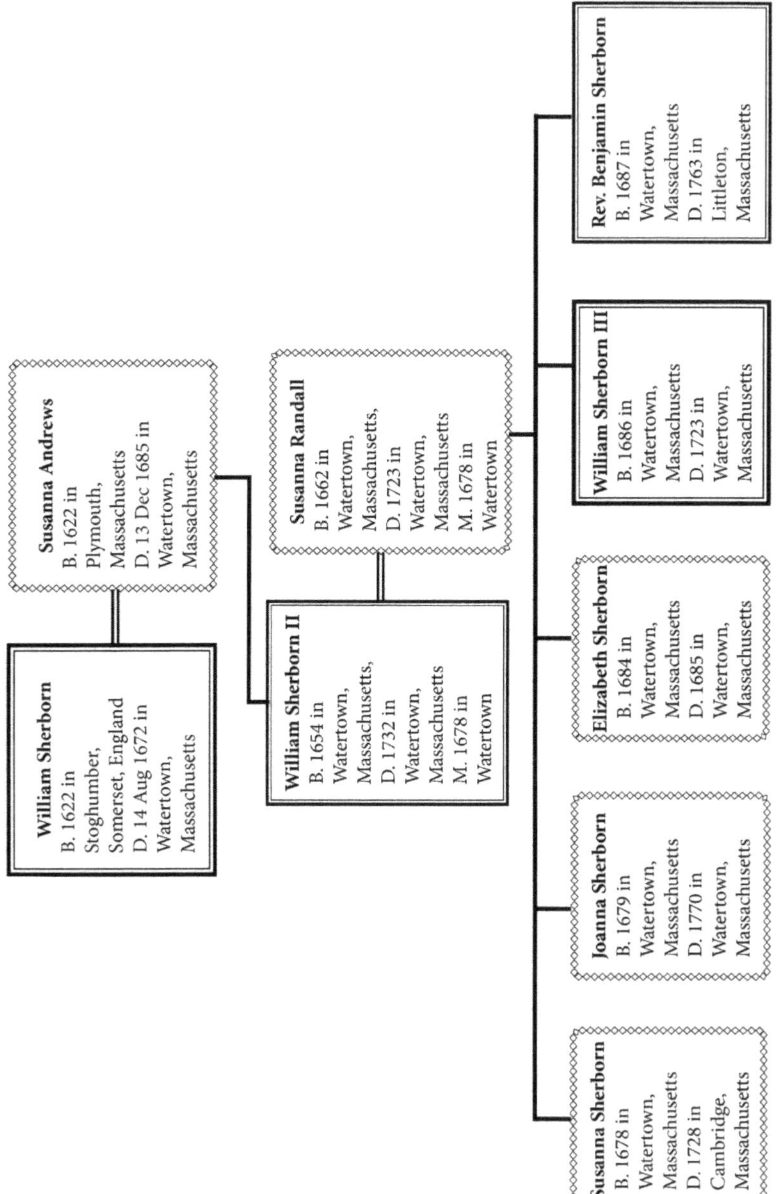

The William (II) and Susanna Sherborn Family - 1

William Sherborn
B. 1622 in Stoghumber, Somerset, England
D. 14 Aug 1672 in Watertown, Massachusetts

Susanna Andrews
B. 1622 in Plymouth, Massachusetts
D. 13 Dec 1685 in Watertown, Massachusetts

William Sherborn II
B. 1654 in Watertown, Massachusetts,
D. 1732 in Watertown, Massachusetts
M. 1678 in Watertown

Susanna Randall
B. 1662 in Watertown, Massachusetts,
D. 1723 in Watertown, Massachusetts
M. 1678 in Watertown

Susanna Sherborn
B. 1678 in Watertown, Massachusetts
D. 1728 in Cambridge, Massachusetts

Joanna Sherborn
B. 1679 in Watertown, Massachusetts
D. 1770 in Watertown, Massachusetts

Elizabeth Sherborn
B. 1684 in Watertown, Massachusetts
D. 1685 in Watertown, Massachusetts

William Sherborn III
B. 1686 in Watertown, Massachusetts
D. 1723 in Watertown, Massachusetts

Rev. Benjamin Sherborn
B. 1687 in Watertown, Massachusetts
D. 1763 in Littleton, Massachusetts

The William (II) and Susanna Sherborn Family - 2

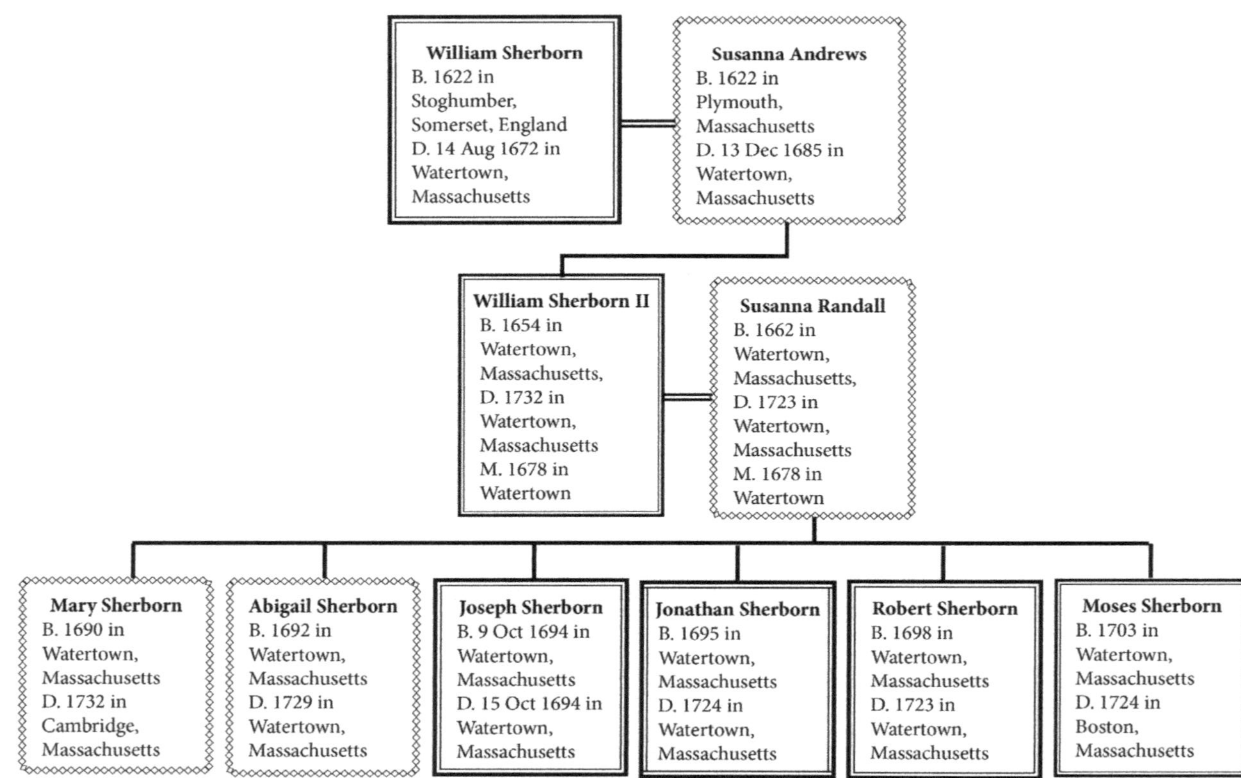

The Rebecca and Samuel Church/Abraham Davis Families

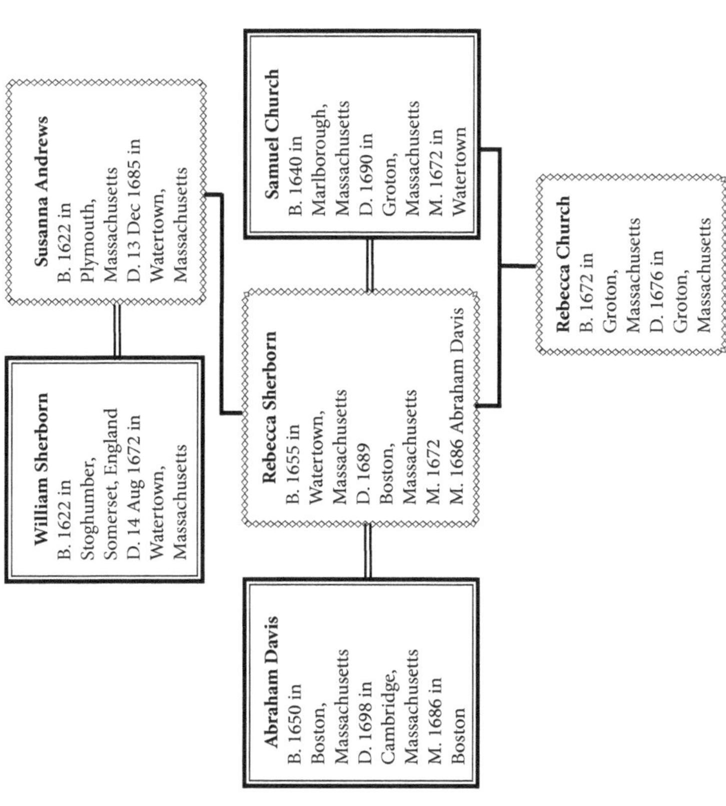

The Abigail and Jonathan Morse Family

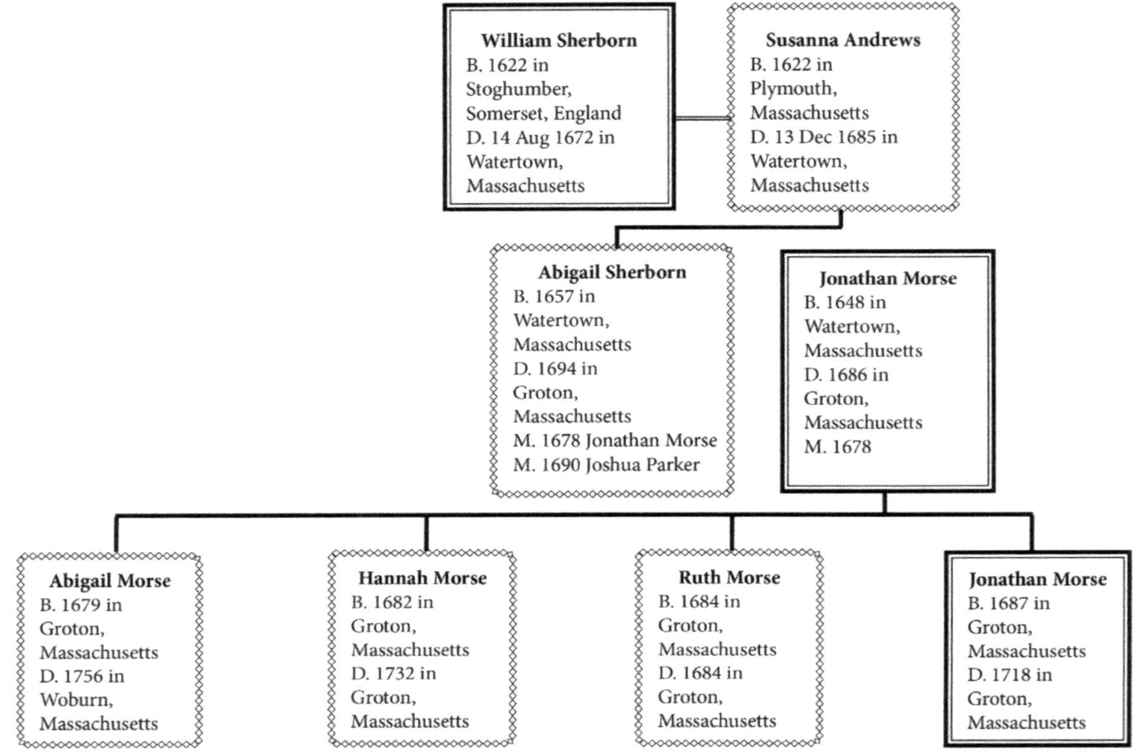

The Abigail and Joshua Parker Family

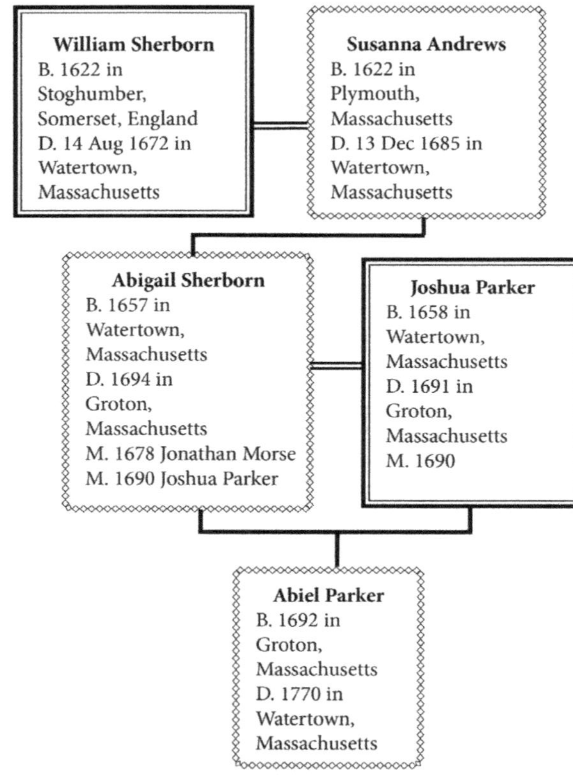

Benjamin Sherborn's Family Tree

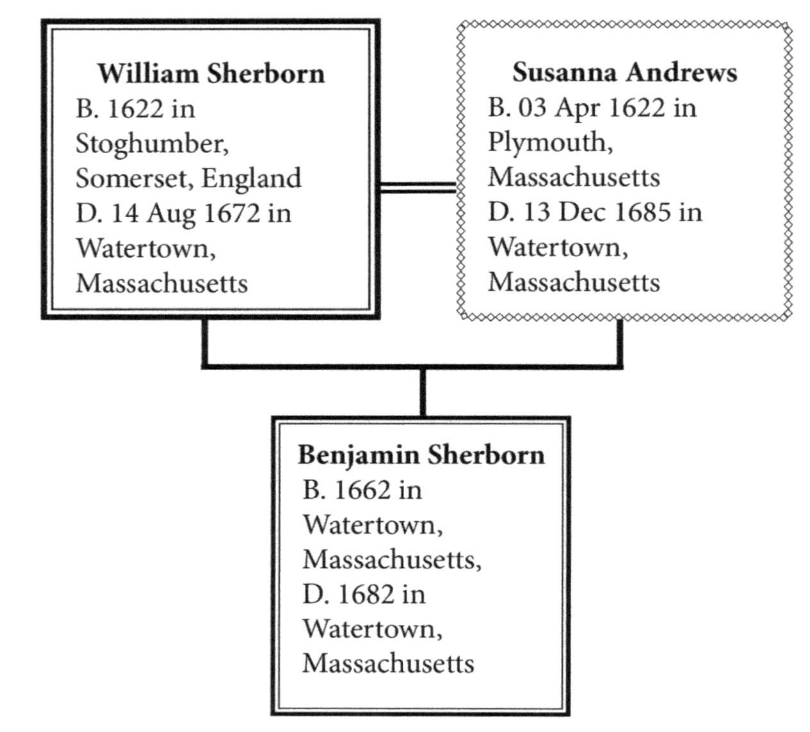

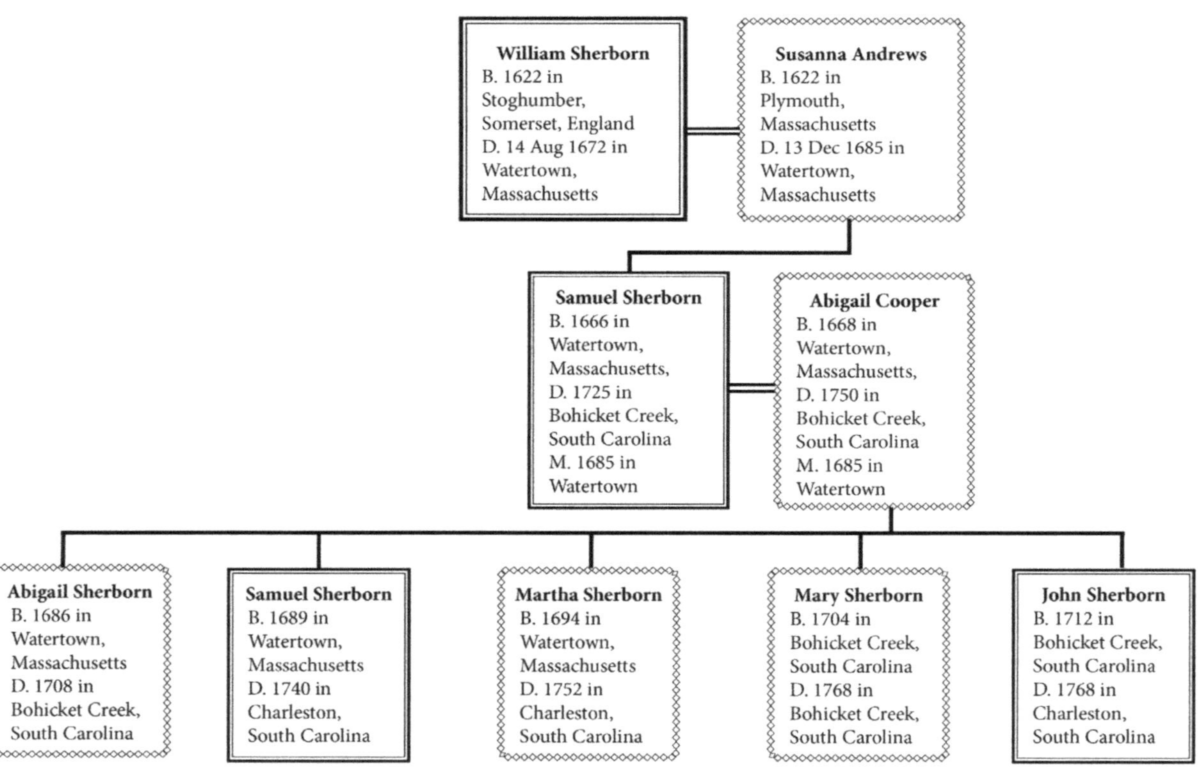

The Samuel and Abigail Sherborn Family

William Sherborn
B. 1622 in Stoghumber, Somerset, England
D. 14 Aug 1672 in Watertown, Massachusetts

Susanna Andrews
B. 1622 in Plymouth, Massachusetts
D. 13 Dec 1685 in Watertown, Massachusetts

Samuel Sherborn
B. 1666 in Watertown, Massachusetts,
D. 1725 in Bohicket Creek, South Carolina
M. 1685 in Watertown

Abigail Cooper
B. 1668 in Watertown, Massachusetts,
D. 1750 in Bohicket Creek, South Carolina
M. 1685 in Watertown

Abigail Sherborn
B. 1686 in Watertown, Massachusetts
D. 1708 in Bohicket Creek, South Carolina

Samuel Sherborn
B. 1689 in Watertown, Massachusetts
D. 1740 in Charleston, South Carolina

Martha Sherborn
B. 1694 in Watertown, Massachusetts
D. 1752 in Charleston, South Carolina

Mary Sherborn
B. 1704 in Bohicket Creek, South Carolina
D. 1768 in Bohicket Creek, South Carolina

John Sherborn
B. 1712 in Bohicket Creek, South Carolina
D. 1768 in Charleston, South Carolina

MORE ABOUT THE SERIES

The second book, *Mary, The Clairvoyant*, relates the churches' influence on colonial rule and explores the suspicious mind-set of the colonists, which fed the ferocity of the Indian war with King Philip (Metacom). Immigrants to the Americas carried the legacy of the German and Swiss Protestant movement that split the atom of Christian religious thought: three centuries of wars and witch trials in Europe preceded the immigrations. Millions had been executed in these conflicts. Mary, the second oldest child, is psychic, and the seventeenth century is a difficult time for anyone who shows paranormal ability when such skills are considered witchcraft. Mary's position in the town is secure; she has married power and wealth, but can she claim that security given the conflicts between her gift and her religion?

The third book in this trilogy, Suzanne, the Midwife, recounts the story of the oldest daughter, who is a certified midwife and healer. The story begins when Suzanne and her husband move to the remote frontier town, Groton. It explores the complex relations between tribal peoples and settlers, when Suzanne meets the formidable Nashua shaman Dancing Light. Suzanne must negotiate legitimacy for her midwife practice through the approval of the enlightened Puritan, Reverend Willard, while taking in the knowledge she gains from her Native American friend and mentor. She handles the rising tensions between the natives and colonists until the war reaches their small settlement, and in the heat of a siege, her neighbors turn on her. Her family now homeless refugees, Suzanne must find love and friendship anew in Watertown.

Look for future releases in the Watertown series:

Book Four – *Susanna, The Matriarch*
Book Five – *John, Carpenter, Miller, Soldier*
Book Six – *Philip, The Doctor*
Book Seven – *Rebecca, The Dressmaker*
Book Eight – *William, The Weaver Warrio*r
Book Nine – *Joanna, The Hunter*
Book Ten – *Abigail, The Pioneer*
Book Eleven – *Benjamin, The Farmer*
Book Twelve – *Samuel, The Prophet*

A RETROSPECT

The fictional Sherborn family is modeled from the Shattucks of Watertown, Massachusetts. William Sherborn's prototype William Shattuck arrived at the Massachusetts Bay Colony around 1640. He originated in west Somerset, in and near the Tone Valley. The 130-square-mile area in Southwest England was the home of all the Shattocke family, Celts who migrated from the foothills of the Alps north of Italy. Ever wanderers, from England, they scattered to English colonies on three continents: Europe, Australia and North America, even New Zealand in Oceania. William's progeny account for more than half (around 8,000 out of a total 14,000-to-15,000) of all Shattocke's alive worldwide today. See www.shaddock.ca/ for an account of the Shaddock, Shattuck, Shattocke diaspora.

William Shattuck Senior emigrated from Stogumber, Somerset, England, that area of England where Samuel Coleridge wrote his well-known work, *The Rime of the Ancient Mariner* and visitors can now walk a forty-mile Coleridge Trail. Although we have no records of his crossing, William was around eighteen years old and a weaver. The Watertown Council meeting minutes dating back to 1630 record his land grant from 1640. He was successful, becoming a full member of the Puritan church and voting freeman; he was a selectman several years, acting as both highway assessor and hog greave. He eventually amassed the property of three neighbors and a farm near present-day Waltham. He died at fifty in Watertown, and the will he filed in 1672 was published.

Susanna Norcross, Widow of William Shattuck gave birth to ten children by William before he died in his fiftieth year. She married a widower, Watertown's teacher RICHARD NORCROSS and occupied the

Shattuck main home until her death. When she remarried, she became mother to her six children still at home and Norcross's seven children. She is known to have written the first prenuptial agreement in Massachusetts when she married the widower, who survived Susanna by five years. Her son William Shattuck Junior bought title to the homestead bequeathed to Benjamin and Samuel when they came of age.

Susanna Morse, Nee Shattuck, William's oldest daughter was widowed twice, and left with 14 children: seven with Joseph Morse, five with John Fay, and three from John Fays' first marriage. She and her first husband settled in Groton, but Indians burned it to the ground in King Philip's war in 1676. Refugees who'd lost everything, the pair returned to Watertown, where her husband died a year later. Another refugee who had fled to Watertown from Marlborough, which Indians also destroyed the same month, married her, and the pair returned to Marlborough. The seven Morse children and the Fay children became prominent in Marlborough. She remarried a third time to Brigham, also from Marlborough.

Mary Brown, Nee Shattuck, lived a long and venerable life with one husband. When her husband of 55 years died, she never remarried, living 87 years in the Waltham area of Watertown. She bore ten children.

John Shattuck Senior, the author's direct ancestor, is William Shattuck's firstborn son, who also has the distinction of siring the most Shattucks from William senior's branch. Though John was drowned in a ferry accident during King Philip's War, he left a widow, three sons, and a daughter.

We also note that John's father, William, slights him in the will; John never joined the church. John's name and the names of his issue show in colonial archives and histories, but the stories leave questions regarding their character. In one story, John accused a neighbor of improper behavior with a young woman. The case ended up in the Boston court, where Reverend Sherman, the minister, advised the court 'don't trust his word.' Another story of John Shattuck's descendants in Groton paints them as bullies. When the residents of the new subdivision, Pepperell, are trying to decide where to build the new meetinghouse, the Shattucks pressure the community to build the church close to their landholdings, which are extensive. Justice prevails, and the townspeople move the half-built structure to land that is more centrally located—the lumber, too—while a two-person-deep line of Shattucks lines the road in protest.

John Shattuck's name turns up in Captain Daniel Gookin's defense of the Christian Indians in King Philip's war as a story of retribution. Gookin's defense of Christian Indians shows a clear bias: he opposed the war and those engaged in it. Unlike many colonists who thought Christianized Indians had joined King Philip, he insisted they were loyal to the English.

Daniel Gookin was the official Superintendent of Praying Indians in The Massachusetts Bay colony. As such, he was the counsel for fifteen Marlborough Indians then on trial in Boston. He was critical of anyone who spoke against them, though two were eventually convicted.

Gookin records John Shattuck's response during that meeting and judges his character in his history of the ferry accident following it. Gookin omits from his story that John Shattuck had been sent to rescue the very settlers the fifteen Indians allegedly attacked. Seeing his fellow soldier's heads on spikes and the charred countryside on the chilling ride to Boston must have fueled John Shattuck's response. Gookin wrote:

> About this time a person named Shattuck, of Watertown, that was a sergeant under Capt. Beers, when the said Beers was slain near Squakeage, had escaped very narrowly but a few days before; and being newly returned home, this man being at Charlestown, in Mr. Long's porch, at the sign of the Three Cranes, divers persons of quality being present, particularly Capt. Lawrence Hammond, the Captain of the town, and

others, this Shattuck was heard to say to this effect:
"I hear the Marlborough Indians, in Boston in prison,
and upon trial for their lives, are likely to be cleared
by the court; for my part," said he [Shattuck], 'I have
been lately abroad in the country's service, and have
ventured my life for them, and escaped very narrowly;
but if they clear these Indians, they shall hang me up
by the neck before I ever serve them again.' Within a
quarter of an hour after these words were spoken, this
man was passing the ferry between Charlestown and
Boston; the ferry boat being loaded with horses and
the wind high, the boat sunk; and though there were
several other men in the boat and several horses, yet
all escaped with life, but this man only. I might mention
several other things of remark here that happened to
other persons, that were filled with displeasure and
animosity against the poor Christian Indians but shall
forbear lest any be offended.

Daniel Gookin attributes the accident to God's
punishment.

John Shattuck's widow Ruth married Enoch Lawrence,
of a prominent Groton family and occupied the land that
John had received as grants and bought from John Morse
in 1666. (John Morse was the uncle of the two Morse
men that Susanna and Abigail Shattuck married.) Enoch
Lawrence didn't adopt Ruth's children; the three boys kept
the name Shattuck.

Ruth's firstborn son JOHN SHATTUCK JR., also
lived in Groton, married Mary Blood, and had children.
When Indians again burned down the town of Groton,
the Shattuck brothers decided to abandon it. However,
John Shattuck changed his mind and stayed. (The Bloods
were the largest property owner, with acreage equivalent to
half the town.) Then, on May 8, 1709, John Shattuck Jr and
his oldest son, John, a young man of nineteen years, were
killed by the Indians while returning from fields on the
west side of the Nashua River. A suitable stone placed by

the site bears the inscription: "Near this site John Shattuck a Selectman of Groton (MA) and his son John were killed by the Indians May 8, 1709 while crossing the stony ford way just below the present dam." (Stone erected 1882)

These deaths at river crossings that eerily reflect John Shattuck Senior's drowning while crossing the Charles River, might call up Gookin's inference of divine retribution. At the very least, they suggest self-fulfilling prophecies. Consider the following report:

> A remarkable fatality seems to have followed Mrs. Mary Blood-Shattuck's kindred. Her husband and eldest son [mentioned above] were killed by Indians. Her father, James Blood, was killed by Indians Sept. 13, 1692. Her uncle, William Longley [was] also killed by Indians; so was his wife and five of their children - on July 27, 1694. The remaining three were carried off as captives. A relative, James Parker, Jr and his wife were killed in this assault and their children taken prisoner. Her stepfather, Enoch Lawrence received a wound by the Indians probably [in] the same attack, July 27, 1694, which almost wholly disabled him. The three Tarball children carried off to Canada June 20, 1707 were cousins of Ruth Shattuck. John Ames the father-in-law of her niece, Ruth (Shattuck) Ames was shot by the savages at the gate of their own garrison July 9, 1724. Lastly, her son-in-law Isaac Lakin the husband of her daughter Elizabeth, was wounded in Lovewell's fight at Pigwacket, May 8, 1725. These calamities covered a period of only one generation extending from 1692 to 1725.

Source: Epitaphs of the Old Burial Ground, Groton, MA. by Dr. Samuel A. Green

While we might err to speculate on divine retribution or a self-fulling prophecies for this family, we can agree it's an uncanny history

Philip Shattuck, became a doctor in Waltham, and he and his wife fostered his younger brother, Samuel, from age seven. (Samuel's mother had married Richard Norcross and the pair apprenticed Samuel to Philip to learn a trade.) His first wife, Deborah, died after nine years, leaving him with four children and his brother Samuel, then thirteen. Oddly, he married his second wife seven weeks later. His second wife bore ten children. He was prominent in Waltham, serving as assessor, treasurer, and other offices of public trust and responsibility. He might have become the head of a long line of doctors if his son, Dr. BenjaminShattuck (the second) had seen his issue follow his lead.

William Shattuck Junior, survived his service to Captain Prentices cavalry during the Great Swamp Battle and the Hungry March of King Philip's War and lived to be 79. He is buried in the Waltham cemetery along with his sister Mary and his brother Philip. He sired eleven children by Susanna Randall, who died ten years before William. Oddly, William's son became the first in the line of Boston doctors, once referred to as "Boston Brahmins," and Shattuck Avenue, a Harvard Medical school address, is named after one of William's line. William served the Watertown council in many positions of public trust and lived at the family homestead on the road to the pond, now known as Washington Street.

The Massachusetts Bay Colony had promised land grants in payment for the attack on the Narragansett fort (Great Swamp Battle) but didn't give out the land until 1725, the year before he died. The thirty-acre Narragansett 2 (later named Westminster) grant to William Shattuck was in northwestern Massachusetts, where some of his issue moved. Others who moved to New Hampshire sired Aron Draper Shattuck, known for his Hudson-River-style landscape paintings.

Rebecca Church, Nee Shattuck, was sixteen when she married Samuel Church, a man of thirty-two years, in January 1672. She bore one child in 1672, after which the family disappears from all records; however, a Samuel Church land grant is recorded in Groton.

Benjamin Shattuck died in his 20th year, leaving no issue or history. We know he suffered from a long disabling illness because his brother Philip petitioned the court for money from his inheritance to pay the medical costs. Benjamin was apprenticed to his brother William junior, who had just turned twenty when his mother married Richard Norcross, and his trades might have been weaving and farming if he had survived.

Joanna Shattuck never married and died the year she turned twenty-three, eight months after her father's death in 1672 and seven months before her widow mother married Richard Norcross in 1673.

Abigail Morse, Nee Shattuck, married her brother-in-law, Joseph Morse's brother, Jonathan Morse after the war. The pair moved to Groton two years after Indians had sacked the town. Abigail outlived Jonathan Morse after bearing four children (the first cousins of Ruth Shattuck-Lawrence's four children), and a second husband, Joshua Parker, after bearing one child. She died at thirty-seven, two years after her second husband died. She was survived by five children, ages five to sixteen. So far, we have no records of these Morse and Parker issue.

Samuel Shattuck: We have no record of where Samuel went after the Indian wars of 1694-95. We know that when his mother married Richard Norcross, she sent seven-year-old Samuel to his brother Philip to learn a trade. He lived with Philip for eleven years before he married at eighteen, but we don't know if he became a doctor or used his brother's skills. Samuel, who was the youngest of William's children, married Abigail in Watertown, but after three children are recorded in the church records— Abigail, Samuel, and Martha are the issue—the family disappears.

Abigail was a covenanted member of the church in Watertown. We have no records of Samuel, Abigail and the three children being involved in King William's war, and it's more likely he sought land grant opportunities that were opening up in the south. There is a record in 1709 that a Samuel Shaddock and his wife Abigail bought land in Bohicket Creek, South Carolina, and DNA research also reveals that the South Carolina Shaddocks are genetically linked to the patriarch, William Shattuck instead of other, later arrivals from England. It is certain that this Samuel Shaddock was William Shattuck's son. Philip Shaddock, who has been tracing family lines genetically, proposes that Samuel may have changed the spelling of his name to be consistent with the southern pronunciation when he moved south.

ABOUT THE AUTHOR

Nancy Shattuck was inspired to write this series when she discovered her direct ancestors had lived through King Philip's War in 1675-76. Exploring their history, she was so impressed by the complexity of the colonial experience that each family member began to tell a different story. No longer a novel, the "chronicles" were born. Nancy earned a master's degree in Comparative and Japanese Literature at Washington University (WU) in St. Louis and completed the classwork for two separate doctorates, in Comparative Literature at WU and American Literature at Wayne State University. Previous publications include a children's fable, *The Fishers*, and a travel memoir, *Travel Wings: An Adventure*, in addition to short stories and poetry. She is the recipient of an American Academy of Poets award in 1978; Tompkins awards for poetry and fiction in 2004, 2005, and 2007; a John Clare award for poetry in 2005; a Judith Siegel Pearson's award for poetry in 2005; and a Heck-Rabbi award for drama in 2006.